ABOUT THIS BOOK

Three novellas (books 13-15) in the **Legends of Havenwood Falls** historical fantasy series, sharing the legacies of our town's supernatural residents.

Changing Fate by Char Webster

During World War I, vila warrior Jerina Ventus's life irrevocably changed when she saved a wounded soldier's life and helped him return to his hometown in Colorado. Twenty-five years later, she's restless and longing for another adventure beyond her forest. Thane Beltaine grew up hearing stories about the beautiful and fierce immortal warrior who saved his father's life. When Jerina's sister Kosa shows up in his hometown on the arm of a wicked mage, Thane volunteers to find Jerina and bring her back. He never expected to meet the woman who was more legend than real and definitely didn't think they would clash about every little thing.

Rise of the Witch Hunters by Morgan Wylie – Sequel to *Dawn of the Witch Hunters*

Marie Blackstone is settling into her new life with Judson Carter in the beautiful box canyon they now call home. On a constant quest to prove her legitimacy—especially to the witches—Marie goes to great lengths to follow a feeling she's only encountered once before and hoped never to again. Someone's practicing the dark arts, but she can't quite discern who. When witches begin to disappear or turn up drained of their magic, suspicion and fear grow. And some are looking at Marie, the resident witch hunter.

The Drowning Bride by Seven Jane

For generations, Noelani has lived in the forest of Havenwood Falls, bestowing blessings and good fortune on all who drink from the waters of her well. She has been visited by hundreds of blushing brides and aging widows who crave her magic, but never has she met a heart as pure as that of Stella Malloy—or as dark as that of her fiancé, Peter Heilen. After hearing stories of Noelani's well, Stella believes it may be the only way to save her love from his dark path and return Peter's heart to her. But the wish she casts at the water's edge may doom them all.

LEGENDS OF HAVENWOOD FALLS VOLUME FIVE

A LEGENDS OF HAVENWOOD FALLS COLLECTION

CHAR WEBSTER   MORGAN WYLIE   SEVEN JANE

LEGENDS OF HAVENWOOD FALLS BOOKS

Lost in Time by Tish Thawer

Dawn of the Witch Hunters by Morgan Wylie

Redemption's End by Eric R. Asher

Trapped Within a Wish by Brynn Myers

Blood and Damnation by Belinda Boring

Fated Beginnings by E.J. Fechenda

Emeline by Katie M. John

Released From a Curse by Brynn Myers

A Pack of Lies by Kallie Ross

Kiss the Ashes by Desiree Lafawn

Hidden Truths by Colleen Nye

Wrath and Retribution by Belinda Boring

Changing Fate by Char Webster

Rise of the Witch Hunters by Morgan Wylie

The Drowning Bride by Seven Jane

Also try the signature New Adult/Adult series, Havenwood Falls, and the YA series, Havenwood Falls High

Stay up to date at www.HavenwoodFalls.com

CHANGING FATE

CHAR WEBSTER

~ A Legends of Havenwood Falls Novella ~

HAVENWOOD FALLS

LEGENDS

CHANGING FATE

USA Today Bestselling Author

CHAR WEBSTER

ALSO BY CHAR WEBSTER

GIFTED SERIES

Discovery, Book One

Exploration, Book Two

Transformation, Book Three

Acceptance, Book Four

Experiments, A Gifted Series Prequel

MYSTIC UNIVERSE: STOLEN MAGIC, BOOK ONCE OF THE MYSTIC MAGIC SERIES

Forgotten Magic, Book One of the Mystic Darkness Series

HAVENWOOD FALLS

Changing Fate, Havenwood Falls Legends Book 13

Saving Tannor, Havenwood Falls Holiday Anthology

To Briella
Love is worth fighting for.

CHAPTER 1

Obnoxious laughter followed Jerina's ungraceful and rapid descent to the ground from the thick branch she had been perched upon. With a wave of her hands, gusts of wind pushed up against her free fall, slowing her plummet to a slight drop and landing her lightly on her feet.

Her sister, Kosa, was still cackling like a hyena when Jerina stalked over to her. Scooping up a handful of snow, she dumped it on Kosa's blond head in retribution for the snow blast her sister sent to knock her out of the tree. The icy shower coated her soft leather handmade jacket.

Kosa shook the snow from her long straight hair. "I've never caught you unaware! You should have seen your face when you fell."

Jerina growled at Kosa. "You should be patrolling, not messing around!"

The sisters faced each other with the same graceful height, same lithe build, and same long blond hair. Even though there were a few years separating them, they could nearly pass for twins.

"My shift is finished. You would know that if you hadn't been pouting in that tree!" Kosa prepared herself for Jerina to attack. This was a fight that had been brewing for years.

Jerina swung out with her fist, but Kosa ducked out of the way while thrusting her leg out to trip her sister.

The girls ended up in a tangle of long arms and legs as they rolled across the forest floor, kicking up snow and leaves in their fury. They ignored the fierce growl that continued to gain in volume but were pulled apart when sharp teeth sank into the soft leather of Jerina's left boot.

"Damn it, Rela! If you tear my boots, I'm going to send you off to the next country!" Jerina yelled at the regal mountain lion that was still growling and showing lethal fangs. Rela was not intimidated in the least by her outburst. The mountain lion shook her head while still grasping Jerina's brown suede boot, making sure the girls knew she wasn't going to let go until they stopped fighting.

Jerina raised her hands, and wind started to whip through the trees, blowing the mountain lion's fur, but she stood firm. Sighing dramatically, Jerina released Kosa and fell back onto the forest floor, breathing heavily.

Rela dropped the boot with what sounded like a snort, but she stood close to the sisters, making sure they didn't continue to brawl.

Kosa ruffled the velvety tan fur of their good friend. "You could have waited a little longer before interrupting us."

Jerina glared at her sister. "Why are you picking a fight today, Kos?"

"You have not been yourself for years, not since you returned from your trip, but lately it's become far more severe. What is the matter?" Kosa wasn't the only one to notice the change in Jerina. Their mother had begun to ask questions, and that was never good.

Rela's head was leaning over Jerina's shoulder as she sat up, so she pushed it out of the way. It sounded like Rela was laughing at her. She was about to reply that nothing was wrong but decided to speak the truth. "I find myself restless."

"You've always been content here in our forest." Kosa was the one who would seek adventure whenever possible.

Rela settled down on some soft moss, not minding the patches of snow, and closed her eyes, ignoring them since they had stopped fighting.

"I love it, but . . ."

"You need something more," Kosa finished for her.

"Yes!" Jerina whipped her hands up, creating a cyclone of leaves, sticks, snow, and wind around the three of them. "I feel as if I should be doing something, but I do not know what."

"We could venture into town and find some humans to have fun with." Kosa had been sneaking off to town whenever she could, but she didn't want her sister to know how often.

Jerina narrowed her gaze. "What have you done?"

"We are not speaking about me. We are discussing your melancholy mood." Kosa was not going to let Jerina intimidate her.

"You know we cannot become attached to humans."

Kosa rolled her eyes. "We cannot get involved with anyone." Kosa spread her hands out wide, and the cyclone stopped. Everything rained down to the ground in a flurry of debris. "No one is around to hear us. You don't need to draw unwanted attention to this area."

"Kosa, I've seen the little gifts that are left for you."

Kosa's eyes grew round, but she smoothed her shock away and tried to act casual. "I have happened upon a few trinkets. They don't mean anything. They could have been left for anyone."

Jerina raised an eyebrow. "Who is he?"

Kosa had no idea how the conversation shifted to Jerina interrogating her. "I don't have any idea what you're talking about."

"Kos."

"Maybe you should go back and visit Tannor."

"Your attempt at diverting the conversation will not work. Tell me about him." Jerina didn't like the dreamy look in her sister's eyes. She also didn't want to talk about Tannor and her trip across the world. She felt drawn to Colorado but not romantically. She had developed a friendship with Tannor, and that was it. No deeper feelings were involved. Tannor loved his wife more than anything, and Jerina had helped him get back to her when he had been seriously injured.

"There is nothing to say." Kosa began to bounce in place, something she did when she was nervous and not being entirely truthful. She forced herself to stop and face Jerina. "I'd rather talk about you and why you have become insufferable lately."

Jerina thrust her hands toward her sister, and hurricane force winds blasted Kosa back several feet before Kosa diverted the gust upward. Jerina's glare would have scared some of the warrior trainees.

"Do not trifle with me." She stopped the wind when Rela roared.

Kosa cracked her neck back and forth. "You have been horrid to everyone, and you have been drifting off alone whenever you're not on duty."

Jerina sank down onto a fallen tree trunk. Her first reaction was to argue, but her sister's tone stopped her. "You should not exaggerate."

"Mother has noticed." Kosa had told their mother that some of the newer trainees had been goofing off instead of working hard, and that was the reason for Jerina's moodiness. It had only been half of the truth, but it had satisfied her.

Jerina pulled a stick from the log and picked at its bark. "I've been feeling a pull toward Colorado. I do not know why it's so strong after all these years."

Kosa sat down next to Jerina.

"I've been longing to travel." She knew it was the wrong thing to say as soon as it came out of her mouth.

"Tell me about the gifts and the man." Jerina narrowed her eyes at Kosa.

Kosa growled silently, cursing her big mouth. "You cannot let anyone know about this."

"Tell me at once." Jerina knew that a man had been leaving little things for her sister, but those gifts had become more frequent and more elaborate.

Kosa took a deep breath. It was time to explain everything to Jerina. Out of all the vila warriors, her sister was the only one who went out into the world and returned. Others had left, but only to find tragedy and heartache. Men were the downfall of the vila.

"I've been watching the humans in town. They fascinate me."

Jerina inhaled quickly. "Were you seen?"

"Not at first, but then I found a note pinned to the tree I take shelter behind."

"What did it say?" Jerina stood and began to pace the small clearing, scanning the area for anyone who might be listening to their conversation.

Kosa sighed wistfully. "It said, 'I thought only angels had the power to stop a man's heart.'"

Jerina rolled her eyes. "He was trying to charm you with pretty words."

"It was sweet." Kosa sighed again. "The next day, a white camellia was tied to the tree with another note. This one said, 'My destiny is in your hands.'"

"That sounds ominous." Jerina was starting to get worried. Something didn't feel right.

Kosa laughed. "That is what the flower means."

Jerina frowned at her. "How do you know that?"

Kosa picked up a stick and began to twirl it through her fingers. "I read the books in the village library."

Education was extremely important to the vila. Even though most never ventured into the world, all the women were required to master many subjects and numerous languages.

"I don't understand your obsession with books." Jerina had been more interested in world history, government relationships, politics, and the world wars that had been plaguing their forest.

"You have not read anything for pleasure. I would not care for books either if all I ever read about was warfare." Kosa could talk about this topic forever.

"I wish to hear more about him." Jerina always had to get her sister to focus on one topic at a time. "What happened next?"

Kosa groaned. "A few days later, he left me a gold silk scarf softer than a rabbit fur. This time the note said, 'No flower as delicate, no scarf as silken, no earthly creature as ethereal.'"

"Have you spoken to him?" Jerina couldn't believe her sister had been fooled by gifts and pretty words.

Kosa pulled a gold chain from under her tunic and twirled the star that was dangling from the chain. "Yes. Two days ago, I found this star necklace with another note. 'It is not in the stars to hold our destiny but in ourselves.'"

Jerina raised an eyebrow and frowned, not commenting.

"It's a quote from William Shakespeare." Kosa sighed. "I spun around, scanning the area, only to find luminous golden eyes focused on me. He nervously shifted from foot to foot and ran his hands through his sandy-colored hair. He was waiting for me to find his gift. We talked for hours."

"You can't be that foolish. Kosa, you didn't tell him who you are, did you?" Jerina's anger was making the wind whip around the trees. Rela roared her displeasure.

"Jerina! Stop! He's sweet and kind, and he loves nature." Kosa twirled around with her arms out. "I'm going to see him tonight. Come with me. You can meet him and see how wonderful he is."

Jerina grabbed Kosa's shoulders with both hands. "You are acting like you are in love. You must remember the vila curse!"

As vila warriors, Jerina and Kosa were sworn to protect their vila sisters and their forest. As descendants of wood nymphs and fae, the vila were volatile magical women who shunned men and society.

"I am not in love with him." *Yet*, Kosa thought. "I am having fun and *living* life. We are so isolated here. I want to see the world and experience what it is like to mingle with humans and other supernaturals. Travel, like you did. He said he would take me anywhere I want to go."

Jerina wiped her hands down her face and tried to calm her raging emotions. "You don't know him. He could be dangerous!" She was shouting and couldn't seem to stop.

"I knew you would react this way! That is why I didn't tell you!"

Rela growled loudly and moved to stand between the girls.

Jerina ran her hand across Rela's fur, trying to calm herself. Kosa was always too trusting.

"Please do not see him anymore." Jerina rubbed her temples. Vila hardly ever became ill, but their conversation was causing her head to ache. "If you want to leave here for a while, I will take you away."

"I knew you wanted to leave here, too. You should visit Tannor and his family." Kosa needed her sister to focus on something else.

"I've already told you that I don't remember where he lives. He told me that I wouldn't remember, but I didn't believe him. Everything is clear up to the train station in Colorado and from leaving on the train to come home. I have a vague recollection of a small town, but that's it."

"Then that is the perfect reason to go back there." Kosa crossed her fingers.

Jerina grasped the idea. "If I take you there, will you promise me you won't see that man again?" Jerina pressed. "It will only end in heartache for you. If he is your true love, he will die, and you will never be the same. You cannot risk your heart like that. Remember we're immortal."

Kosa kicked the dirt and uncrossed her fingers. Jerina never gave up on something once she set her mind on it. Her shoulders slumped. She didn't want to end her romance, but she knew it was probably for the best. "I need to tell him goodbye."

Even though Kosa had said what Jerina wanted to hear, her entire body filled with dread as she watched her sister disappear from view.

CHAPTER 2

"*J*erina! Jerina!"

Dropping down from her perch on a boulder looking out over the valley, Jerina landed in front of the novice warrior. "What's happened?"

The girl looked terrified, shifting from foot to foot. "Kosa is gone!"

"What do you mean, gone?" Jerina started jogging toward their village. The girl needed to run to keep up with her.

"I saw her get into a vehicle with a man!" The girl didn't follow Jerina into her house. Novices had to be invited inside their superiors' homes.

Jerina cursed. "I'm going to wallop her!"

She went directly to her weapons cabinet, pulling out several knives and sheaths. Jerina needed to be fully armed when she went hunting for her sister.

***

A storm had been brewing for three days, the same amount of time that Jerina had gone without any sign of her sister. She was going to have to tell the vila elders that Kosa was gone. She dreaded that conversation with their mother.

Jerina had been searching for Kosa for two weeks. At first, it had been a series of near misses, but it seemed as if something was keeping Kosa just out of reach. The Second World War had also made things difficult for Jerina. Traveling was more challenging and everyone was secretive with the German army everywhere around.

Jerina had tracked them through Poland, but had lost them. There hadn't been a sign of Kosa or her companion for the last few days. She was losing hope.

As leader of the vila warriors, she couldn't abandon her responsibilities. The vila were sworn to protect their forest and all who resided in it.

Her training duties and patrols could not be missed. When the vila had too much free time, they became bored and their more mischievous and malicious tendencies came out. Jerina needed to make sure her warriors focused their energies on strengthening their skills instead of causing trouble with humans. The elders had forbidden the vila from mingling with humans and revealing their secrets. Times had been changing too much, and magic was no longer something the humans believed in. Their secrets needed to be protected.

Jerina had been scheduling double shifts for all her warriors due to the increased war activity and fighting in the area. The vila had been successful at keeping soldiers from staying too long in their forest, but the war was all around them.

Twenty-five years before, Jerina and Kosa had stumbled upon two soldiers during the First World War. One of the soldiers was shot while saving squirrels and his selfless act caused Jerina to attempt to heal him. When that didn't work because the man had been fae and was shot with an iron bullet, Jerina vowed to help him return home to a mysterious town in Colorado.

Jerina smiled. She hadn't thought of the soldier Tannor in a while.

Pulling her sword from the leather sheath strapped to her back, she prepared to make a sweep of the area with her warriors. A flash of light and a disturbance in the air signaled the beginning of a portal. A supernatural was invading her forest.

Two young warriors circled the intruder. He quickly pulled a matched pair of short swords from inside his coat and parried the warriors' attacks. Jerina noticed that he was simply defending himself, not attacking. His moves were fluid, smoothly arcing the swords back and forth, dueling with the warriors.

Vila warriors were usually tall, five feet eight or more, but the man had several inches on the two warriors. Jerina guessed he was about six feet two. His muscles rippled across his back as he moved his swords, stretching his shirt across his shoulders.

Jerina had to admire his skill and energy. She should end the battle and rid her forest of the intruder, but she found herself mesmerized by him. Even though they were moving too quickly for Jerina to see his features clearly, she felt a familiarity from him. She needed to know more.

One of her warriors stumbled on a branch that the other vila had kicked up and was sliced across her arm by the man. She dropped back from the fight, clutching her wound. Jerina swore she heard him apologize to the warrior.

Before Jerina could engage in the fight, the man expediently disarmed the remaining warrior, flinging the sword into the air and catching it. He faced the two defeated warriors and bowed, swords out to the sides in a sweeping gesture.

Jerina stalked toward the tall, lithe man with golden brown hair, her sword ready to defend her warriors and her forest. The man sheathed his swords and drove the one he had claimed from the vila into the ground.

She stopped before reaching him, stunned at his display. She wasn't sure what to do next. Was he toying with them or was he trying to lead her into underestimating him?

"I've put my weapons away. Won't you?" The man sounded playful in a situation that should have been tense.

"Stop where you are!" Jerina called.

Jerina nodded to a warrior that was in the tree above the man. The vila tossed a net from above, covering him. Jerina approached quickly, placing the tip of her sword at the back of his neck. She nodded to her warriors to move away from her capture.

"Turn around slowly." Jerina poised to take him out if he made any kind of aggressive move, but he seemed much too relaxed to be a threat.

He took his time turning toward her.

"Is this slow enough for you? Have you gotten a good enough look?" he mocked, his hands in the pockets of his long coat.

She was tempted to prick him with her sword. He was dressed as a human, but most supernaturals dressed to fit into society. When he faced her, she dropped her sword with a gasp.

"Tannor?" Jerina motioned to her warriors. "Leave us." With confused expressions and backwards glances, they left the area.

When he realized that she wasn't going to run him through with her sword, he pulled the netting off him and tossed it aside.

The man tipped his head and appraised her, his cerulean eyes twinkling. "No. Tannor's my father. My name is Thane." He continued his survey, absorbing every detail. "You look exactly the way he described you, Jerina."

Jerina counted the time since she had seen Tannor. It had been more than twenty-five years. The baby that Tannor had been rushing home to meet was standing before her as an attractive and arrogant man. He may have been a man, but he was certainly not human. He radiated magic and power. If she remembered correctly, he would be half Seelie and half elf. "What are you doing here? We could have killed you! Why did you engage my warriors?"

Raising an eyebrow, he took his time answering. He couldn't believe he was standing before the famed vila warrior. "Your warriors attacked me first. I could have knocked them both out, but you should have been able to tell that I didn't want to hurt either one of them." His eyes drifted over her once more. "And I'm here because my father sent me with a message."

That got her attention. "What message?"

Jerina wanted to knock the smirk from his face. His father, Tannor, had not been that smug. She ignored his comment about beating her warriors. They would have to train harder. Both had newly completed their apprenticeships. Maybe they needed additional instruction.

"He said to tell you that Kosa was seen in town."

Jerina rushed him with her sword drawn, bringing it just under his chin. "You'd better tell me everything you know right now."

Thane hadn't reacted to her outburst or to the sword pressing into his skin. He was fairly confident that he could hold his own against her. His father had warned him of her temperament, but also of her amazing compassion. He knew that Jerina wouldn't hurt him. Well, he hoped she wouldn't hurt him badly.

"I can't explain it to you here. You're going to have to come with me."

"How do I know you're not lying?" Jerina wanted to believe him, but she didn't know the man before her.

Thane winked at her. "You'll have to trust me."

Jerina pressed the blade a little bit more, but not enough to draw blood. Yet. "Where did you see her, and who was she with?"

"I can't tell you. You have to see it for yourself." Thane shrugged one shoulder. He wasn't in a hurry.

Leaves began to swirl around them. Jerina clenched her fists, remembering that Tannor couldn't speak of his hometown. It was magically protected.

"Are you sure it was my sister?" She pulled the sword away and dropped her arm.

"Yes. He was positive it was Kosa." He needed her to come with him. His father had been concerned about whom Kosa was with.

Jerina wanted to rush off and get her sister, but she had responsibilities. It was troubling that Kosa had ended up in the town that seemed to be plaguing her thoughts for months. "You got here through a portal. If I go with you, can we use that to travel back?"

Maybe the trip wouldn't take very long.

Thane leaned against a tree, waiting for her to make the correct decision to accompany him home. "We can get close, but we can't breach the protective barrier."

Jerina nodded absently, mentally planning all the things she had to do before she left her warriors.

"Are you going to keep pointing that at me?" Thane motioned with his chin.

She hadn't realized she was aiming the sword at him again. Jerina slipped it behind her back and into its leather sheath. If Jerina stuck him, she might get blood on her sword and then she would have to spend time cleaning and polishing it.

"I need to get a few things before we can leave. I also need to put someone in charge until I return." Jerina started to jog toward her house.

Thane began to follow after her, but stopped when she swung around to face him.

"You need to stay here. You can't come into our village. Men are not allowed."

Thane raised an eyebrow, but moved closer to a tree and leaned on it with his arms folded across his muscular chest. "Should I get comfortable?"

Jerina didn't answer. She continued on her way, trying to ignore the eyes she felt trailing her until the path curved from view.

CHAPTER 3

"We're going to be a couple of miles from town. I left a car there so we don't have to walk in." Thane muttered a few words and waved his hand. A shimmering portal opened in the air between a couple of trees.

Jerina shifted her small leather bag higher on her shoulder and followed Thane, pausing only slightly to examine the flickering disturbance. She had never traveled by portal before, but she knew a few of the vila elders had used them.

Thane stepped into the portal but turned once on the other side, waiting for her to step through.

Jerina hesitated, suddenly feeling as if her life was about to change once again.

"Are you coming?" Thane called.

With a groan, she stepped through to a wooded area along a quiet mountain road. She saw Thane head toward a cream-colored vehicle with large black tires with white rings along the silver wheels. He told her they were called white wall tires. Jerina wondered where the top of the vehicle was.

"Isn't she swell?" Thane asked, running his hand over the polished fender.

"She?" Jerina glanced around, looking for a female.

Thane grinned. "My car."

"You call your car a she?" Jerina frowned at him.

Thane shrugged, but pulled open the door for Jerina to slip inside. "It's a Delahaye 135 convertible."

She sank into the soft red leather seats and ran her hand over the matching dashboard. The last car she had been in was so different from this one. Nowhere near as luxurious. Glancing behind her, she was surprised that there was not another bench for sitting.

Jerina considered him, confused by his reference to the car. Shaking her head, she asked, "Are we going?"

Thane started the vehicle with a roar and pulled out onto the road. Jerina loved the way her hair blew out from behind her as the car moved faster. She could get used to traveling like this. The wind was a little cold on her face, but it was thrilling.

The view was amazing and somewhat familiar. She had loved the snow-covered mountains before. They surrounded the valley on all sides, protecting the town and hiding it away from the world. It reminded her a little of her mountains in Poland.

After several moments, Jerina felt a pressure building around them and a sudden intense headache. Her skin tingled and itched from the cascade of magic drowning her as they crossed the barrier. Jerina grabbed her head with both hands and tried to breathe deeply to get past the pain.

Thane slowed the car to a stop and turned toward her, concerned. "Are you feeling poorly?" He reached out and cupped her cheek. "Supernaturals don't usually react that strongly to the wards." He brought his hands up to her temples and began to massage slow circles.

She didn't say anything, just concentrated on breathing. When the ache started to recede, she leaned away from him.

Thane smirked as he wiggled his fingers. "I knew that would make you feel better."

Jerina glared at him, turning to face the front of the vehicle with her hands fisted. One minute he was being nice and then he had to open his mouth.

Thane chuckled and put the car in drive once more. They drove for a few minutes through the woods and passed by a stone sign with big, bold metal letters. "Welcome to Havenwood Falls, Jerina."

Her head began to ache again, but differently. Flashes of things and bits of memories scattered through her mind, but nothing fit together. She blinked a few times to clear her head, but the partial scenes continued to swirl.

Thane watched Jerina closely. "The memories from your time here before will come back. Sometimes they come back all at once, but with others, it might only be pieces. Don't try to focus on the memories too much. It will only make your head hurt more."

Jerina nodded and rested her head against the seat. She wasn't used to the rush of magic she felt from this town. It was much stronger here than in her forest. "Are you taking me to Kosa?'

"No. We're stopping at my parents' house first." He continued quickly when she looked like she was going to argue. "They made me promise I would bring you there before we do anything."

"Aspen." Jerina smiled slightly. "Your mother's name is Aspen."

Thane nodded. "Yes. Your memories are returning already. It usually takes a little longer."

They drove through a quaint town with Victorian-style homes and huge shady trees that lined the road on both sides. Jerina was happy when Thane slowed down so she could absorb everything they drove past.

She remembered a little bit of the town square, but didn't recollect the majestic gazebo in the center. It was someplace she would like to explore more. The ice cream shop had her sitting up on her seat. She knew that she had been there before and hoped to return once again.

"I had ice cream there!" Jerina pointed to the Charms Soda Shoppe.

"Their sundaes are keen." Thane watched her wide-eyed excitement with amusement.

Jerina's forehead crinkled, not understanding.

Thane gave her a lopsided grin. "The sundaes are really good."

After a couple of quick turns, they stopped in front of a large cottage with a wraparound porch. A swing and several hanging plants decorated the front of the house.

Thane hopped out of the vehicle and approached her side. She remained in her seat with her hand on the door handle.

"I didn't think vila were afraid of anything." Thane opened her door, but she stood and pushed by him.

She frowned when she heard his mocking chuckle. Her response was cut off by the front door opening and a couple walking outside.

"Jerina!" Aspen called as she hurried to the steps and down the walkway. "It's so good to see you!" A tall woman with dark brown hair wrapped her thin arms around Jerina and hugged her tightly.

Jerina pulled back. "Hello, Aspen."

A brilliant smile lit her face. "You remember me?"

"A little. My memories are coming back in pieces." Jerina glanced toward the porch and saw Tannor standing next to Thane. They looked amazingly similar.

Jerina knew that Tannor and Aspen were nearly immortal, so she hadn't expected them to look different, but it was still a slight shock.

Their clothes were the most different. Aspen had on an A-line dress that reached below her knees with buttons running down the length. It was in a dark blue color with tiny flowers printed on it. Tannor was in navy trousers and a light blue button-down shirt. He had his sleeves rolled up.

Tannor bounded down the stairs and scooped Jerina up in a tight embrace. "I'm happy to see you. Please come inside."

They all filtered into the house and took seats in the living room that was just off the foyer to the left. Jerina scanned the inside of the house, trying to remember it from the last time she had visited, but nothing triggered any memories.

Thane watched his parents and Jerina speak excitedly with each other, catching up on many things that had happened over the years since Jerina had last been in town. He had heard the stories before, but he was intrigued to hear about them from Jerina.

"I'm sorry your forest has soldiers in it again." Tannor put his arm across the back of his chair. "At least you didn't have to bring a wounded officer home to his pregnant wife."

Jerina smiled. "I was happy to help you return to Aspen."

Jerina had witnessed Tannor return a couple of baby squirrels to their nest and get shot when World War I had entered her forest. She had been moved by his selfless act and tried to heal him, only his fae nature had prevented him from fully recovering from the iron bullet.

Aspen put her hand on her husband's knee and addressed her son. "If it wasn't for Jerina, we wouldn't have your father with us. I'm so thankful for her."

Tannorsmoothed his wife's hair. "Jerina spent Christmas with us and even saved the Caroling in the Square that year. A strong storm had rolled in, and she blew it over the mountains so we could continue the night."

Jerina laughed. "I had forgotten about that."

Thane loved watching how happy his parents were with each other. He wanted to have a relationship like theirs someday.

Their stories turned to things that had happened during their time apart. Thane was chagrined that many of the stories featured some of his more embarrassing antics.

Aspen excused herself for a few moments and returned with tea and pastries that she set on the coffee table.

Tannor sat forward with his forearms on his knees. "Jerina, I'm thrilled you're here in Havenwood Falls, but I know you aren't here for pleasure."

Jerina leaned back in her seat and gave Tannor her attention. "Kosa disappeared a few weeks ago. She had been receiving gifts from a man and spent time with him. I thought I had talked her into ending their acquaintance, but she ran off with him instead."

Tannor clasped his hands in front of him. "Kosa is with Perun. Do you remember him from your time here? He was the mage from the Green Coven whom you met at the Christmas Caroling in the Square."

"The leech who leered at me?" Jerina tried to remember Perun clearly, but she was only getting images.

Aspen tried to stifle a laugh. "He's the one I told you not to kill, because it would have turned the snow red."

Thane had been quietly listening up until then. "You were going to kill Perun? I would have liked to see that."

He had seen the trouble Perun caused, knowing he would never be punished for any of it. That was part of the reason Thane honed his fighting skills. He wanted to protect his family and Havenwood Falls.

Jerina scrunched her nose. "How would he and Kosa end up together?"

Tannor frowned and rubbed the back of his neck. "I have a suspicion, but I'm not sure."

"What is this suspicion?"

Aspen gave her husband an encouraging nod.

"When you left, Perun asked dozens of questions about you and the vila. He was especially interested in where we met." Tannor rubbed his neck again, but continued quickly when Jerina opened her mouth to speak. "I would never betray you, Jerina."

Jerina smiled kindly. "I know you would not." She began to fidget with the leather string on the top of her knee boots. "Why was he so interested in me? We keep to ourselves."

Tannor rubbed the back of his neck, massaging the tension that was building there. "Not much is known about the vila. That makes some people want to discover more. I think Perun was intrigued by your strength and power."

Jerina frowned at him. "Wasn't Perun a mage?"

Thane leaned against the wall next to the fireplace. "He's not a strong one. He has always wanted more power and a higher status in the Green Coven. Ada is currently the head of the Green Coven, but Perun has always wanted the position."

Jerina scrunched up her nose, not making the connection. "I do not understand what that has to do with Kosa or me."

Thane chuckled. "He needs more power to control the coven. Only the strongest lead them. Perun has ambition, but not the magic he needs."

Jerina turned white, and her eyes grew into large saucers.

Aspen moved next to Jerina and patted her arm. "I don't think he would hurt her. He can be charming when he wants to be."

Jerina didn't want to say her thoughts out loud for fear they might be true. "Would you please excuse me for a moment?"

Without waiting for them to answer, she fled to the front porch.

He wants more magic and power. He couldn't know. It's not something many people know about. Closing her eyes, she prayed that Perun hadn't discovered their weakness. *This could be worse than I thought.*

Aspen stepped outside. "What's the matter, Jerina?"

Jerina whipped around, startled. She usually didn't get caught unaware. "I'm worried about Kosa."

"Let's go back inside and get ready to leave. I'm sure Tannor and Thane would love to walk us into town so we can meet with the Court of the Sun and the Moon. All supernaturals must register with the Court within twenty-four hours of coming to Havenwood Falls," Aspen reminded her. "We should take care of that matter before we do anything else."

Jerina nodded, a few more memories flooding back. "I had to wear a medallion the last time I was here."

Aspen motioned toward the door. "They don't use those anymore. Now they give visitors a temporary tattoo infused with a little magic." Aspen pulled the collar of her dress away from her neck and pushed her hair back. "It doesn't have to be large, just something small. They usually mean something to the person wearing it. Since I'm a resident, mine is permanent."

Jerina leaned closer and saw a delicate flower with a butterfly perched on the top of it. "Do I get to choose my design?"

Aspen nodded. "Yes. Do you know what you would select?"

Jerina thought for a moment. "A snowflake with wind around it."

Jerina stepped inside and stopped abruptly when she heard Thane's voice.

"After all the stories about how fierce she was and how powerful, I'm not very impressed. I walked right into her forest and took down two of her warriors. I probably could have slung her over my shoulder and carted her back here." Thane's back was toward the door, so she didn't think he had seen her walk inside the house.

Tannor watched his son fly through the air and land in a heap on the floor against the wall across the room. Jerina stood over him with her sword pressed into his neck once again.

"You need some new moves. You've already tried this one out," Thane mocked, seemingly unconcerned.

Tannor moved closer. "Let him up."

Jerina glanced over her shoulder at Aspen and Tannor. Neither of them seemed too worried about their son. She took a step back, but decided not to sheath her sword yet. "I don't have time for your games. I need to find my sister."

Aspen nudged Tannor with her shoulder. "Jerina, we know you want to find Kosa, but you need to be a little patient. First, we need to get you registered and settled."

Jerina scrunched her forehead. "Settled? I can't stay. I have duties at home."

Aspen approached her carefully. Jerina had raised her sword absently. "You can't barge into the Green Coven and demand your sister. Doing it that way will not end well."

"What do you suggest?" Jerina didn't want to waste time, but she also didn't want to scare her sister into leaving town.

"We can walk to the town square, take care of business, and come back here to form a plan." Tannor knew that Jerina wouldn't want to wait.

Jerina slid her sword back in place and started for the door, but

Aspen stopped her. "You might want to change clothes so that you don't stick out in town."

Jerina glanced down at her soft leather pants tucked into her worn boots. Both were handmade by one of the vila novices and probably not what human women wore. They probably didn't have leather vests and swords strapped to their backs either. Jerina used to wear long dresses, but since her trip to Havenwood Falls the last time, she had adopted wearing pants.

"Thank you, Aspen. I hadn't thought about my appearance." Jerina walked over to the coffee table and picked up a magazine. She flipped through a few pages until she opened to a young woman in a navy-blue dress that buttoned up the front and reached mid-calf. She loved the open collar, puffed shoulders and three-quarter sleeves.

With a snap of her fingers, she was wearing the dress, along with low kitten heels and a wide-brimmed hat. She even turned her leather bag into the same dark blue clutch purse the model had.

"How is this?" Jerina caught Thane's appraising stare, but he quickly looked away.

Jerina wanted to bring her sword, but didn't think a back holster would be appropriate for town. She twirled it in her hand, and it shrunk down to fit into her purse.

"You look spiffy!" Aspen beamed. "Let me get my hat and handbag, and we can be on our way."

CHAPTER 4

$\mathcal{T}$he walk to the town square was uncomfortable and tense. Aspen and Tannor stayed in front of Jerina and Thane. The couple linked arms and whispered quietly to each other every few minutes.

Thane and Jerina kept a few feet between each other in painful silence. Neither would back down from their stubbornness. Aspen acted as their tour guide, pointing out things as they passed. Some of it Jerina recognized, but most of it was new. Things had changed so much since she had been there last.

The courthouse was the same as she remembered and so was the way they had to enter the Court of the Sun and the Moon. The front doors of City Hall were for the humans; the rear door that led down to the basement was for the supernaturals. That was the door they used.

Sheriff Ric Kasun greeted them before they could pass the threshold. "Come in. I want to speak with you before you meet with Saundra."

He stepped aside, allowing them entrance, but stood stiffly, his muscles tense and ready to act.

Aspen and Tannor shared a glance, but didn't say anything.

Thane passed the group and flopped down in a seat next to the door.

Sheriff Kasun didn't even glance at Thane. He focused on Jerina. "I'm warning you, I will not stand for any kind of trouble from you. I have already been warned that you are here to force your sister to return home with you. I will not tolerate kidnapping or coercion."

"Pardon?" Jerina couldn't believe what she was hearing. "She is *my* sister and a vila warrior under my command!"

"You're not in your forest any longer. This is Havenwood Falls. We have our own governing body and our own laws. You either abide by them or you will be escorted out of here."

Papers on the desk began to blow across the room, and Aspen's hair lifted from her shoulders.

Sheriff Kasun's gaze narrowed. "Do you want to leave now?"

Tannor stepped next to Jerina, placing a hand on her shoulder and nudging her. "Jerina was caught off guard. She won't cause any trouble."

Jerina's chest heaved. She wanted to blast the sheriff into the next state. She opened her mouth, but Tannor squeezed her shoulder to get her to stop.

"Well?" Sheriff Kasun asked.

"No. I'm not going anywhere without my sister. I'll follow your laws."

He gave her a skeptical look. "I'm not convinced."

"Neither am I," a voice from the hallway called.

Jerina saw an elegant woman in a dark business suit glide into the room. Her hair was tinged with silver streaks that made her look distinguished and polished, not aging. This was a powerful woman. Jerina remembered a little bit about her from her visit before, but not much.

"Hello, Jerina. It's been quite some time. I don't know if you remember me. I'm Saundra Beaumont." She stuck her hand out for Jerina to shake.

Jerina stared at the hand in front of her for a few seconds, before reluctantly clasping it. "My memory is returning in pieces, but I do remember you a little."

Saundra raised an eyebrow. "Good. Then you will remember that I don't play around."

Saundra's hair lifted momentarily, but Jerina managed to make it stop before she got herself kicked out. "Neither do I."

Exhaling with distaste, Saundra moved closer to Jerina. "We don't know you very well, and we don't trust you yet. Your sister is staying with a resident of town and has not caused any trouble since her arrival. She expressed a fear of you."

Jerina made a strangled sound, but Saundra continued.

"We do not get involved in family squabbles unless it becomes a danger to Havenwood Falls."

Jerina folded her arms across her chest, seething and afraid to respond. The only thing she could think to do would be to send everyone flailing away from her with a burst of wind.

Tannor moved closer. "I can vouch for her."

Sheriff Kasun shook his head. "She needs an escort while in town. I don't have a deputy to spare right now. We are short-staffed."

Jerina's face turned red, and her fists clenched. She was having difficulty controlling her emotions. "I don't need an escort."

Saundra eyed her. "Unfortunately, that is the only way you can stay in town."

"No."

Jerina was ready to argue more, but surprisingly, Thane stood up. "I can babysit the vila while she's here."

Aspen's eyes lit up. "I think that is a brilliant idea!"

"Absolutely not!" Jerina would rather spend time with the sheriff and all his deputies.

"Are you sure you want to take on this responsibility?" Saundra asked Thane.

Yawning and stretching his arms out in what appeared to be boredom, Thane shrugged one shoulder.

Saundra took that as confirmation. "It's settled. Jerina will not be permitted to remain in town without Thane being at her side." She faced an irate Jerina. "If you disregard our dictate, you will be banned from town."

~

Jerina was in a daze. Somehow, she managed to keep her mouth closed long enough for her temporary tattoo to be placed on her shoulder and for Aspen and Tannor to suggest that she stay at Whisper Falls Inn since it was closer to Thane's house. Saundra and Sheriff Kasun both agreed to the location. Jerina thought they liked the idea of more people watching her.

Thane held the door for Jerina to step out into the afternoon sunshine. She turned her face up to the warmth and soaked in the renewing energy. She had no idea how she had ended up in such a mess, and now she had to spend time with an arrogant ass.

Thane grasped her elbow to lead her toward a tall Victorian mansion on the corner facing town square. "Come on. I'll take you to Whisper Falls Inn."

Jerina could only nod from the numbness spreading through her body.

They strolled past the gazebo and the couples who were taking advantage of its shade. She wondered if she would ever be as carefree as they appeared to be.

Thane noticed her eyes watching the people meander around the square and the longing look in Jerina's eyes. "Are you too tired to continue on to the inn? We can rest, if you require it."

Jerina kicked him in the shin and stomped toward their destination. She was drawn to the inn's gingerbread trim and majestic turrets. It reminded her of the castles in the books Kosa would read. That thought made her feel sick. Her sister didn't want to see her and was afraid of her?

"Jerina?" Thane's mocking tone had changed to concern.

"We should continue."

As soon as the stepped onto the wraparound porch, the door

opened, and a man and woman stepped outside. They moved so smoothly that Jerina could tell that they were otherworldly, but wasn't sure which type of supernatural they were. Their grace and poise showed in their every motion.

Thane smiled at the couple. "Good day to you, Mihail, Irina. I've brought you a guest. This is Jerina Ventus. She will be staying with us for a few days."

Thane enjoyed spending time with the Petrans. Mihail had helped Thane develop his fighting skills and taught him how to win against supernaturals with superior speed.

"Jerina, this is Mihail and Irina Petran. They own Whisper Falls Inn."

Jerina recovered her manners and greeted the couple.

Mihail reached out to shake her hand. "Saundra called to let us know you would be arriving. It's a pleasure to meet you. I hope you enjoy your stay here with us."

He shared a glance with Thane that Jerina couldn't interpret, but she dismissed it. There had been too many weird things happening for her to worry about another odd look. "It's nice meeting you."

Irina reached out toward Jerina. "I'll show you to your room." She scanned the area. "Do you have any luggage?"

Jerina knew that it must look odd to be traveling without a suitcase. "No. I didn't bring much with me."

Irina smiled caringly, her gray-green eyes sparkling. "It's all right. I have a few things that past guests have left behind. We can also walk into town to one of the shops to get some things you might need."

Jerina felt comfortable for the first time since arriving at Havenwood Falls. "Thank you."

Thane called after them. "I'll be back for dinner!"

Jerina could hear his laughter all the way inside.

Irina patted her hand. "Things are not always as they seem. Don't let first impressions guide you down the wrong path."

Jerina scrunched her nose. "I don't understand."

"I know you don't now, but you will. Havenwood Falls is a magical place. Remember that." Irina stopped before closing Jerina inside her room. "We serve dinner at six. Madam Luiza does not like tardy guests."

"I'll make sure that I arrive early. I appreciate your kindness." Jerina paced around her spacious room, not focusing on any of the elegant but comfortable furnishings. She was restless and basically on house arrest for the next hour before Thane would return for dinner. She didn't know how she was going to deal with him being around her so much.

Jerina flopped down on the soft bed and ran her hand over the cover. She had never slept on anything so fluffy. The bed she had at home was more functional and stiff than anything.

She glanced at the pale yellow flowers on the wallpaper and bedcoverings, which gave the room a springtime feel. "Ughhh," she groaned.

She couldn't go anywhere without Thane, but maybe she could explore the inn. Jerina followed the aroma of freshly baked bread and found a woman with dark brown hair cutting vegetables at a large wood table that looked well-used.

"Hello, Jerina. I'm Madame Luiza."

"Uhh, hi. I uh . . ."

"There is a huge pile of potatoes that need peeling."

Relieved at having something to do, Jerina hurried to the sink to wash her hands and get to work. "I didn't mean to be a bother."

"I'm happy for the company."

Jerina smiled as she picked up her first potato.

They chatted about the town and the tourist attractions that everyone should see while visiting. She didn't remember having a nicer time working.

Thane hurried back to his parents' home. He needed to speak with his father before meeting Jerina for dinner.

He jogged up the street, jumped over the white picket fence, and leaped onto the porch. Tannor was waiting for him in a wicker chair.

"Are the Petrans looking after her?" Tannor asked.

Thane laughed. "I don't think anyone needs to look after her."

Tannor leaned back and stretched his long legs in front of him. "She's a fierce warrior, but she's also been completely sheltered her entire life. I remember how wide-eyed she was when she experienced everything for the first time."

Thane took a seat next to his father. "You're worried about her?"

"Yes. I'm afraid that she will relinquish her freedom to join her sister." Tannor rubbed the back of his head. "She's going to give you a hard time."

Thane grinned. "I'm looking forward to it." He lost his smile when his father scowled at him.

"If Perun gets control of them both, we are all in danger. There could be no stopping him." Tannor sat up and stared at his son.

"I'm not going to let Perun get Jerina, and I will save Kosa." Thane stood from his chair. "I need to change for dinner. I'll stop by later."

"You're covered in flour." Thane popped his head inside the kitchen.

"I see you left her here in a hurry. Were you afraid I would get you to help too?" Madame Luiza teased.

"No, ma'am. I had a few things to do before dinner."

Jerina noticed how good he looked in his dark gray pinstriped suit with a matching vest. Her dress was covered in flour and a few wet spots.

Madam Luiza walked over to her. "Shoo. Go get ready for dinner. I'm sure Thane will help with setting the dining room."

Thane sighed, and Jerina hurried off to her room. She still didn't have any changes of clothes with her, so she had to use magic again. Surprisingly, she had to concentrate on her magic for it to come forth. She wondered if the tattoo was hindering the flow. Dismissing that thought, she busied herself with fixing her appearance.

Ten minutes later, Jerina jogged down the stairs toward the dining room but almost stumbled on the last step. She hadn't realized Thane was waiting at the bottom for her. She stopped when she noticed his approving appraisal.

Thane inclined his head and held out his arm for her. "Truce?"

She wasn't sure what to do, so she hesitated.

He took her pause as a rejection of his peace offering. "Or not."

He dropped his arm and spun around. Jerina hastily caught up with him and linked her arm around his. He stiffened at first, but then relaxed and smiled down at her.

"You look lovely." He winked at her when her eyes grew large.

"Tha-thank you," she stumbled, not expecting the compliment. Jerina wanted to keep up the conversation, so she searched for a safe topic. "Did Madame Luiza ask for your assistance?"

He chuckled. "Of course she did." He turned a corner and led her into the dining room. "It wasn't too bad. She let me snitch a cookie from the oven."

"I have a feeling it isn't the first time that's happened."

Thane grinned devilishly. "I can't help it if women want to give me treats."

He harnessed his best manners and pulled out her chair for her and then circled the small table to sit across from her. He selected a table by the windows, away from the rest of the room. He wanted a little privacy with her.

Jerina wasn't used to formal dining, so she sat quietly with her hands in her lap. They usually sat around a fire in the center of the village back home. They had houses now, but they still held on to past traditions.

Madame Luiza stopped by her place at the table. "Don't you worry yourself. We're not fancy around here. Just enjoy the food you helped me make."

She glanced around at the other guests, but no one seemed to be paying attention to her. She sighed with relief.

Thane was waiting for more sparks from Jerina. She didn't seem to be the shy type of woman, so her quietness was worrisome. He twirled the wine in his glass. It was a particularly flavorful vintage from the Stone Falls Winery.

"You're staring at me like you're waiting for something to happen." Jerina dug into her mashed potatoes. They were creamy and buttery and delicious.

"I am. You're too quiet and reserved. It's like a volcano just waiting to erupt or the calm before the hurricane."

She tilted her head and studied him. "I could create a hurricane."

"Madame Luiza would be upset if you interrupted dinner." Thane liked teasing her. Her cheeks turned pink, and her eyes brightened. It was a good look for her. "Have you ever made a hurricane?"

She shook her head. "No, but I caused a massive blizzard when I was young. It's still spoken about."

"How much snow?"

She grinned. "About forty inches. I threw a bit of a tantrum, and the elders had difficulty trying to put a stop to it."

Thane gazed at her quizzically. "Don't all vila have power over the weather?"

"Yes, but some are stronger than others." Jerina didn't want to seem like she was bragging, but she had more control and power over the weather than all the other vila.

"You are the strongest." It was a statement. He could tell by her confidence.

Jerina shrugged with a small smile and took a sip of the red wine. She hadn't noticed that Thane had poured it for her. Jerina scanned the room over the rim of her glass. No one was looking her way, so she felt comfortable to be more herself. With a sparkle in her eye, she dug into her baked chicken and roasted vegetables.

"Do you like the wine?" Thane asked.

"Yes. It's different from what we have back home, but I like the mild taste." Jerina was used to heavier wines.

"It's from the Blackstones' winery. They have been making wine for a very long time here in Havenwood Falls." Thane hoped to take her on a tour of the town and would be sure to stop there.

"Would you like to take a walk around the square? It's a beautiful night," Thane asked when dinner was finished. He was shocked to have enjoyed himself as much as he had. "You don't need a coat."

Jerina glanced around the lobby of the inn, trying to decide. She had nothing to do except return to her empty room. Normally, she could patrol or train with some of her warriors, but those were not options. Thane had been charming all through dinner, so she didn't mind continuing the evening in his company. "Yes. I would love to see how much things have changed since the last time I was here."

CHAPTER 5

Thane draped his coat over her shoulders. He offered his arm to her, and this time, she accepted without a second thought.

As soon as they stepped off the porch, Jerina tipped her head up to look at the sky. She waved her hand, and the clouds cleared so that they could see the stars.

"That's a handy trick." Thane loved stargazing. His mother had taught him about the constellations and the stories people had created about them. It was always something he enjoyed.

Changing the clouds had been easy for Jerina. She wasn't sure why her other magic was sluggish, but at least she could still change the weather without any problems. "It can be. Some vila use their powers to toy with humans or to destroy things. They rage against their lot in life."

Thane led her to the gazebo so they could people-watch and continue their conversation. He wanted to hear anything she was willing to tell him. He didn't know much about vila. No one did.

"Many people are not happy with their life, but they don't lash out." Thane sat on the bench inside the gazebo and stretched his legs out in front of him.

Lots of people were strolling around the square, mingling and enjoying the night. Jerina took everything in, learning about the world once again. "Vila are different. All vila are women."

Thane interrupted. "Well, that explains it."

She caught on to his sarcasm. "Funny. There are no men in our lives or in our village."

"None?"

"No. There are none. Anyway, some are born vila, like Kosa and me, but some are created."

That got Thane's attention. "Created? Are you saying they are made? And how are vila born without men?"

"Vila might not live with men or settle down with a male, but that doesn't stop them from taking pleasure when it suits." Jerina knew she shouldn't have brought up men. There were some things she didn't want to discuss with him or anyone.

"That's interesting. So, whenever the mood strikes, you pick the first man you see?" Thane wiggled his eyebrows.

"No. Not talking about that." Jerina groaned. He was not going to let that go.

Thane wanted to ask her more about men, but he was afraid she would shut down and not be so open with him. He felt an uncontrollable need to know more. "Continue. The vila select the first man that piques their interest and then have little baby vila." He paused in thought. "What happens to any boys born?"

"Vila only have girls."

"Hmmm."

Jerina rolled her eyes. "Other vila are not born and grow through life. Young women who are killed while engaged or before they are married sometimes have the choice to be turned into a vila or to cross over to the afterlife. Some of them select becoming a vila for revenge."

"That's a scary thought." Thane could imagine the damage a scorned woman could create. "None of the vila ever want to settle down with a man? Don't any of you want to have a family?"

Jerina knew these questions were coming and prepared to answer him, but another couple entered the gazebo.

The woman's blond head was leaning on the man's shoulder while his arm was around her back, holding her close. Their heads were so close together, she couldn't see their faces.

Jerina wondered what that would feel like, then quickly dismissed the thought. It was too dangerous. Thane stiffened next to her, setting her on alert. She scanned the area for danger, but didn't see any. He seemed to be staring at the couple that just joined them.

Thane took her hand and pulled her to her feet. He hadn't expected this to happen and wasn't prepared for the fallout. He only prayed that not too much damage would occur and that Jerina wouldn't break Havenwood Falls' laws by revealing her magic.

He knew the moment Jerina discovered the identity of the couple before them. The clouds began to gather in the sky, and a distant thunder roared. Thane squeezed her hand to try to keep her calm.

"Kosa!" Jerina shouted. "What are you doing? Why are you here? With him?"

Kosa's eyes became saucers as she faced her sister, but she didn't speak.

"Why, Jerina, how lovely to see you," Perun crooned. He tightened his hold on Kosa, who stood just a couple of inches shorter than him.

"Sister, have you nothing to say?" Jerina couldn't believe Kosa was simply standing there mute.

Kosa lifted beseeching eyes to Perun, but didn't answer Jerina. His light brown hair blew in the breeze Jerina was creating.

Thunder grew closer and louder. Jerina switched her heated stare to Perun. His hazel eyes were filled with malice. "What have you done to her?"

Perun sneered. "You'd better watch yourself, vila. Too many weather changes will cause the humans to wonder what is happening. You wouldn't want to get yourself banned from town."

As Jerina's rage intensified, so did the weather. Thane grabbed both of her shoulders and turned her toward him. "Do you want to save your sister?" Thane glanced to Perun. "I'll get her out of here so you can enjoy your night."

Perun snickered. "Babysitting duty? There are ways of controlling her. Let me know if she gives you any trouble, and I'll let you in on the secret."

Jerina threw her hands toward Perun, but Thane encircled her with a shield, cutting her off from everything.

"I'd advise you to continue your night elsewhere, my friend. She's volatile tonight," Thane called out as he struggled to contain Jerina's magic.

He wished he could open a portal to whisk her away from there, but there were too many humans around. He knew that as soon as he released her, power would explode from her. Thane hoped he could calm her down before that happened. The Court of the Sun and the Moon would have a difficult time containing something like that.

Perun led Kosa away, laughing loudly and watching Jerina with calculating eyes.

Thane began to shake slightly from the force of magic she was pushing outward. The skies had settled, but he knew a torrential storm would rage once she was fully unleashed. He stepped close to her, nearly touching. He bent his head toward her so that he could whisper in her ear. He didn't want anyone to overhear.

"If you wield your power here, you will never save your sister. They will ban you from this town, and she will be lost to you forever. Perun will make sure you never get to her."

Jerina's eyes were blazing fire, and Thane didn't know if he was getting through to her. "You need to calm down so I can release you. I can't do that until I know you won't lose control. I can feel your powers pulsating."

She took a deep breath, and he could feel her power lessen.

"That's it. I can't help you and hold your powers back at the same time." Thane's tone was soft and soothing, much like someone speaking to something wild and untamed.

"He's controlling her!" Jerina shouted. She couldn't get her emotions under control. She had thought her sister was acting out over a man she wanted to be with. Jerina never considered that her sister would be under his complete control.

"Yes. But you can't do anything about that until you let the power go." Thane hoped he could get her to listen to him.

Jerina closed her eyes and centered her power, drawing it into herself. Even though the jerk was going to turn her into the sheriff, she knew he was right. She couldn't save her sister if she was kicked out.

Several deep breaths later, she opened her eyes and focused on Thane. "Are you going to turn me in now?"

Thane pulled back some of his shield to test her. He felt her power withdraw, but he knew she could throw it back out instantaneously. "No."

"How can I trust you?"

"You don't have a choice. You have to trust someone." Thane wanted to earn her trust, but they didn't have time.

Jerina shook her head, wanting to deny him. Her power was starting to build again, so she forced it back. She hadn't had this kind of trouble since she was a teen, many years ago.

"I know you don't think so, but I'm here to help you. Just give me the opportunity to explain everything." Thane ran a hand through his hair. "Please."

Jerina exhaled and dropped her power completely. "I'll listen."

"This would be considered a bribe," Jerina mumbled as she stuffed another heaping spoonful of ice cream sundae into her mouth. A dribble of chocolate syrup escaped and slid down her chin.

"Is it working?" Thane was too interested in watching her devour her dessert to pay any attention to his own. He was glad he remembered his dad mentioning that Jerina loved ice cream. The Charms Soda Shoppe was the perfect place to take her.

Jerina glanced up from her treat to see Thane staring at her.

Embarrassed, she wiped her mouth and chin and tried to eat a little more politely. "You're watching me eat. Stop."

"I can't. It's cute. I don't remember ever being that excited about food before." Thane leaned over the table, getting closer to her. They were sitting in a corner booth, facing the front of the shop. Jerina had walked up and down every aisle in the place before they were seated. She loved all of the tourist gifts and pharmaceuticals that she didn't have at home.

Jerina shrugged. "We don't have ice cream or candy at home."

Thane's eyebrows shot up. "You don't have dessert?"

"We do, but nothing like this. Mostly a type of flat cake or tarts." Jerina finished her sundae and contemplated licking the bowl but figured that might be pushing things.

"Want to finish our walk?" Thane asked, sliding his unfinished sundae away from him.

"I want some answers."

Thane chuckled. "I'm going to give you some. I thought you might be in a better listening mood after this." He stood and offered her his hand.

"So, it *was* a bribe."

"I never said it wasn't." Thane walked her around the town square and toward Whisper Falls Inn. He knew they could spend time on the back porch without too many people milling about.

Traffic was getting lighter, and many people had returned home, so they didn't have to stop to greet anyone on their way back to the inn. He was not in the mood to share her with anyone.

Jerina spotted the large wooden swing that was covered with soft pillows. She flopped down, causing it to flow backward before swinging forward again.

"No porch swings at home either?" Thane found himself eager to see what she would enjoy next.

Jerina dropped her foot to stop her momentum. "No. But some of the younger girls have swings to play with before they start their warrior training."

Thane sat next to her and pushed them forward to start the motion again.

"Why are you being nice to me now? You haven't been most of the day." Jerina needed to understand this complicated man.

"What, my charm hasn't been up to your standards?" Thane laughed, but stopped abruptly. Deputy Conall Kasun, Sheriff Kasun's son, stepped out of the darkness and onto the walkway leading to the back porch.

"You need to go inside for the night. You can't leave the inn. The Petrans will watch you until I come back tomorrow." Thane stood and pulled her roughly to her feet.

Jerina had no idea what had just happened. One minute he was being sweet, and the next he was rudely ordering her around. Folding her arms across her chest, she stood her ground when Thane tried to guide her inside. She stomped her foot down hard on his toe and spun around to leave the porch. She froze in place when she noticed they had company.

"Is everything okay, Thane? I was checking up on our new guest." Conall moved into the porch light, but didn't climb the steps.

Thane plastered on a fake smile. "Hello, Conall. Thanks for stopping by. I was just saying farewell."

Conall swung his attention to the vila. "You need to stay here at the inn and not wander around by yourself."

Jerina growled low. She was getting really tired of everyone thinking she was a criminal. "I'm not a *dog*."

She knew he was a wolf shifter and couldn't resist the dig.

Conall stepped closer. "What did you say?"

Jerina smiled sweetly. "I said, I'm not *alone*. There are many people who watch over me."

Conall narrowed his gaze at her.

"I'll walk Jerina inside," Thane called over his shoulder as he tried to usher her away as quickly as he could. "You're asking for trouble."

Jerina shrugged his arm away from her. "Why do you care?"

Before he could answer, Irina joined them, carrying a pile of clothes. "Oh good, Jerina, you're here. I was going to put these inside your room." She turned to Thane. "You can run along."

Jerina was happy to escape Thane, so she quickly hurried after Irina.

CHAPTER 6

*J*erina punched her pillow once again. There was no way she could get comfortable or possibly sleep. She had too much on her mind.

Irina had been so nice to bring her all those clothes. She couldn't believe people would leave so many things behind when they stayed at the inn. Jerina could tell that the innkeeper was trying to distract her from her dark thoughts by rattling on about the town and its many inhabitants.

At first, Jerina wasn't sure which type of supernatural Irina and Mihail were, but she quickly determined that they were some sort of vampire. They were nothing like the bloodthirsty ones Jerina had encountered back home.

The nice woman had squeezed her shoulder and whispered low. "Give Thane an opportunity to speak with you tomorrow. Things won't seem so bad then."

Jerina had her doubts, but she refused to be rude to the kind woman. Irina had given her silky pajamas.

Coffee was not something Jerina had at home, but she had

remembered it from before and couldn't wait to try it again. Since sleep had eluded her the night before, Jerina knew she would need gallons of the stuff to keep her awake.

She managed to stumble down the stairs to the dining room and sink into a seat. She was immediately poured some coffee, which she gulped, only to spit out the scorching liquid. She scanned the room to see if anyone had seen; luckily no one had.

Jerina waved her hand over the wet brown stains that were spreading across the white table linen. She watched as the stains dried and disappeared. She was thankful for her father's fae heritage that gave her extra abilities.

"Don't worry about the cloth, dear."

Jerina jumped in her seat, a guilty expression on her face. "You gave me a fright, Madame Luiza!"

The older woman winked at her and flitted away to check on her other guests.

With her breakfast finished, Jerina contemplated exploring the town a little, but knew too many people were watching her. Someone would report her lack of an escort, and she would be kicked out of town.

Groaning loudly, she stomped toward the porch. At least she could spend time outside while she waited for Thane to arrive. If he showed up. They left things unsettled between them, so she had no inkling if he was coming. Jerina hated being at the mercy of anyone.

The tulips and daffodils in the garden drew her attention as they swayed in the light breeze. She felt herself leave the porch and approach the colorful display. It seemed to be reeling her in and capturing her in its beauty. She knelt on the early spring grass by the carefully sculpted flowerbed, running her hands along the petals.

Glancing around to make sure no one was watching, Jerina infused the flowers with a little magic to help them grow. Smiling at her handiwork, she took a few steps backward and bumped into a solid chest. Yelping, she jumped forward, turning quickly to see who had snuck up on her.

"If you want to brush up against me, I suggest turning around first. It's much more fun that way." Perun's leering gaze made her skin crawl.

"What are you doing here, and where is my sister?" Jerina could feel her emotions churning, but she knew she had to keep it together.

Perun continued to undress her with his sleazy eyes. "Would you like me to take you to her? Simply say the words." Perun pulled a tarnished gold pocket watch with a long gold link chain from his vest and ran his thumb over the glass front. "I would never deny the company of sisters."

"You're revolting." The way he fondled that watch made Jerina shiver with disgust. She could feel the dark magic oozing from the timepiece.

Perun stepped forward, attempting to grab her arm. Jerina saw a flash of silver from a small pocket knife clutched in his other hand.

"If I didn't know better, Perun, I would think you were bothering one of my guests, but I know you would never do that. Would you?" Madame Luiza moved around the side of the azalea bush to join them.

Jerina hurried over to Madame Luiza and sighed in relief. She was afraid to even imagine what Perun would have done. Madame Luiza had just saved her.

"Luiza," Perun spit out through clenched teeth. He spun around and marched off the property.

"You need to be more careful," Madame Luiza said, patting her shoulder.

"You have perfect timing." Jerina turned in a circle to make sure Perun had left.

Madame Luiza guided her toward the porch. "Thane will be here shortly. Don't wander around without him."

Jerina flopped down on a wicker chair with an unladylike grunt. She was used to leading warriors and training. She hated taking orders and following directions.

What felt like hours later, Thane jogged up the sidewalk toward her. "I heard you had a visitor this morning."

Jerina shot to her feet and arched a brow. "You heard already?"

"I would have been here earlier, but I had visitors too."

Jerina shrugged, not interested in his visitors or his life.

"Why don't we go somewhere a little more private?" Thane offered his hand.

Jerina shook her head, ignoring his outstretched fingers. "That's not a good idea."

"Sure it is." He leaned closer to her. "There are too many busybodies around here."

She shrugged. "So?"

He leaned even closer and whispered, "A few members of the Green Coven stopped by for a chat. Seems like they wanted to keep me occupied so that Perun could get to you."

Jerina was intrigued. "Let's go."

Thane grinned and led her from the porch and around the back of the inn. Making sure no one was watching, he opened a portal and pulled her through.

Jerina hadn't been expecting him to do that, so she stumbled but righted herself quickly. "I thought you couldn't open portals through the town wards."

"We are still inside of them. I figured it was the quickest way to get somewhere private, and I thought you might like to see the falls." Thane watched her closely as she spun around to gape at the rushing water.

"Wow! I can feel the magic of this place. It's exhilarating!" Jerina held her arms out to her sides and soaked in the feel of the magic.

Thane grinned. He knew it was a good place to bring her. "You like it here?"

She twirled with her arms out. "I love it."

Thane slid a backpack off his shoulder and removed a blanket, spreading it on a flat-topped rock. "Here. We can sit and . . ."

"And you'll explain everything?" she challenged.

He grinned wickedly. "Yes."

Jerina settled on the blanket, folding her legs under her. "Why are you being nice today?"

Thane ran his hand through his hair. "I never wanted to be rude to you. I had to be."

Jerina started to rise, but he placed his hand on her arm to stop her.

"Give me a chance to explain," he pleaded.

She leaned back, folding her arms in front of her. "Go on."

"Perun has been setting things up for a long time now, convincing people that he is an upstanding citizen. He's been donating to the town, helping with things that need doing, and taking care of problems. The Court likes having him around. He doesn't mind bending or breaking the rules for them."

"What does that have to do with you?" Jerina was happy for the information on Perun, but she wasn't making the connection to Thane.

"My family loves this town and will do anything to protect it. I grew up learning magic, defense, and weaponry so that I could protect my family and Havenwood Falls. I help out Sheriff Kasun and the Court."

"Great. So, you brought me here for a lecture. Save it." Jerina slid off the rock and stomped to the edge of the water.

He followed after her. "No. I'm trying to explain everything to you. Please listen for a few more minutes."

She nodded, twisting around to face him.

"My dad has been watching Perun for a while, suspecting that he was up to no good with his obsession with vila. We knew he had been making trips all over Europe looking for you and your people. He wants your power."

"We're not so easy to find." Jerina kicked at a small stone with the toe of her boot. She was thankful Irina had provided a pair of sturdy pants, boots and a lightweight jacket. She knew most women didn't wear pants often, but she preferred them.

"No, you're not. He searched for twenty-five years."

"Until he found my sister."

"Yes. When my dad saw Perun in the town square with Kosa, he knew something wasn't right. He had approached them to say hello to Kosa, but Perun wouldn't let her speak. When my father asked to speak to her alone for a moment, Kosa looked to Perun, who refused. The behavior was not what he remembered, so he watched them."

"She doesn't listen to anyone. She would have spoken with Tannor. We both had fond memories of him." Jerina's suspicions were becoming stronger. Perun had control over her sister.

"One of Perun's servants told my dad that Kosa wasn't allowed to leave the house without his permission and then only with him. She must ask for everything. The servant also claimed to have seen Perun order her to use her magic when it seemed as if she didn't want to do it." Thane wasn't going to go into detail of how much her sister had been mistreated. Jerina didn't need to hear that.

Jerina wanted to cover her ears to block out what he was saying, but she needed to know. Somehow, Perun discovered one of the vila secrets.

Thane's scrutinizing stare bored into her. "You don't seem surprised about the level of control he has over her."

She ignored his comment. "Why are you telling me this? You wanted to turn me in to the Court last night."

He picked up a smooth pebble and skipped it across the water. "Perun had already gotten to the Court. Your sister made a complaint against you and asked for their protection. I couldn't seem to be on your side. I had to make you and everyone else believe that I agreed with them. It was the only way I could help you. They would have never allowed me to be your escort in town if they thought I was sympathetic to you."

He skipped another pebble. "It's all been an act. I needed you to dislike me and not want me to watch over you." Thane ran his hand through his hair again. "I needed you to not want to be around me. It was the only way to assure that I would be assigned to you."

Jerina sank onto the grass, suddenly feeling exhausted. Could she believe him? His arrogance and disdain were an act? She wiped her hands down her face. "I don't know what to believe. How do I know this isn't a game to get information from me?"

Thane clasped her hand and pulled her to her feet. "The grass is damp. Come back to the blanket."

Jerina followed along numbly. "How can I trust you?"

Thane held her gaze. "I'm going to help you rescue your sister."

Jerina was skeptical. "How?" She didn't trust him with what she feared.

"I'm going to help you get your sister's lock of hair back."

CHAPTER 7

*J*erina jumped to her feet, pulling her magically shortened sword from her pocket and willing it to its full and deadly length.

"How do you know about that?" she shouted.

Thane had been expecting her outburst, so he had a shield ready for when she advanced on him. "Easy."

"I'll make things really easy!" She imagined skewering him with her sword.

"We've been spying on Perun. He acquired a dark-magic-infused pocket watch from a dealer who doesn't worry about selling items legally. He bragged to the dealer that he needed it to hold a lock of hair that he didn't want to lose," Thane rushed out. "We started to do some research into vila legends. That's when we discovered your weakness."

"We don't have a weakness!" Jerina couldn't believe this was happening. She slid from the rock and backed away.

"Everyone has a weakness. I have a low tolerance for iron. All fae do. Every supernatural has something. Vampires can't tolerate the sun. Wolf shifters have trouble with silver. The vila just happen to have a weakness that can be exploited. You're immensely powerful, but can be controlled by a simple lock of hair." Thane shrugged. "Perun is keeping Kosa's hair in his pocket watch, and we are going to get it back."

Jerina dropped her arm, pointing the sword to the ground. "How do I know you're not telling me this to get close enough to steal my hair?"

"I could have taken it from you many times, but I didn't. I won't." Thane was still in the same position, but he had dropped his shield. "I want to help you, but you need to start trusting me a little."

Jerina slumped. "What do you suggest we do?"

"We're going to break in to Perun's house and talk to your sister." Thane grinned at her when her mouth dropped open.

"Just like that? Go to his house, break in, and try to talk to my sister who is under his complete control?" Jerina growled her frustration. "You're insane!"

"Maybe a little." Thane stood and gathered up the blanket. "Come on, we need to start planning."

"You cannot be serious."

"Are you afraid of a little adventure?" Thane challenged.

Jerina narrowed her gaze. "Not at all. Let's go."

Four days later, Jerina was about to walk into the enemy's lair. She knew Thane had been working on a plan, but never expected it to be a trip into hostile territory dressed to kill.

"Now I know you're crazy," Jerina muttered as Thane tightened his hold on her hand, pulling her along the sidewalk leading up to Perun's Havenwood Heights mansion. "We're just going to walk up to the door and go inside?"

"How else do you suggest we enter? We could scale the ivy and crawl into the second-floor window, but I don't suggest you doing that in your evening gown." Thane was enjoying the red streaks across her cheeks and the fire in her eyes.

Jerina couldn't believe Thane's brilliant idea was to attend an upscale party at Perun's house. *What was he thinking?* "We're going to a ball at his house?"

"It was the perfect idea. Perun is hosting this year's spring Flower Ball fundraiser. Every supernatural in town will be in attendance. It would look odd if I didn't go, and I can't leave you unattended, so you had to come along." He gave her a toothy grin.

Jerina glanced down at the shimmering silver gown Thane had bought her from Callie's Trinkets and What Nots. The owner, Calla Lily Mircea, was so nice to Jerina when they arrived at her shop. Without any words, she immediately led Jerina over to a vintage silver dress that sparkled and insisted she try it on. It was exactly her size and the right style for the vila warrior.

Thane agreed that the dress was perfect. Jerina looked like a goddess ready to go to war. He laughed to himself because she *was* ready to do battle. She was carrying her sword with her in the small evening bag slung over her arm. He thought he saw her strap a knife or two under her gown.

Stopping, Thane turned to her and brought her in close to him so he could whisper quietly. "I know you're going to want to grab Kosa and take off or go after Perun. We can't do either. We are here to gather some information and hopefully give you and Kosa a few minutes to talk. If you lose control of your temper and cause a scene, we will be asked to leave, and you will be escorted from town. Can you keep it together?"

Jerina knew he was right, but it still irked her. "Yes. I'll be in control."

"Good." He leaned closer, his breath tickling her ear. "I'll be here to help you. Now let's put on a show." Thane's thumb was rubbing her hand in slow circles.

Jerina shivered, but not from fear. His breath and silky voice were giving her goose bumps. She had to stop herself from leaning into him. She shook herself. *What was she doing?* Vila needed to stay away from men.

Thane tucked her hand around his arm and led them forward. A few others were walking into the mansion. Flowers were everywhere they looked—lining the walkways, hanging from the trees in baskets, around the door in garlands, and on every windowsill. Wonderful fragrance filled the air along with a little magic. There were exotic flowers from all over the world, including many that were out of season. Jerina loved it.

A man at the door greeted them with an iris for Thane's lapel and a flower ring for Jerina's head. Each guest was given flowers to wear on their clothes, in their hair, or as jewelry. They continued through a blossom-covered archway and into the spacious foyer.

Perun, with Kosa on his arm, greeted the guests that lined up to enter the ball. Thane and Jerina stepped to the back of the line to wait their turn to say hello to their hosts.

Kosa's eyes grew large when she spotted her sister, but she quickly looked away. Thane noticed and squeezed Jerina's hand. She leaned closer. "I'm fine. I'm prepared for this."

"That's my girl." Thane winked, pulling her in closer to him. He could have continued their ruse of barely tolerating each other, but he decided it would be much more fun to act like lovers. It would throw everyone off.

The couple in front of them stepped away from Perun and Kosa, and then it was Thane and Jerina's turn. Perun took Jerina's hand and leaned over it, making a show of kissing her knuckles. It took everything she had not to pull her hand away and send him flying through the air.

"I'm surprised to see you here, my dear. I'm so happy you decided to accept my invitation to visit. I'm sure we can arrange for you to spend an extended amount of time here with your sister. You would like that, wouldn't you, Kosa darling?" Perun spoke loudly to all who were listening to the conversation.

Kosa blanched but simply nodded her head in agreement. A single tear ran down her face. Perun's eyes grew hard and dangerous. "Go powder your nose and come back," he whispered in her ear. "You may not speak to your sister."

Kosa glanced at Jerina and hurried off to do what she was told.

Thane tightened his hold on Jerina but was surprised to discover her in complete control of her powers and emotions. He grinned down at her.

"Your home is lovely. I can't wait to see what other flower displays you have," Jerina said loudly for the crowd and turned away.

Thane grinned at her. "Perun." He nodded his head. "Nice to see you."

"Watch her, Thane. Wouldn't want that one to get away from you."

Thane cocked his head to the side. "Don't worry about me. You have your own vila to worry about."

Thane didn't wait for a reply. He shuffled off with Jerina toward the ballroom.

Jerina stopped at a huge display of flowers that were designed to look like a volcano with lava erupting. It was amazing and looked so realistic. She liked looking at the flower art, but her mind was in the other room with her sister.

Jerina spotted Aspen and Tannor across the room. She hurried over to join them. Thane filled them in on what had been happening, and they agreed to help in any way they could. Aspen suggested that Jerina accompany her into the ladies' restroom.

Jerina frowned. "Why? Kosa can't speak to me."

"No, but you can speak to her, and she can answer back to me." Aspen grinned. "There is always a way around the problem. We elves are great at finding loopholes."

Aspen linked arms with Jerina to stop her from rushing off toward her sister. She was so excited at the prospect of speaking with her that Jerina practically ran through the hallways.

A few women were freshening up in the room that was filled with everything a lady might need to refresh at a party. Dozens of perfumes, hair sprays, makeup, and toiletries lined the counter under long mirrors. Jerina ignored it all and ventured into the back, where a secluded sitting area featured two love seats and a small table in between. The area was divided by privacy panels. It wasn't the best place, but it was better than nothing.

Aspen and Jerina approached Kosa, who was slumped over, covering her face with both hands. It was obvious that she was weeping.

"Kos." Jerina reached out and gathered her sister in her arms. "It's going to be okay."

Kosa stiffened and tried to pull away, scanning the room frantically.

"Aspen is here with us. You can speak to her. He said you couldn't talk to me, but he never said that you couldn't speak to me through someone else."

Kosa wiped the tears from her eyes and tried to calm herself. She turned to Aspen. "I'm so sorry. Please tell her I'm so sorry."

Jerina stepped back so the three of them could gather closer together. "I know, Kosa. I'm going to figure out a way to get you out of here. Can you tell Aspen what happened? How he got you?"

Kosa focused on Aspen. "I went to tell him I wasn't going to see him anymore, but he tricked me. He wanted a hug goodbye. As soon as my arms went around him, I felt him tug on my hair. When I pulled away, he was dangling a long blond lock between his fingers. All I could do was stare at it. He was laughing manically, bragging how he now had all the power in the world. He was going to run the Green Coven and his hometown."

Wringing her hands, Kosa continued. "Perun's cousin, Ada, is the current leader of the Green Coven, and he hates that fact. He wants all of the coven's power to be his, but that won't happen unless he gets stronger. He's trying to use my magic and powers to do that."

"We'll get the hair back. He won't be able to control you anymore." Jerina didn't know how she was going to be able to do that, but she swore she wouldn't leave Havenwood Falls without her sister.

The sisters spoke through Aspen for a few more minutes, before Aspen warned that they were taking too long. She was afraid that Perun would send someone looking for Kosa.

Reluctantly, Jerina hugged her sister goodbye and promised to find a way to see her again.

Jerina was quiet when she returned to Thane's side, and he knew that he would have to do something to improve her mood if they were to keep up appearances. They needed to act like there was not a thing in the world wrong.

Saundra Beaumont and Sheriff Kasun were both in attendance, along with several other members of the Court. They all needed to see Jerina behaving herself and having a fun time.

Thane wrapped an arm around her shoulder and led her to the dance floor. Soft music played, and other couples were swaying to songs from Frank Sinatra, Bing Crosby, and Duke Ellington.

Jerina stopped on the edge of the floor and planted her feet, not moving another inch. "I don't know how to dance."

Thane rubbed her check. "It's just like a sword match, only without the blood and gore. Counter my moves, and you'll do just fine."

She considered him for a moment. "I think I can do that."

He leaned in. "You have to let me lead."

Jerina made a face, but moved closer and placed her left hand on his right shoulder like the other women were doing and her right hand in his left. Before she was ready, he began to move his feet. She stumbled at first, but he didn't seem to mind.

"Close your eyes. Feel what I'm doing and where I'm going. Let your body react naturally." Thane knew she would pick it up easily. She was so graceful when she moved and held a sword. Dancing was just more complex fighting steps.

A few minutes later, she opened her eyes and grinned up at him. "I like this."

"I knew you would. Wait until they play faster music. You'll love it even more." Thane would have liked to hear some of the faster big band tunes, but he was content to hold her and sway to the softer sounds.

"You don't seem to be having any more trouble," Perun

remarked with Kosa in his arms, dancing alongside of them. "You must have discovered my secret for dealing with difficult women."

Thane's warning squeeze stopped anything Jerina might have said.

Thane smirked at Perun. "It's all about charm, my friend. The ladies love my charismatic wit and personality."

Perun laughed. "We'll have to talk after the festival tomorrow. I'm sure there is much to discuss."

Jerina wanted to zap him with some lightning, but she managed to turn away and pull Thane to a different area of the dance floor.

Thane leaned in to speak quietly in her ear. "You are doing amazingly well tonight. I'm proud of you. I know it took a lot of control not to go after him."

She didn't know why, but his praise thrilled her, and that scared the hell out of her.

Colorful tents and booths filled the town square, displaying crafts, clothing, trinkets, jewelry, and floral designs. Areas were set up for flower-arranging lessons, seed swaps, children's crafts, gardening tips, and tons of food that were either made with plant ingredients or shaped to look like flowers. Another section held a stage where residents could vote on their favorite flowers and artwork.

Aspen was excited that her fuchsia-and-light-pink lily had been selected as a finalist. She had proudly displayed the plant in a hand-painted pot with a pink ribbon around it. Judging would continue throughout the day, and winners would be announced at the end of the festival.

Jerina scanned the crowd for her sister, but so far, Perun and Kosa had not made an appearance. "I thought Perun told you he would be here today?"

Thane glanced around. "He'll be here. He wants to know if I control you." Thane got a twinkle in his eyes. "We could always make him believe that I do. Are you up for a little acting?"

"No. Not happening." Jerina put her fists on her hips. She was not going to let him get away with bossing her around. He would have too much fun with it.

Tannor's arms were filled with items his wife had selected, while she only carried one bright yellow bouquet. "It might work, Jerina. I know what you're thinking. Thane won't take advantage of the situation, but Perun might speak more freely to Thane if he thought they were both reaping the same benefits from stolen hair."

Aspen piled another item on top of the others her husband held. "If he does step out of line, I'll help you get even with him."

"Mother!" Thane couldn't believe his own mother would side with Jerina.

Aspen chuckled, then stiffened slightly. "Perun is over there."

She shifted nervously and nibbled on one of the leaves of the blue Forget Me Nots she held in a pot in her arms.

Thane grinned when he saw his mom eating the flower. "Aren't you going to plant that?"

Aspen looked down. "Oh! Yes. It's going to be a part of the rock garden out back."

Tanner took the flowerpot from her. "You won't have anything to plant if you keep eating that." He turned to Thane and Jerina. "She was so nervous earlier, I had to take her flower entry away from her so she would still have something for the contest."

Thane leaned closer to Jerina and whispered in her ear. "Mom's an elf. They love to eat all kinds of plants. She starts snacking on leaves when she gets upset."

Jerina gave Aspen a half smile, but kept her eye on Perun.

Aspen shrugged. "I can't help it."

She nudged Tannor, and they left to find more flowers.

Jerina wanted to throw up. Kosa was clinging to Perun's arm, and he was parading her around like a trophy. He made a huge show of stopping to speak with everyone he passed in the crowd.

They were slowly making their way closer to Thane and Jerina. She knew she would have to act the part, so she gritted her teeth and wrapped her hand around his arm, staring up at him obediently.

"Don't blow a fuse, okay?" Thane joked. "Wouldn't want your head to explode."

"You fracture me." Jerina smiled sweetly. She had heard the Petrans use that word when they thought something was funny and made them laugh.

Thane's eyebrows raised, surprised at the comment. She was beginning to fit into his world. "You're going to get even with me, aren't you?"

"You can count on it."

Thane rubbed his hands together. "Looking forward to it."

They watched Perun pass a few booths to get to the place where Thane and Jerina were standing. Thane pulled her a little closer. "Showtime."

Jerina plastered on a phony sweet smile and turned to face her sister, who looked terrified, and Perun, who was sporting a sinister smirk. Neither one of them had any flowers or crafts. It was clear to everyone that they had only attended the festival for social interaction. They were not supporting the local crafters and businesses.

"Good afternoon." Thane reached out his hand to shake Perun's.

"It's good to see you both enjoying the festival." Perun ran his knuckles across Kosa's cheek, watching Jerina for a reaction.

Thane was pleasantly surprised that Jerina did not attack Perun for touching her sister. He knew her restraint would not last too long if he didn't do something soon.

Perun rubbed Kosa's cheek again and licked his lips, all the while never taking his eyes from Jerina. "We should take a stroll through some of the judging tables."

Thane noticed the challenge in Perun's eyes, so he decided to test out the plan he and Jerina had created. Watching Perun from the corner of his eye, he addressed the vila on his arm. "Jerina, please go get the scoring sheets for the contests and bring them back quickly. Don't stop to speak with anyone. Run along now."

Kosa glanced between the two men in confusion.

Thane held his breath, hoping Jerina didn't zap him into the next county. With fire burning hotly in her eyes, she stomped off to do as he asked.

"NO!" sobbed Kosa, who slumped against Perun. He hadn't expected to support her weight, so she nearly sunk to the ground.

Jerina ground her teeth and trudged on. She hated the broken sound of her sister, but she knew they needed to play things right.

With her head down, she didn't make eye contact with anyone. She needed to do what he asked and return. Grabbing four score sheets and a few small pencils, she hurried back.

Kosa was sniffling beside Perun, who was scowling at her.

"Quiet down at once!" he hissed.

Thane wanted to punch the man, but he needed to keep his cool. Jerina was headed back to their group, and the next part of their plan needed to go perfectly. "I didn't know selecting the best flowers and crafts would be something you would want to do."

"I only like the best," Perun commented flippantly.

Thane grasped the opportunity.

"That's too bad, because it looks like I have the best this time." Thane reached his hand out to Jerina, who allowed him to pull her into his embrace. He held his arm around her back, locking her in place.

Jerina handed Thane the score cards. "Is there anything else you need?"

Thane scanned the crowd. "Yes. Do you see that man over there, across the square? I want you to blow his hat off his head but not have any wind blow across the booths."

Jerina raised her eyebrows in question, but did what he asked. She hoped he knew what he was doing. Raising her hand slightly, she focused on the man and directed a small amount of wind to whip by him, knocking his hat from his head. She hadn't done anything like that in a while, so she had a little fun with it. Once he bent to retrieve his hat, she blew it away again.

"That's enough," Thane chastened. He knew she enjoyed doing that, but he couldn't let Perun know that he wasn't in control of her.

Jerina cut off the wind and lowered her head to gaze at the ground. This meek act was driving her crazy.

Perun clapped his hands slowly and forcefully. "Congratulations. You have yourself a powerful weapon."

Thane didn't answer.

Perun stopped clapping to place his hand around the back of Kosa's neck. "We need to see a few more people before the festival is over."

Perun led Kosa away.

Jerina's eyes shot up with hatred flaring in their depths. Thane squeezed her side to offer the support he knew she must need from him. Seeing her sister in that situation must have been awful.

"You were amazing." Thane didn't know if his compliment would be met with hostility.

"It's a good thing you didn't ask me to do anything else. You would have been flying around with that man's hat." Jerina watched the crowd move, blocking her view of her sister.

"We needed to make him believe. My bet is he sends someone to my house to try to steal the hair he thinks I have. He wants control of both of you." Thane guided her toward a booth with displays of jewelry to distract her.

A snowflake with silver swirls around it caught her eye. She bent closer, drawn to the delicate charm.

"That reminds me of you." Thane picked it up carefully and held it to the light, watching it sparkle. He turned to the woman behind the table. "We'll take this."

Jerina's eyes shot to his. "You don't have to do that."

"I want you to have it. Someday, you'll be wearing it and I hope you'll think about me." Thane paid for the necklace, but didn't turn it over to Jerina. Instead, he stepped behind her to place it on her neck.

Jerina lifted her long blond hair so that he could secure it. She looked down and smiled. "Thank you." She sighed loudly. "Now what do we do?"

"We need to gather more information. Your sister should have it, if we can get to her."

"I've seen that look in your eyes. You are planning something." Jerina studied him.

"How would you feel about being bait?"

CHAPTER 9

"*P*lease explain." Jerina wasn't afraid to put herself in danger. She just had to know all the details.

"The Green Coven meets once a month in a different coven member's house. After the meeting, several of them will go to one of the local pubs for a few drinks. Perun usually goes to flirt with the female tourists or human residents. It might be the perfect time for you to distract him while I sneak in to speak with Kosa." Thane had tried to think of as many things that could go wrong as possible.

Jerina's eyes grew into saucers. "You think that's safe?"

Thane didn't love the idea of splitting up from Jerina, but he needed to get inside Perun's mansion without him being there. "I don't want you to go alone, but it's the only way we can keep Perun distracted and still get to speak with your sister."

Jerina frowned. "I cannot go anywhere in town without someone coming with me."

Thane guided her toward another booth as they made their way to the food vendors. "I thought of that. Calla Lilly was just telling me that she needed a night out."

"She would do that for me?" Jerina couldn't believe that someone she barely knew would help her so much. Then she looked at Thane and realized that he was helping her more than she had any right to expect. They were playing a dangerous game, and he had no thought for himself. He only wanted to help her.

Thane noticed the change in her expression. "Is everything okay?"

She stared up at him. "Yes." She tried to pull her eyes away from him, but he held her captive.

Thane cupped her chin. "We'll get your sister back."

She nodded. "I know. I trust you."

Fire ignited in Thane's eyes, and he tightened his hold on her, his eyes glued to hers. He slowly bent his head toward her, but stopped inches away, waiting to see her reaction.

She tilted her head toward his, aligning their lips, daring to take what he was offering. Just as his mouth was about to settle on hers, they were jostled apart by a group of teens pushing past. Jerina hastily stepped back and shook herself out of the spell he had cast on her.

A blush streaked her cheeks, but she didn't look away from him.

"Come on. I want to show you something." He linked his fingers through hers and pulled her along as he weaved through the crowd.

Slipping into an alley between two of the large buildings, he crossed behind Whisper Falls Inn and continued jogging a few blocks until they reached Danzan Park. He had a sudden need to not share her with anyone else.

The park was empty, with most of the town residents at the flower festival. Thane led her past a few trees and backed her against a large trunk that blocked everyone from view.

A warning was flashing in Jerina's head, but she was too tempted by Thane to heed it. She wanted to explore things with him a little bit. Surely the curse would allow her a few minutes of passion.

Thane's predatory gaze should have made her nervous, but it thrilled her instead. She wasn't sure what he had planned, but she was ready for whatever happened.

He had been holding back, waiting for her to show some faith in him. To trust him. He could still hear her saying those words.

Sliding both hands into her hair, he held her gently, giving her time to push him away. She didn't. She fisted his jacket and pulled him closer to her.

Thane dipped his head down, nudging her nose with his as his lips inched closer to hers.

Jerina's heart thundered in her ears as she waited for his mouth to settle over hers. She'd had a few kisses in her life, but they were simply to sate her curiosity about men. She had never found any particularly interesting enough to dally with.

Thane couldn't wait any longer. He claimed her lips in a searing kiss that was sure to burn him into her memory forever. His teeth grazed her lip, nipping it playfully, before his tongue swept inside her mouth to meet hers.

As soon as his mouth laid claim to hers, Jerina wrapped her arms around his neck and held on as wave after wave of emotion burst forth. If a kiss was this amazing, what would more be like?

Thane shifted his hold, pulling her closer and deepening the kiss. He knew it would be good between them, but he never dreamed it would be this intense.

Jerina broke the kiss, breathing deeply, chest heaving as she fought for control.

Thane leaned his forehead against hers and closed his eyes. "I won't apologize for that."

Jerina smiled. "I won't ask you to."

He caught her eye. "It's going to happen again."

Jerina placed her hand on his cheek. "We can't let this go too far."

Thane straightened and took a couple of steps back. "Why not?"

Covering her face with her hands, she struggled for control of her raging emotions. The wind whipping through the trees was growing in intensity.

Thane pulled her hands away from her face.

"Why not?" he repeated.

Jerina sucked air into her lungs. "Because we are cursed."

Thane shrugged. "I know that."

Shaking her head, she backed up a couple of feet. "No. Not about our hair. We have another curse."

Thane dropped his shoulders. "I'm not talking about your hair."

Jerina wanted to stomp her feet. He needed to listen to her. "Thane, you don't understand! You could die! I don't want anything to happen to you! Vila are cursed to never find true love. If we do, our true love will die a terrible death."

Thane closed the distance between them and framed her face with his hands. "I already know that is the legend. The vila believe it, but I don't."

Jerina grabbed his wrists to pull his hands from her face, but she just held him in place. "You know our legends are true. You've seen the power Perun has over Kosa by just having a lock of her hair. This is true too."

Thane's thumbs caressed her cheeks. "Haven't you ever heard that true love conquers all or true love's kiss breaks the spell? There is nothing stronger than true love. I believe it. True love brought my father back to my mom after he was wounded in World War I."

Jerina dropped her hands to his jacket. "True love didn't bring him home. I did."

He slid his hands farther into her hair. "How do you know that true love didn't send you to help him?"

"We can't let this go any further. I like you too much. I don't want anything to happen to you." Jerina wondered if it was already too late. She was growing attached to the charming, arrogant male.

"I'm not going anywhere, and I won't let you push me away." Thane wrapped his arms around her and hugged her tightly.

"I can't push you away right now. You're my assigned escort while I'm in Havenwood Falls." Jerina clung to him, absorbing some of his strength.

Since she was still in his arms, he kissed her again to remind her just how good it was between them.

After what seemed like hours, Thane walked her back to the inn and stopped at the bottom of the staircase. "Good night, Jerina. Sweet dreams." Thane winked at her. "Of me."

~

It had been three days since Thane had kissed her in the park and two days since she had seen her sister in town on Perun's arm.

Jerina had met Calla Lily for a drink at the Fallview Tavern. It was the hangout of the Green Coven since Ada Daryn, the coven's leader, controlled the sirens who ran the place. They entered the building with high ceilings, wooden beam supports, and hardwood floors. Everything seemed to be covered in earth tones with a large iron chandelier hung over the sitting area in front of the stone fireplace. Iron was everywhere, so she understood why Thane didn't step inside.

While they were waiting for Perun to arrive, they discovered that the Green Coven meeting had been postponed. It had been a nice night with a new friend, but it hadn't accomplished what she wanted.

Thane stayed outside Perun's mansion for hours until it was clear. He wasn't leaving Kosa alone. He wondered if Perun had discovered their plans. He wasn't sure how that would be possible, but it was too coincidental for his liking.

The next day, they had heard the Green Coven was going to meet. They prepared once again to distract Perun so Thane could speak privately with Kosa.

Jerina was supposed to only let Perun see her, but she would do whatever was necessary to give Thane time to do what he needed to do. Once again, she was wearing a vintage dress from Calla Lily's shop. This one was a little more daring than she normally wore, but Thane assured her that she looked amazing in it. The bright red A-line dress barely reached her knees, and its open collar dipped lower than any of her other clothes.

She kept glancing down to make sure the top of her dress was where it was supposed to be. Madame Luiza had told her it was not indecent and that it was designed to make a man wonder what the clothes were hiding. Jerina could picture the leer spreading across Perun's face when he saw her.

This time, Jerina was going to the Fallview Tavern with Irina and Mihail Petran. Normally, she would hate tagging along with a couple, but it would work to her benefit if Perun noticed her.

Thane stopped by before they left to wish her luck and to warn her not to engage Perun without him there. She didn't plan to take on Perun herself, so she agreed.

The tavern was crowded, but the three of them found a few soft chairs around a small table next to the bar where they could survey the entire place. They had been there for half an hour when Perun strode in with two other men who Jerina could tell were also mages. They oozed much more power than Perun.

Jerina understood where his obsession began. Perun wanted to be like his coven mates, but his level of power didn't come close. He wanted to use her sister to compete with the others. Disgust filled her.

Mihail drew Irina from her chair and brought her to the dance floor, leaving Jerina by herself. They had planned to do this as soon as they knew Perun was in the bar. It had been Irina's idea, and Jerina readily agreed. They also suggested that no one mention the change of plans to Thane. He might not like the risk Jerina was taking.

Jerina sipped on a gin and tonic, watching the single patrons flirt and the older gentlemen sway on their stools from too many alcoholic beverages. She loved to people-watch, and the tavern was a great place to do that.

She was going to pretend not to notice Perun, but she decided to be bold and stare him down. Perun was attracted to the strong and powerful. He would seek her out.

"Where is your keeper?" Perun demanded.

"He left someone else to watch over me, as you can see." Mihail and Irina stopped dancing to stare over. They were waiting for

Jerina to let them know if she needed their help. "Where is my sister?"

"Locked in her room," he sneered. "Want to join her there?"

Jerina laughed. "And be under your control?"

"I know you're here to see me." Perun's eyes were glued to the V neckline of her dress.

It took every ounce of willpower to not smack the leer from his face. "Of course I am. I am drawn to you." Jerina couldn't stop her eyes from rolling.

Perun's leer intensified. "I should have held out for the fiery one. Maybe Thane will make a switch." He stepped closer to her.

Jerina saw her shot and decided to go for it. She leaned a little closer to him. "You think you could handle me?"

Perun licked his lips. "I look forward to proving it to you."

Jerina placed her hand on his chest. "Thane would never give you the chance." She slipped her hand lower.

Perun adjusted his stance, moving the bulge in his pants. "We might share you both. He seems to like a variety of women."

Jerina swallowed her disgust. She could do this. "He doesn't share, but I do."

She slid her hand lower still. She rested it just above Perun's vest pocket. She could feel the evil power radiating from the watch. Her hand was so close.

She fluttered her eyelashes at him like she had seen women do in the movie that Thane had taken her to a few days before. Jerina had no idea how to flirt, but Perun seemed to like what she was doing.

"I've never had sisters before. Do you and Kosa share everything?" He was leaning into her and breathing harder.

Jerina wanted to gag, but she kept a slight smile on her face. She licked her lips to keep his eyes on her face and slid her fingers into his pocket.

Perun grabbed her hand, crushing her fingers until they felt like they would break into a million pieces. "Do you think I am that stupid? Did you think you could fool me with that poor attempt at flirting?"

He pushed her away from him, toppling her chair and leaving her sprawled out on the floor. Perun stormed from the tavern in a rage.

Jerina jumped up and ran from the bar to follow him. She knew he would go directly to her sister.

CHAPTER 10

Thane crept up to the historic mansion in the heart of the old-money district. He was sure hoping that none of the founding families on the street saw what he was about to do. He would be brought in front of the Court, and then he would have to answer a whole bunch of questions he wasn't ready for.

He had been teasing Jerina at the ball about climbing up the ivy and crawling into a window, but that was exactly what he was going to do. The trestle that supported the vines reached up to the second floor of the majestic home. He knew Kosa was staying on the higher floor in a servant's room. Perun didn't want her to get any ideas that she was anything but a servant to him.

He was purposely dressed in all black so he would blend with the night and wore sturdy climbing boots. Thane could hear someone listening to the radio loudly, which served his purposes. No one would hear him if he fell off the ivy.

A night watchman strolled down the street whistling, assuring that any criminal would hear him approaching and hide away safely. Thane chuckled to himself. The guy had no plans to look for anyone up to no good, and if he did unwittingly run into a crime in progress, he would probably turn and run the other way.

Shaking his head, he began to climb the greenery. Between the trellis and the twisted vine, climbing was way easier than he thought it would be. He reached the second-floor window that he was told would be open by the servant that had been feeding him information about Perun. The window raised with ease, and Thane was able to slip inside the room. He dropped down to the floor and paused to listen to the sounds of the house.

All was quiet, so he continued on to the hallway. According to the servant that his father paid, Kosa would be locked in a room one floor up and just down the hall to the left. He needed to be careful to avoid any servants who were ordered to stand guard.

He hoped there weren't any outside her door. He was prepared to deal with it if that turned out to be the case, but he would rather not have to.

Thane made it to the servants' steps at the back of the house without seeing anyone. He had heard a few voices inside rooms, but no one had ventured out into the hallway. He knew at least two of the servants had been rather busy with each other from the sound of it.

As soon as he reached the top floor, he leaned out quickly to see if anyone was there. Cursing to himself, he realized someone was just outside Kosa's door. He would have to throw a sleeping spell on the guard and hope it lasted long enough for him to get to Kosa, speak with her, and leave.

Thane leaned out again and saw the large man leaning against the wall, listening to the radio and not paying much attention to anything else. Thane was thankful he wouldn't have to confront the man who was at least a half a foot taller than Thane's six-foot-two frame. The man had about fifty pounds on him too.

Thane whispered some words that would put the man to sleep and waited for a thump. It never came. Thane leaned out again, and the man was still in the same position as he was before, wide awake.

Frowning, he said the spell again, but with more power behind it. He didn't hear the man slump to the floor.

"What the hell?" Thane mumbled to himself. He was going to have to find another way inside her room.

Returning to the second floor, he counted the rooms and stopped at the one just below Kosa. He listened at the door, but didn't hear anything. He slowly twisted the knob and entered the room. It was a guest bedroom that didn't look like it had been used in years. The furnishing and decor were from decades past.

Thane approached the window and slid it open to look out. The trellis didn't reach that high, but the ivy did. He would have to take a chance at climbing it to her window. He just hoped Kosa was awake and not completely freaked out to have someone at her window at night.

The climb was relatively uneventful. He managed to slip only twice, but the ivy was so thick he was able to find another foothold quickly. Being half elf, he had an affinity with plants, so he encouraged it to grow and strengthen to help his climb. The ivy was happy to oblige.

He reached her window and was thankful that she was sitting up in bed with her nightstand lamp on. Thane tapped lightly, trying not to draw too much attention. Impatiently waiting, he tapped again. He saw Kosa stiffen and hop out of bed to investigate. She cautiously approached the window and frowned at him, ready to knock him off the ivy.

"What are you doing here?" she hissed.

Thane held up his hands in surrender. "I'm here to help. Your sister sent me."

Kosa moved closer to the window. "How do I know that's true?"

"She told me to tell you that she hasn't forgotten you pushing her out of the tree, and when you both get back home, you should beware." Thane repeated what Jerina had told him. "She also said that I might be an arrogant crumb, but you should listen to me. I'm here to help." He shrugged. "She's not entirely correct about that part. I'm not a crumb."

Kosa arched a brow in an expression that was so much like her sister. "Are you in control of her?"

Thane chuckled. "I don't think anyone would ever be in control of Jerina."

She was satisfied enough with his answers. Kosa unlocked the window and slid it open so he could enter. Kosa held a finger in front of her lips. "We need to be quiet. Someone is right outside the door."

Thane nodded. "I saw him. I tried to spell him to sleep, but my magic wasn't working."

Kosa sat him down on the floor on the window side of her bed so they were somewhat hidden. "Perun bragged that he was immune to magic and had some sort of innate protection against spells. That was why he was put there. My magic won't work against him."

"How do you know that?" Thane asked.

Kosa shrugged. "We have a drink together every night. He likes to share."

Thane looked thoughtful. "Interesting. You've got moxie. I'll give you that." He sat on the floor, facing the door. He was ready to defend them if necessary, but had a feeling she could take care of herself. "I'm Thane. We haven't been properly introduced. I'm helping your sister."

Kosa growled at him. "You'd better be helping her, because even the gods won't be able to help you if you're lying to me."

Thane loved how fiercely loyal they were to each other. "I would never hurt her. I'd do anything to make sure she was happy and safe. Even scale a building to gather information to save her sister."

Kosa studied him, suddenly understanding. "You're falling for her, aren't you?"

Thane didn't answer.

"Do you know about the curse?" Kosa asked gently, terrified for her sister. They could never have true love.

"Yes, but I don't believe it." Thane crossed his arms over his chest.

"You should. We've seen it happen before." Kosa tried to shift to a more comfortable position, but the floor was hard.

"I'm not here to discuss a curse. I'm here to talk to you about

Perun. Do you know where he keeps his pocket watch?" Thane leaned back against the wall.

"When it's not in his pocket, it's in a box on his dresser. I've seen it before a few times." Kosa didn't think there was any way to get the watch.

Thane grinned. This was the information he needed. "Describe it to me. I need every detail you can remember."

Kosa had her first smile in a long time. "I can show you."

One of her gifts was sharing memories. She could connect with someone and allow them to witness something she had seen or done. It was never something she valued until now.

Kosa closed her eyes and pictured what she wanted Thane to see. Grasping his wrist, she drew him into her vision.

Just as her memory ended, they heard Perun's raised voice down the hallway. Thane quickly slid into her closet. There was not enough time for him to open the window and climb outside.

He heard Perun enter Kosa's room and pull her forcefully into the hallway. He waited a few minutes to make sure he wouldn't be seen or heard and left through the window. He was going to follow after them.

CHAPTER 11

The darkened street was deserted, with most of its residents already asleep. Jerina hadn't expected to be caught following Perun home and never imagined that he would drag Kosa outside to punish her in front of Jerina. He was taking his fury out on Kosa when it should have been directed at Jerina.

Jerina was the one who had attempted to flirt with him to steal the pocket watch, and she was the one who had been caught in the act.

"I know you're watching, Jerina! Step into the moonlight so I can see you. I wouldn't want you to miss this," Perun taunted, pulling Kosa along after him.

Kosa stumbled twice but managed to keep up with his punishing pace.

"Come see what happens to Kosa when you defy me!" Perun backhanded Kosa across the face, sending her sprawling into a row of hedges.

"No! Leave her alone!" Jerina screamed, losing all control over her emotions. She knew she should walk away and find Thane, but she wouldn't leave her sister to this despicable mage.

Leaves began to rustle, thunder roared in the distance, Jerina's hair blew back, and she was gathering lightning. She wished she could simply blast him, but his mage magic and her sister's powers would block any attempt she made. She would have to catch him without Kosa around and without him realizing what was happening.

"I knew you were here." He turned to Kosa. "Come here. I'm not finished with you."

Jerina watched Kosa slump over and gather something in her nightgown. Kosa stomped up to Perun and faced him unafraid.

Kosa's eyes met Jerina's seconds before Kosa grabbed the branch she had hidden in her nightgown and attempted to whack Perun in the head. He might have control over her, but she would fight him until the end. She would not accept her fate.

Perun's temper flared out of control when he blocked the strike. He swung his fist back and let it fly into Kosa's cheek, nearly knocking her out.

Kosa grabbed her throbbing cheek and sobbed her frustration and pain. Perun roughly pulled her up and led her from the street and away from Jerina, laughing the entire way.

Jerina was left on the street alone.

Wind whipped through the trees, lightning blazed across the sky, and a torrent of rain and hail crashed down on the entire region. Jerina's scream of outrage echoed through the valley as she watched Perun lead her sister away.

A hurricane was forming over their valley, and there was nothing Jerina could do to stop it.

Strong arms circled her from behind, and at first, she struggled until she heard his soft murmurs in her ear. "It's going to be okay. Jerina, you must stop this. They'll know it's you. I figured out a way to rescue her. Kosa won't be with him much longer, but I need your help!"

Jerina's whole body shook from uncontrollable rage.

"Please, babe, you need to listen. I know how to save her." Thane pleaded, but his words were not getting through to her. There was only one thing he could think of that might work.

Thane twisted her around and claimed her mouth in a searing, branding kiss that was designed to curl her toes. He slanted his mouth over hers, taking ownership and demanding that she participate.

The rain soaked through their clothes, but neither of them paid any attention to it. She was unresponsive at first, but he claimed victory when her arms wound around his neck and the wind died down. As he continued to kiss her and his tongue explored her mouth, the external storm dissipated.

Thane's hands ran up and down her back, getting to know her every curve. When he pulled her closer and considered exploring her body more, he pulled away panting.

Jerina's pupils were dilated and her breath ragged, but she no longer affected the weather. "He hit her."

Thane hugged her harder. "I know. I saw." He rubbed her back in soothing circles. "We're going to rescue her and make sure he pays."

"How?" The rain turned to a drizzle that eventually stopped. Jerina was regaining control.

Thane winked at her. "I have a plan."

His plan was simple. Executing it would prove to be a little bit harder. Everything had to be perfect, or it wouldn't work. He knew magic would play a big part and so would an elaborate illusion, but they also needed a fairly big distraction and lots of luck.

Thane was thankful that Kosa was able to share her memories of the box that Perun kept on his dresser and of the pocket watch itself. Those recollections were key to his plan.

A stop at Simple Treasures Pawn Shop—owned by Lawrence Mills, a dragon shifter and Court member—gave him a little bit more to think about, but he was sure things would work out. He purchased a couple of items he would need to pull off his plan.

An hour later, Thane picked Jerina up at the inn and led her across the town square.

"Where are we going?" Jerina fidgeted nervously, not liking the direction they were headed.

"We have an important meeting."

Jerina stopped dead. "I'm not going in there!"

Thane pulled on her hand to get her moving. "You don't have a choice. They're waiting for us."

Jerina groaned. "This won't go well."

Sheriff Kasun met them at the back door of City Hall once again. Instead of scowling, he simply nodded. Jerina had no idea what to make of that.

"Follow me." Without waiting for them to respond, he turned and headed down the steps to go into the basement of the building.

He stopped before a set of double doors that led to the main meeting room. Jerina didn't want to go in there.

Thane rubbed her hand with his thumb. "You trust me, right?"

Jerina took a deep breath. "Yes."

"Good. Let's go."

The members of the Court were already assembled in their seats. They were speaking quietly amongst themselves, but stopped all conversations when Thane and Jerina entered.

Thane inclined his head. "Thank you for agreeing to meet with us. As I was explaining before and with evidence from a reliable eye witness, Perun has stolen a lock of Kosa's hair and has taken control of her."

Jerina shifted from foot to foot. She didn't think they would listen to what they had to say and would simply kick her out before she could get Kosa away from the evil mage.

Thane continued. "I provided information on vila from our town library, and we have a vila warrior here to answer any of your questions."

Saundra leaned forward. "Why didn't you explain all of this when you arrived?"

"I didn't know he had control of her then. I had hoped she was only angry with me for wanting her to discontinue seeing an admirer." Jerina met Saundra's stare with ease. She was not afraid of the truth.

"And after you discovered the truth?" Saundra continued.

"I didn't think you would believe me. You made it very clear that you thought I would be a trouble maker so I didn't hold much faith that your opinion of me would change," Jerina countered. She heard a few grumbles, but no one said anything about her statement.

Jerina continued. "The vila keep to ourselves, so not much is widely known about us. We also don't like to announce a weakness, so I didn't think Perun would know about it. He must have done a lot of research."

"How do you know he has her hair?" Saundra and the Court wanted to hear it from her even though they had already received information from Thane.

Thane nodded to her to keep going with her story.

"He orders her around and demands she do things that she ordinarily wouldn't do. He told her she couldn't speak to me, but we figured out a way to do it through Aspen."

Another Court member, Roman, made a disbelieving sound. "That's not proof."

Jerina glared at him. "He made her go sit down by herself and not talk to anyone. He demanded she use her powers when it was obvious she didn't want to, and he also beat on her in front of me and she had to stand there and take it!"

Saundra shifted uncomfortably. "He abused her?"

Jerina was shaking with rage, but she was keeping it together enough to not affect the weather. "He backhanded her and then punched her in the face. As he pulled her away with him, he yelled at her to stop crying."

Thane rubbed the small of her back. "I have spoken with Kosa, and she confirmed that Perun has her hair."

Saundra sighed. "Thane, please tell us what you have planned."

Jerina interrupted. "You'll help us?"

Roman leaned forward to glare at her. "No. We will not."

Saundra frowned. "What Roman means is that we won't interfere with your rescue attempt, but we also cannot offer you any assistance."

Jerina turned to walk out of the meeting room, but Thane grasped her arm to stop her. "Just wait a few minutes," he whispered.

"Why?" she demanded in a normal voice.

"Please. You trust me."

"I knew I'd regret telling you that." Jerina kicked him in his calf and returned to standing next to him.

Saundra cleared her throat, not happy with the disruption.

Thane stood straighter. "We need a little assistance with some spells that will mimic dark magic and that will also contain it."

Saundra looked stern. "That could be arranged."

Thane held up a wrapped package. "It would be great if you could do that now."

Saundra narrowed her gaze but waved them closer.

The sun had barely risen when Jerina ventured outside of the inn and into the back gardens. She couldn't sleep and had too much nervous energy, so she needed to find something to do. It had been so long since she practiced with her sword, so she pulled it out and began to swing it in sweeping arcs.

Jerina shifted back and forth with her moves in a combination of arm and foot work. Having her sword in her hand gave her comfort.

"You're up early."

Jerina hadn't seen Thane enter the garden. He smirked as he pulled his two short swords from a sheath on his back.

She grinned up at him, readying her sword.

"Something told me you would want some fun this morning." Thane twisted his swords in an elaborate pattern.

Jerina admired his graceful movements and was mesmerized by

the way his muscles rippled and pulled across his arms and chest. Caught staring at his body, she didn't see the sword coming toward her until it was right in front of her face. She swung her sword up to catch it, and the sparring was on.

Parrying across the grass and pathways, and through the flower beds, they clashed swords and strikes. Jerina had seen him fight her younger warriors, but he had been holding back. Fighting him was thrilling and challenging. She hadn't had a match like this in years.

After a while, they both decided to end things before their competitive streaks took over and one of them got hurt. As it was, Thane had a cut across his thigh, and Jerina's shirt sleeve had a couple of torn spots with beads of blood seeping through.

Thane replaced his swords and sat down on the dirt path, trying to catch his breath. Jerina had been the best opponent he had ever had. He couldn't wait to practice with her again.

"How did you know I was out here?" Jerina asked, wiping sweat from her forehead with her sleeve.

"I know you." Thane grinned at her.

"You think you know me so well?" Jerina teased.

He nodded, rising to reach her side. He only wanted to brush back some of the strands of hair that were sticking to her cheek, but he ended up caressing her neck down to her shoulder.

Her shivering response was all the encouragement he needed. Bending his head, he nipped at her lip before pressing his mouth gently against hers. The kiss was feather soft and sweet, intended to only savor the moment, but once he started, he craved more.

Jerina tugged on his shirt to get him closer. She knew she shouldn't allow him to kiss her, but it was too intoxicating and wicked to stop.

Thane broke his mouth away from hers but placed a quick peck on her forehead. "We need to get cleaned up. We have a big day. I'll be back in a couple of hours."

Jerina nodded and watched him walk off. She had a ton of things to do before they executed their plan that night.

CHAPTER 12

Thane had snuck in to see Kosa again to explain what they had planned. She was more than willing to help and even offered a suggestion as to how they should distract Perun. She had been gathering as much information about him as she could in hopes that she would one day be free of him. She knew Jerina wouldn't give up on her, but she never expected Thane to be just as dedicated to saving her.

Every night after she was locked inside her room, she would peek under the bed to see if Thane had left anything for her. The first night, she found a key that seemed to be infused with magic. She discovered that it unlocked every door she tried. That would be a handy thing to have.

She found a spell to counteract the dark magic in the pocket watch enough for her to take it. They were not sure if it would be powerful enough to allow them to destroy it.

The next night, she found a small corked glass bottle with instructions on how to use it to make the guard outside her door fall asleep. It was a strong sleeping draught that doctors used on humans. If he was immune to magic, maybe pharmaceuticals would work. There was enough for two times. Once to test it out and once to use on him when they planned their rescue, if it worked the first time. She would slip it into his drink and hope for the best.

Kosa could hardly wait for her next instruction.

～

Thane and Jerina had made sure that Perun and Kosa were occupied at one of the restaurants in town before they broke into his house. They needed to leave a package for Kosa.

It had been anticlimactic and disappointing to Jerina. They had walked up to the back door, recited an open spell, entered the house, and ran up the back stairs without seeing anyone. She didn't want any trouble or danger, but she had expected something a little more interesting.

They left a carved wooden box trimmed in gold swirls with gold hinges and lock. It was an exact replica of Perun's box. Even if it had slight differences, the magical illusion covering it would assure that he saw only his box.

Inside the box was a gold pocket watch that was spelled to look and feel just like Perun's. Saundra had helped to make the watch carry a dark magic signature so that it would give off the same energy as his.

It was vital that when Kosa switched out the boxes, he believed that he still had his originals.

～

Thane picked up the white silk wrap and stepped behind Jerina. She twisted around to view him, surprised at the gentlemanly gesture. She had never experienced a man helping her do anything. She allowed him to place the wrap around her shoulders and was thankful she could suppress a shudder when his fingers brushed her neck as he pulled her hair from beneath the wrap.

Thane shrugged. "Since we are all spiffy, I figured I'd better pull out my good manners."

Jerina glanced at him, at a loss.

Thane grinned at her discomfort. "It's just a short walk to Glitz. We have reservations for the ten o'clock show. We have a little bit of time to walk around the town square."

"What is Glitz?" Jerina linked her arm through his as they left the inn.

"It's a restaurant with a big band and two couples that sing and dance. Some say that one of the girls is a better dancer than Ginger Rogers." Thane knew his parents enjoyed going there on a night out on the town. He would have liked to take Jerina out on a real date, but that wouldn't happen until Kosa was safe.

"Who is Ginger Rogers?" Jerina crinkled her forehead.

Thane smiled. "She's an actress and one of the best dancers today. My mom will have a photo of her in one of her magazines."

Thane and Jerina walked through the town square as if nothing was wrong in the world. They meandered through the crowds, window-shopped, and chatted with people as they walked by. No one would ever suspect that in an hour, they were going to break into Perun's house, steal the watch, and rescue Kosa.

Jerina paused to glance inside Charms Soda Shoppe, her favorite place to get ice cream. She wished they weren't on a mission and had time to enjoy themselves with dessert.

They had decided to sit in the gazebo for a few minutes to calm Jerina's emotions enough for them to continue on with their plans.

Glitz was a couple of blocks off the square, sitting majestically up on a hill. Valets waited in front of the circular drive to hop into the convertibles and luxury vehicles of the town's exclusively wealthy.

Jerina watched as glamorous women in sparkling gowns and high heels clung to the arms of dashing men in suits and fedora hats.

"Do they always dress like this?" Jerina asked, feeling a little out of place.

Thane turned her toward him as they watched a maroon

Pontiac Streamliner pull up to the valet station followed closely behind by a shiny red DeSoto sedan.

"Most of the people that come here do." He brushed hair from her cheek. "Don't worry. You look beautiful."

She simply smiled, not knowing what to say to the compliment. Bright lights lit the entire area, making it almost like daylight as people filtered into the restaurant. Jerina glanced at the two-story glass front of the building that sparkled and gleamed in the brightness.

Jerina caught the eyes of two young human men who were trailing behind an older couple.

"Check out the dish over there," she heard one of them say to his friend.

"She's a looker. Too bad she's with that tall fella." The other guy was not hiding his blatant stare.

Thane placed his hand at the small of her back and guided her inside and away from the men. He focused on Jerina and not the two outside.

"Thane?" Jerina called for the third time.

He smiled sheepishly. "Sorry. It's taking all my self-control not to go out there and brain those two."

"Brain?" His words sometimes confused her.

"It means hit on the noggin." Thane pointed to his head.

"There's no need for that." Jerina turned toward the two women waiting to greet them. One of them approached and helped Jerina remove her wrap, and the other took Thane's hat and overcoat. The lobby was filled with lounge chairs in cozy clusters, allowing for privacy while patrons waited to be seated.

Thane had phoned ahead and arranged for them to have a table at the side of the room that offered a little privacy. They left the lobby, venturing down a few steps into the vast main ballroom. A large low stage covered the back wall, with a raised platform off to the right that held the big band. White linen tables with crystal wine glasses rimmed the dance floor in the center of the room.

Jerina was captivated by everything she saw. They were led to a table at the edge of the room that was set for two. Thane pulled out her chair and waited as she took her seat.

"Thank you," she said nervously. They would be sneaking out of the show soon, but she was determined to enjoy things while they lasted.

"I'm sorry we can't stay and see the entire show. I will bring you back here after we save Kosa." Thane was busy watching Jerina as she took everything in with the innocence and wonder of someone experiencing everything for the first time.

She bestowed him with a dazzling smile. "I would love that."

The lights turned low, and music filled the room. Thane knew they could stay for a few minutes of the show before sneaking off.

Jerina sat up in her seat with her eyes glued to the stage. A couple of women danced into the center of the stage from the sides, swirling their long gowns to the beat. Their dance partners swept them into their arms and continued to twirl them around so many times, Jerina would have become dizzy.

After a couple of songs, Thane reached over and laced his fingers with hers. "We have to go."

Jerina nodded and slowly stood, sliding along the wall to the rear exit. Thane followed behind quietly. Thankfully no one was paying attention to the dimly lit outer area. It would be easy to leave while the performance was underway.

Thane unlocked the door with magic, and they hurried into the alleyway.

Step one of their plan had been completed.

The walk to Perun's hadn't taken much time at all, so they arrived before Thane had anticipated getting there. That gave them extra time to make sure everything was in place.

Kosa left the curtains to her room open and the light on so they could see inside. She walked past the window twice but didn't look outside. They knew once she knocked the guard out cold, she would signal that she was ready.

"I hate waiting," Jerina mumbled. "It makes me antsy."

Thane leaned over and kissed her forehead. "I could come up with something to keep your mind off of things."

She glanced sideways at him. "No, thank you."

"Your loss." Thane purposely ran his hand down the length of her arm as he reached around her to look into their bag. They had brought a few weapons with them in case things turned out badly. They hoped it wouldn't happen, but they needed to be prepared.

Kosa stood at the window, looking out for several moments and then turned out the light. That was the signal.

"How do we know if Perun is asleep?" Jerina asked.

"He won't be. It's still early enough that he will be in bed, but not asleep. That's where my part comes in." Thane kissed her cheek and jogged off toward the front door.

It was an indecent time to call on someone, but Thane was counting on that. He needed Perun to be already dressed for bed and annoyed at having to answer the door.

Thane knocked loudly on the front door for several minutes. A haggard looking man answered the door with a sharp, "May I help you, sir?"

Thane brushed by him and into the foyer. "I must see Perun at once. It's urgent."

The servant seemed torn between rushing off after his employer and ejecting Thane from the house.

"Hurry!" Thane insisted. He even made a show of pacing back and forth.

Perun appeared at the top of the staircase, wrapping a silk robe over his cotton pajamas. "What is it? This had better be important, Thane!"

Thane tried extremely hard not to grin. His plan was working out perfectly. "I needed to speak with you at once."

"What is it?" Perun's exasperation was clear.

"I found a loophole with controlling vila with their hair. It's a way out for them. I needed to warn you immediately."

Perun narrowed his gaze at Thane and exhaled a deep breath. "Why are you sharing this with me?"

"Jerina escaped. I'm going to get her back. I figured she would probably go for her sister so I wanted to warn you before they both get away."

Perun threw his head back and laughed. "So, this isn't about helping me, but getting your plaything back." He walked into the study off the foyer and poured himself a whiskey. He threw it back in one gulp.

Thane followed him into the room but stayed by the door. He didn't trust the mage.

"It's not just about power to you. I see how you look at her." Perun poured another inch in his glass. "You'd better watch yourself with that one. You'll end up dead. The curse is real."

"I can take care of myself." Thane backed out of the room, keeping Perun in his view.

"You never had any intention to tell me about this loophole. You only came to see if she was here." Perun narrowed his gaze at Thane.

Thane shrugged one shoulder and walked toward the front door. "Let me know if you see Jerina."

Thane hoped he gave Kosa enough time to switch boxes. He couldn't stay any longer or Perun would suspect something was up.

He took his time walking across the street and let the shadows close around him.

Jerina was waiting for him just up the road behind a large bush. He knew she had been watching the door to Perun's. He could feel her eyes on him.

As soon as he cleared the streetlight and stepped behind the bush, Jerina's arms wound around his neck.

"I was so worried!" She hugged him tightly, her chest aching with fear for him. "Do you think he suspected anything?"

Thane squeezed her to him. "No. Not at all. He was more concerned with me losing you than anything."

He left out the part about the curse. Jerina was worried enough about it. He didn't need to add that Perun was convinced that it was real.

"How long do you think it will take Kosa to sneak out?" Jerina wanted to storm inside and get her sister, but she knew they would have a better chance if Kosa came out on her own.

Twenty excruciatingly long minutes later, they spotted Kosa at the window of her bedroom. She slid the panes up and leaned out. She was holding something in her hands.

Jerina squinted to see what she was doing. Kosa struck a match and was placing it over the open pocket watch. As soon as the fire touched the watch, a horrifying scream shook the night. It sounded like the watch was being burnt alive.

Thane and Jerina ran toward the house. Kosa held the screaming watch helplessly, not knowing what to do. They had not anticipated the watch being a trap.

Kosa leaned out of the window. "The spell allowed me to take the watch, but I can't destroy it."

Lights flickered on through the house. Thane knew they had to get Kosa out of there immediately. "Throw it down to me. I'll burn it, while you climb down the ivy!"

Kosa tossed the watch to Thane.

"I can't leave the house until it is destroyed!"

The watch stopped screaming when Kosa dropped it, but once Thane created fire magic, it began to screech again. Thane intensified the fire, but it resisted.

They were running out of time. Jerina joined Thane and added her magic to his, making the fire roar with strength. The watch's back compartment opened, and the hair went up in flames quickly.

Kosa leaned out of the window, trying to force herself to climb out, but unable to do so. Once the hair began to sizzle, she felt the invisible barrier break, and she was able to slip from the room.

She reached the ground at the same time Perun flew out the front door with a gun in his hand.

"What have you done?" Perun demanded. He pointed the gun at Jerina. "You have been nothing but a problem to me since you first entered this town!" Perun stalked toward them, closing the space.

Jerina clenched her fists. "You will not control another vila. Ever!"

She took her sister's hand and backed up a few steps. They needed to get away from Perun. He was looking a little unhinged.

"You lost, Perun. Give up. No one should be enslaved by another." Thane wanted to direct Perun's rage at him and not the girls. He needed to get them to safety and away from the gun.

"She is MINE! She belongs to ME!" Perun bellowed into the night.

Jerina stepped back again, but Perun followed. She didn't know how to get away from him while he was waving that gun. She had heard that guns didn't work well in Havenwood Falls and especially around supernaturals, so she was surprised he had one. The vila never used guns. They would not work correctly around all their magic.

"Kosa! You get back here right now! You are mine! MINE! You'll always be mine! I'll find you no matter where you go. I *will* find you. You'll never escape me."

Thane glanced at Jerina and Kosa. "I'll distract him. You two run for help."

Jerina shook her head. "I'm not leaving you. We're in this together."

"I'll be fine. Just go!" Thane needed them out of the way. He threw magic at Perun, but the mage was good enough with spells that he blasted it away from him.

Thane tried a stunning spell, but that too was reflected. His swords were not a match for a gun, so he needed to keep Perun talking and hopefully push him over the edge to do something stupid. "You're not man enough for a vila."

Jerina's jaw dropped. "What are you doing?"

Thane ignored her. "Yeah. The vila warrior couldn't wait to get away from you. And look where she ran. Straight to me."

Perun swung the gun toward Thane. "You're trying to steal them both for yourself! I won't let you get away with that."

Thane turned to glance at Jerina. "Run!" he mouthed.

Jerina was terrified for Thane. He had just turned the monster's attention solely on him. She needed to do something.

"You're nothing, Perun! You had to steal my sister to be a stronger mage. You didn't have enough power on your own to compete in your coven, so you decided to steal Kosa's," Jerina taunted. "You're a fool!"

Perun screamed inhumanly and flipped the gun toward Jerina. When he saw her smile, he pulled the trigger with a sneer. A deafening blast shook the street as the gun fired. Jerina's eyes grew huge as she saw the bullet head directly toward her.

Seconds before it was to hit her chest, Thane jumped in front of her and was shot in the chest.

"NOOOOOOO!" Jerina screamed in agony, her arms going around Thane as he fell to the ground. Red was spreading from the middle of his chest, soaking through his clothing.

Manic laughter filled the street after Jerina's scream ended.

"I win." Perun moved closer but was suddenly surrounded by members of the Court, who took him into custody.

Jerina ripped open Thane's shirt and gasped. The hole was huge and was rhythmically expelling blood. He was shot through the heart.

Jerina's hands began to shake as she tried to heal him, sending every ounce of power she had into him. His skin was closing up, but it didn't seem to be enough.

Thane lifted his hand to Jerina's tear-stricken face. "It's not going to work. The bullet was made of iron."

"No! No! It has to work. I won't let you die." Jerina sobbed as she continued to try to heal him.

Thane's grip was growing weaker. "It's okay. You're safe. He won't hurt you or Kosa again."

"Don't you dare give up, Thane! I won't let you!" Jerina gripped the edges of his shirt.

Thane smiled sadly. "I guess you were right. The curse is real. I love you."

"I love you too," Jerina sobbed, and then Thane's heart stopped beating.

Jerina's scream of outrage could be heard throughout Havenwood Falls. She unleashed her emotions all at once, creating a storm unlike ever before. Hurricane-force winds ripped through the valley. Thunder shook the houses, and lightning lit up the sky. Rain pelted down on the street, drenching anyone brave enough not to take cover.

Kosa sobbed as she watched her sister hold the man she loved. Damn the curse! She hated being a vila.

She watched her sister look up at the sky and knew she was asking the gods why they would do this to her.

Lightning struck a tree near where they were, throwing sparks into the air. The flash drew her attention and gave her an idea. Kosa let her power surge through her and reach for the storm. She didn't know if it would work, but it was worth a try.

Kosa connected with a bolt of lightning and guided it toward Thane, striking him in the chest.

Jerina's head whipped toward Kosa. "What are you doing to him?"

She lay across his chest, protecting him from everything, sobbing his name.

She felt him twitch, making her sit up and stare at his beautiful face, wondering if it was her imagination. Just then, he inhaled deeply and began to cough. The storm died down, and Jerina pulled her power back.

Kosa was at their side in an instant, her healing powers running through her hands. Jerina snapped out of her shock and joined her sister, locking their hands together.

After a moment, Thane opened his eyes and focused on Jerina.

She threw herself into his arms and kissed him hard. "Don't ever do that to me again!" She cried and laughed at the same time.

Thane hugged her to him. "We changed fate. You're stuck with me now."

Jerina pulled back so she could face him. "Forever?"

"Forever."

EPILOGUE

ONE WEEK LATER

The roar of the rushing water didn't drown out Jerina's thoughts, but she had hoped they would. She had too much on her mind and no idea what to do about it all.

She stared out at the falls, hoping answers would suddenly manifest. All that had appeared were four pixies playing in the underbrush near the falls. They seemed a little skittish, so she didn't try to speak with them.

Perun had been held in the basement of the courthouse in a magical cell that kept him from escaping until the Court of the Sun and the Moon decided his fate. It took them the entire week to deliberate before they finally decided that he would be banished from Havenwood Falls for fifty-five years.

Jerina had no idea how they came up with fifty-five years, but at least the residents of the town wouldn't have to worry about him for a long time. Warning her vila sisters to be on the lookout for him would be vital. She had a feeling he would be relentless in an attempt to seek revenge on her and Kosa.

She began planning everything they would need to do to

prepare. Some camouflage around their village would have to be put in place so that he would never be able to find it again.

"Ugh," she muttered to herself.

She had responsibilities to her vila, but she knew her heart would remain in Havenwood Falls. It would be so easy to make a life with Thane. They loved each other, and they changed fate. That meant everything.

"I knew you would be here," Kosa called out as she approached her sister Jerina. A light breeze ruffled her blond hair.

Jerina pulled her focus from the falls and greeted Kosa with a big smile. "I love it here. There's so much magic in the falls and around this area. It—"

"Almost feels like home?" Kosa finished for her. She sat on the flat boulder next to Jerina, bumping her shoulder purposely.

Jerina nodded. "Yes. It does."

It was spring in Colorado, but the air around the falls was chilly, causing her to tug her jacket tighter.

The sisters sat quietly, each lost in their own thoughts as they gazed at the rushing water. Jerina watched a few fish jump from the waves, splashing down and disappearing from view.

Kosa took a deep fortifying breath. She couldn't delay any longer. "I'm not going back."

Jerina continued to stare into the falls.

"Did you hear what I said? I'm not returning." Kosa twisted to face Jerina.

Jerina blinked slowly and shifted around to her beloved sister. "I know." Grasping Kosa's hand, Jerina gently squeezed and then released Kosa. "I knew you would want to remain here." She paused. "Things will never be the same."

Kosa's shoulders dropped. "You're going back?"

Jerina slipped off the large rock and stepped toward the bank of the river. "I'm the leader of the warriors, and I must protect every vila. I can't abandon our sisters."

Kosa stormed over to Jerina. "You aren't an elder. You don't rule over the vila. Think about yourself for once."

"Who would train the warriors? How could we both leave?" Jerina pulled at her hair. Their mother would be furious, and not because she would miss her daughters. She would be afraid of the scandal and how it would affect her.

Kosa put her arm around Jerina's shoulders. "There are many who could, and would want to, step into your role as leader of the warriors."

Jerina crossed her arms over her chest and hugged herself. "Yes, but I need to make sure everyone is safe before I could even consider anything else."

Kosa tried to control the quaking in her legs at the thought of Perun out in the world somewhere. "We are safer from him here."

"Yes, we are, but our vila sisters need to be as well." Jerina wanted to stay, but didn't know how it could possibly work.

"It wouldn't take much to make them safe." Kosa loved the vila. But she needed this, and she knew Jerina did too. "What about Thane?"

"What about him?" Jerina shifted, suddenly uncomfortable.

"I know you love him." Kosa raised an eyebrow. "Don't try to deny it. Don't you want to stay here and see what happens with him? You love him, do you not?"

Jerina sighed. "It's not that simple."

"Yes. Yes, it is." Kosa bounced on her toes. "Has he asked you to stay?"

"She hasn't given me an answer yet." Thane strolled out of the woods and into the clearing by the waterfall.

Jerina's breath caught as she watched him move closer, his muscles rippling with each step.

Thane nodded at Kosa but continued to focus on Jerina. "I'm still waiting." He stepped into her space, crowding her, but she didn't seem to mind. He heard her breath catch and couldn't prevent a dazzling smile from brightening his face. "I came up with a solution."

Jerina had to clear her throat to answer him. "A solution to what?"

Kosa crossed her fingers and moved back to give them some privacy.

Thane leaned closer. "To everything. I know you don't have much in today's currency because the vila don't need it, so living independently here would be extremely difficult. You wouldn't be happy staying with my parents or at the inn and letting me pay for it."

Jerina frowned and retreated a step. "I already know all this."

Thane followed after her. "You didn't let me finish. I've been thinking about this a lot." He rubbed his hand down her arm, causing her to shiver. "There is a human gentleman who is getting ready to retire. He doesn't have any family to leave his business to and doesn't need any money. He wants his business to continue, but doesn't have anyone to take it over. I spoke with him, and he would love to take on two lovely exchange students who wanted to stay in Havenwood Falls and not return to their war-torn country."

Kosa couldn't pretend to give them a private moment any longer. "Really? What business?"

Thane didn't take his eyes off Jerina, but answered Kosa. "Mr. Scoop remembered how much you love his sundaes. He's looking forward to showing you how to make them."

Jerina's eyes lit up. "Charms Soda Shoppe?"

Thane grinned. "Yes. Perfect, isn't it?"

Jerina threw herself into his arms and hugged him tightly.

Thane crushed her to him. "Does this mean you're staying?"

Jerina pulled back a little and looked over at her sister. "What do you think?"

Kosa grinned widely. "I think we need to make sure you leave some ice cream for our customers."

Jerina rushed to her sister, and they embraced, laughing.

Kosa squeezed Jerina and stepped back. "I'll see you two in a little while at the inn. Madame Luiza is going to show me how to make cookies."

Thane watched the sisters' joy and knew that they were going to end up very happy in Havenwood Falls.

"Thank you so much for arranging this." Jerina would have to make a short trip back to the vila village, but it would no longer be her home.

Thane brushed hair out of her face. "I would do anything for you."

"I would do anything for you, too." Jerina's eyes twinkled and became a little watery. She'd never felt that way about anyone before. "I love you."

"Good. You're going to have to love me for a really long time, because I'm not letting you go." Thane slid his hands into her hair and sealed his vow with a toe-curling kiss.

ABOUT THE AUTHOR

Char Webster weaves suspense, mystery, romance, and humor into all of her books. She strives to make the paranormal world fit perfectly into real life, where anything seems to be possible.

Reading and getting lost in a story have always been Char Webster's favorite things to do. She has also had a love for writing, which led her to her daytime career in public relations and marketing. After years of writing for others, Char decided to write something for herself.

Her writing fulfills a lifelong dream of creating a world where people can escape reality for a little while. Char Webster adores living in South Jersey because she feels like it is in the center of everything. She loves pizza, hot sauce, French fries, dancing, photography, and trying new things.

Stay in touch with Char:
Facebook: www.facebook.com/CharWebsterAuthor
Twitter: www.twitter.com/JustaGirlinSJ
Instagram: www.Instragram.com/Char.Webster
Website: www.CharWebsterAuthor.com

ACKNOWLEDGMENTS

It's an honor to be a part of the Havenwood Falls family, and I am so very thankful to Kristie Cook for bringing me into her incredible shared world. There are so many talented authors who have contributed to Havenwood Falls, and I get to be one of them. A special thank you to Kristie Cook, Kallie Ross, Brynn Myers, Randi Cooley Wilson, and Amy Hale for allowing me to include their awesome characters in my story. It was so much fun to include them.

I love the cover to *Changing Fate*, so I definitely need to give a big thank you to Regina Wamba at Mae I Design for creating great covers for this universe.

A HUGE thank you to all family for all their support and love and putting up with my crazy writing schedule.

I want to send lots of love to all of the readers out there. You are amazing. Thank you all for reading my books and showing me so much love. I also want to give a very big thank you to the Havenwood Falls Book Club and to Char's Gifted Society for being awesome and supporting me and my books.

RISE OF THE WITCH HUNTERS

MORGAN WYLIE

A Legends of Havenwood Falls Novella

HAVENWOOD FALLS LEGENDS

RISE OF THE WITCH HUNTERS

USA TODAY BESTSELLING AUTHOR

MORGAN WYLIE

BOOKS BY MORGAN WYLIE

YA FANTASY

Silent Orchids (Book 1)

Veiled Shadows (Book 2)

Daegan (Novella 2.5)

Fractured Darkness (Book 3)

Fading Light (Book 4)

The Sol-lumieth (Book 5) (Winter 2019)

The Rise of the Paladin (An Alandria Short Story Prequel) (Free with
Newsletter subscription)

YA PARANORMAL/SUPERNATURAL

HAILEY: The Necromancer (A Shadow Realm Novella 1) (previously
released as Supernatural Chronicles: The Necromancers Novella #7)

JAX: The Doppelgänger (A Shadow Realm Novella 2)

WILLOW (A Shadow Realm Novella 3) (Coming soon!)

SOLANGE (A Shadow Realm Novella 4) (Coming soon!)

NA/ADULT PARANORMAL ROMANCE

RYLEN (The Tangled Web Book 1)

MATHER (The Tangled Web Book 2)

JET (A Tangled Web Novella)

HAVENWOOD FALLS

Reawakened (A Havenwood Falls High Novella)

Dawn of the Witch Hunters (A Legends of Havenwood Falls Novella)

Redefined (A Havenwood Falls Novella)

Rise of the Witch Hunters (A Legends of Havenwood Falls Novella)

Rediscovered (A Havenwood Falls High Novella)

To the Havenwood Falls Book Club and readers . . . You ROCK!
Thank you for reading our stories and loving our town as much as we,
the authors, do.

CHAPTER 1

1858 WHISPER FALLS

*M*arie Blackstone meandered down an aisle, passing through new shoots of grape vines in the oldest section of the Blackstone vineyard. The aroma of the sticky sweet fruit wafted into her nose as she passed by. As she approached the large outbuilding, she expected to run into the waiting arms of her husband, Judson. Except he wasn't standing with the barrels of wine where he was supposed to be. Noting her bare feet, Marie paused and slowly turned her head, realizing she was not alone. She took in the faces of a small crowd of townspeople around her, but something strange happened. Faces distorted and blurred. Her pulse quickened, and she looked around with panic.

Where's Judson?

Beyond the blurred faces, trees slowly enclosed around them. Within the trees, Marie spotted something—something she couldn't quite define. Dark wispy shadows of swirling masses wrapped around the trees, moving closer, stretching out tendrils of smoke, and invading the town and the people within it. Marie doubled over. Her stomach hurt so bad with the effects of dark magic she thought she would be sick. Her hands shook. Her head swam with visions of darkness, and dizziness took her down to her knees.

Judson! Where are you? Marie screamed but no sound came from her mouth. Her words were trapped in her mind.

Soon the townspeople faded from her view, consumed by the darkness as it moved closer toward her. Silhouettes emerged but not enough to recognize who or what they were. Were they supernatural? Were they creatures of some kind? Were they the souls of people she knew?

Out of nowhere Judson shot out in front of Marie, holding some kind of tool—a small sword with a glowing stone, her family dagger—sending a jolt of light toward the darkness. The light mixed with the power Judson had somehow infused it with and pushed the darkness back with hisses of displeasure screeching through the night.

Judson! Judson! Marie called again, but she couldn't seem to reach him with her voice. Instead she reached out her hand to grab his, but he, too, faded away from her with the townspeople. Marie heard words before she also faded into nothingness:

"Release me, Marie."

Then darkness swallowed her.

Marie awoke gasping for air, doubled over in pain. Her brow was slicked with sweat as she opened her eyes and took in the room around her. She pushed back her long blond hair away from her sticky skin. Home. She was in her bed.

A dream. It had all been a dream. Then why did she still feel so sick? Could it also be a warning?

Marie wasn't surprised to not see Judson in bed next to her. Since they'd been married, he'd been busy with blacksmith work. She called out, her voice dry and scratchy from sleep, "Judson? Are you there?"

When Judson didn't reply, she stumbled to her feet and went in search of him. The more she moved, the more she felt herself coming back from the brink of whatever ailment she had experienced. Her heart rate slowed to normal, and her breathing finally caught up with her. She had only felt a feeling so strong once before, when she and Judson had traveled across the country by wagon train with the other original settlers. They had stumbled upon an encampment of witches—witches who had been performing black magic. Unfortunately, her brother Dante and his band of rogue witch hunters had killed them all before she arrived and had the chance to stop him. He had been sending her a message: *This is our calling. This is our destiny: to rid the earth of all those capable of destructive magic.* However, Marie knew he wouldn't stop at users of dark magic alone. No, he would kill any and all witches if he could. He felt it was their birthright.

Marie felt differently.

She wanted to find a way to coexist. She had friends who were witches, and her mother had found peace among them before she died. Marie chose to follow in her mother's footsteps. Plus, she wouldn't have Judson if she went along with the idea of who they thought a witch hunter should be. Judson may not have been a witch, but he was raised by one within an entire coven of witches. So to Dante, Judson was just as evil.

Marie paused in front of an open window and gazed out at their beautiful new surroundings they called home—well, not so new, considering they had been living in the quaint box canyon area for a few years now. The sight of the mountains boxing them in on all four sides still warmed her heart and freely offered her peace, especially when a fresh thin layer of snow had fallen overnight, as it had the past night. Snow was early for September but not unheard of in the mountains. It wouldn't last through the day, however. The sun had just barely begun to make its ascent into the sky, but soft pink still welcomed the coming day.

Marie smiled when she noticed man-sized footprints traveling away from their home toward the shed Judson had set up as a blacksmith's forge. He had earned quite the reputation for his metalwork around town, and he'd been attempting to catch up on orders he had yet to fulfill. She had no doubt that was where he'd been since before dawn, working his heart out. Judson's personal metalwork took a back seat while he worked on orders for the townspeople, early in the morning or late into the evening, to make ends meet.

Marie dressed for the cold winds of fall she was about to face and wrapped herself with a heavy shawl. Theirs was a modest home built right next to the land they had claimed for the vineyard they were cultivating with such love and devotion. The house had just enough rooms for the family who had traveled with them: Marie's human father Hank, her human brother Rodney, her young adult hunter cousins Caroline and Michael, as well as a few other cousins who never fully awakened into their hunter side. Also, Rachael Stronghold—Marie's best friend from the coven Judson was raised in—and Ahote Ahusaka traveled and lived with them. Rachael and Ahote were now married with an emerging toddler named Alo Stronghold Ahusaka, after Ahote's brother and Rachael's maiden name for her mother who died before they had arrived. Needless to say, they were living in tight quarters.

Marie dreamed of one day being able to add additional rooms —perhaps even additional little cabins—to their home not only for family but for visitors who came to the area. The view was magnificent, and she wanted to share the peace and comfort she had found there with others. Then when the vineyard was fully functional and they had enough workers to sustain it, Marie dreamed of a larger, grander home closer to the falls to live out her days with Judson, hopefully raising a family of their own.

For the last several years since arriving in town, the original settlers had begun calling the area Whisper Falls due to the way the falls had beckoned them, whispering into their souls, to come. And when they stood in the center of the little canyon, the falls sounded like a whisper, and so they had begun to build the town in that very spot. However, other names had been bandied about—many wanted to include *haven* in the name, since that was the purpose of the town—and there was still much discussion about it.

As she exited the warm and cozy home—thanks to one of the early risers' forethought to build a fire—she inhaled slow and deep, feeling the sharp sting of the bitterly cold air as it flooded her lungs, and smiled. Though jarring, the feeling reminded her she was alive. She loved fall in the little box canyon. It wasn't unheard of to find snow this early; still, she proceeded with caution as she made her way toward the forge. Marie carefully avoided patches of ice and areas of thicker frost. Loving the squeaking sound her boots made against the snow, Marie paused to listen for the whispers from the falls. This time of morning, the town was quiet and the rushing water could clearly be heard. She closed her eyes and could practically feel the mist spray off the water and onto her face. Such a great sense of importance, of magic, and of purpose she felt next to the waters.

The memory instantly took her back to when they had first arrived. She and Judson had picnicked by the edge of the lower pool. She had just discovered that the stone set into the dagger Judson had given her had immense power when it touched the magical waters, but when it was interlocked with her ancestor's journal, the pages within had revealed much more about who she was as a Blackstone than she had ever known. The secrets and knowledge she had been seeking since her mother died had finally been revealed. It was also then and in that space, Judson Carter proposed to her—again. His action was not necessary, as they had been married in secret back in Virginia before they left, but he wanted to make a symbolic statement of their new life. Shortly after they established their life in the mountains and secured their position, they had asked Raffaele Augustine to marry them again. She wanted friends, not just strangers, to witness their union. And it had taken them some time and experience to gain that trust and companionship she had so longed for.

CHAPTER 2

*A*s Marie approached the shed, she could hear the clanging sounds of iron slamming against metal. She snuck into the forge, attempting not to disturb Judson while he worked with hot metal. Just as she was about to make her presence known, she watched Judson shake out his hand after the last hit with his hammer, only to realize extra sparks ascended into the air. Sparks not from the metal or the hot coals. Surprised confusion lit up his face. Marie cocked her head, wondering what could have caused the sparks, when she considered that perhaps he'd been working on her dagger. Since being infused with the water from the falls, the stone had lit with magic; the sparks could have come from that.

"Judson," she called out from around the wall to announce her entrance. Glancing at him, she saw him quickly put his hand behind his back before he reached for his hammer once more. "Everything all right in here?" she asked.

Moving around to the front of the fire, he briefly frowned, then smiled at her. "You're up early. Everything fine at the house?"

She noticed he didn't answer her question.

"I woke up from a disturbing dream where you disappeared from me again, so I came to check on you."

He came to her and placed his free hand upon her shoulder. His warm brown eyes bored into her soul. "I'm right here, Marie. I don't like you having these recurring nightmares. Sure you're all right?"

She nodded, though the memory of the dream made her shudder. "I know it was just a dream, but I needed to see you awake."

Judson watched her for a moment more before he returned to the fire and picked up his hammer. Judson was tall and muscular. His dark blond hair had grown longer and appeared dirtier than normal, working amidst all the soot and smoke.

"I'm almost finished with the repair work on your dagger. I smoothed out the blade as well." He lifted the dagger that had been in her family for centuries to show her his work. Only in the last several years did she discover that the dagger had originally been in her family for many years—and the Stronghold coven had been keeping it safe—and because of her family's journal, she learned more of the dagger's properties and how it might have worked for her ancestors. Judson had been tinkering with it and found learning about the round stone fascinating. Before they arrived, the stone was colorless. Then Marie infused the smooth rock with a magical aether, turning it to a glowing blueish green, when she mixed the stone with the water from the falls. Inscribed on the blade itself was a Latin phrase: *Elige tibi*. Translated, it meant: Choose yourself.

And that was exactly what Marie had done in order to free what family she could and herself. She chose the kind of witch hunter she and her descendants would have the opportunity to be.

Marie moved around to the other side of the circular stone fire pit containing a raging fire in order to watch Judson put the finishing touches on her dagger before dipping it in the cool water to solidify his work. His actions were smooth and graceful, practiced and perfect for working on even the most delicate piece of metal. Marie's eyes never left him. She watched each movement, evaluating him. Something was wrong, though, and he hadn't shared it with her—and that bothered her the most.

"Jud? Are *you* all right? You seem a little off," she said casually, watching his reaction, waiting for his reply.

He slowed his swing but didn't fully stop. "I woke up a little shaky, but I'm sure it'll wear off. Perhaps I'm just hungry. I didn't eat before coming out this morning. I didn't want to wake you."

"Oh, Judson, you know you need to eat before expending all that energy. I'll go fix you something right now and bring it back." Of course, that had to have been all it was. He burned so many calories and so much energy when he worked in the forge. "I'll see if Rachael and Ahote are up, and we'll all come out for breakfast." Marie headed back the way she entered but looked over her shoulder at him before she left.

"Sounds great, love. I'm famished. But I'll be in shortly—no reason to have them all traipse out here in the cold of the morning." Judson wiped the sweat from his brow, causing the hair to stick up at the top of his head, then he winked at her.

The wind picked up as soon as she left the outbuilding. Marie clenched her wrap tightly around her shoulders, ducked her chin, and dashed back to the house. Upon entering, she heard all the voices joyously chatting in the kitchen. She loved how they all still wanted to live together, but someday soon they would definitely need more room. Marie chuckled to herself and smiled at the heavenly sounds of grease popping on the griddle, eggs cracking in a bowl, and the fire crackling, accompanied by the most delicious smells. Breakfast was already underway.

"Everything smells so good in here!" Marie walked into the kitchen, inhaling with a smile the entire way. "I hope I didn't wake you," she said, putting her arms around Rachael, who stood in front of the cast-iron wood stove, checking the sizzling bacon.

She and Rachael Stronghold had been friends forever. When Marie needed to leave her home and family in Virginia to head out west with a traveling wagon train to get away from her crazed witch hunter brother, Dante, Rachael and some others from their coven chose to join her—plus Dante and his group had pretty much destroyed the Strongholds' entire village, and they had nowhere else to go. Still, Rachael had been Marie's biggest supporter since her mother, Cessily, had died. Since moving out west, Marie wanted to support Rachael in return.

Rachael's mom had died during the raid Dante and his band had inflicted upon their coven. Marie owed Rachael a life debt—at least that was how Marie saw it. And now, Rachael and Ahote's first child was a part of their family. Marie couldn't contain her excitement. She considered all of them under her protection within the new town, and as such, she claimed them as her family—as Blackstones.

Rachael had prematurely gained the leadership of the Stronghold coven at the death of her mother. Since arriving, Rachael had offered her people—those who had remained with them—the opportunity to join the Luna coven while she studied and grew in her own powers and magic.

"Not at all. In fact, I was waiting for you to get up. When I heard you moving around, I got up, but you had already walked outside. Will Judson be joining us?" She smiled and picked up a slice of bacon with a fork and flipped it over.

"Yes, he'll be along shortly. And he's famished, so I'll make some more," Marie said with a laugh.

Rachael turned to look at Marie, cocked her head, and frowned. "What's wrong?"

Marie dropped her arms and took a step back, looking intently at her friend. "How do you do that?"

"What?"

"That thing where you always know something is either wrong or about to go wrong," Marie added, knowing full well Rachael knew exactly what she was talking about.

She shrugged. "I don't know what you mean."

"Of course you don't. It's part of your witchy heritage, and you don't listen to it enough, if I'm honest about it."

"So . . . what is it?"

Marie sighed and looked around the room to see everyone busy with either setting the table, cooking something else, or reading. "I had another dream last night."

"About Judson?"

"Yes . . . and no. It was strange. There was more to it this time, more involvement with the town and something dark creeping in. I couldn't find Judson, and then he jumped in front of me with my dagger shooting light from it, defending me. And a strange voice was calling to be released—for me to release them. At first I thought it was Judson, but then it changed. I didn't recognize it. I think it was a woman, but I couldn't be sure."

Rachael frowned. "I don't like it. Something is going on."

"You don't think it's pre-party nervous dreams?" Marie tried to lighten the moment. Rachael smirked, knowing what she intended.

"Oh no!" Rachael cried, realizing she had let a piece of bread burn. She quickly attempted to put out the small flame and save the toast. But Ahote was immediately at her side, pushing her out of danger and smothering the fire out of the now smoking piece of bread.

Just then Judson came in and burst into laughter. "I leave you for just a little while and you practically burn down the new house," he said with good humor.

"Ha ha, very funny," Rachael threw back at him.

Judson playfully patted Rachael on the shoulder with brotherly affection, then went to see if he could assist Ahote. "You have it under control?"

"Yes." Ahote nodded. "I will go to work with the grapes today, right Atsidi?" Atsidi was a name Ahote and his brothers had called Judson from the beginning. It was a word that meant *blacksmith* in their native language and became a term of endearment for him.

"Yes. Rodney goes with you today, and I will be along this afternoon," Judson replied, turning to Rodney to ensure that was his plan as well.

"I'm heading there after we eat." Rodney nodded, tipping his head back down to what was left of his coffee. "We have a public opening to get that wine ready for!"

"Then we have a plan for today," Judson said, taking a vigorous bite off the end of a piece of bacon straight out of the pan and ending with a big cheesy grin.

CHAPTER 3

*L*ater that day, Marie, Rachael, and little Alo took a slow leisurely walk into the main part of town. The air still held the crisp edge of the beginning of fall, but the sun was out, and the combined mix of warm and cold was a refreshing combination.

"What is on your list for today?" Rachael asked, helping little Alo with dark hair and skin like his father, but with green eyes like his mother.

"I am headed to meet the Trents, Gregory and Charlotte, to commission them to make something for Judson as a gift. They make the most beautiful music boxes and timepieces."

"Oh, what a wonderful idea!" Rachael gushed.

Marie's gaze took in all the new growth in the town. Since they had arrived only a handful of years ago, more buildings had gone up around what was being referred to as the town square. Most of the dirt roads still remained except for the ones they had paved with cobblestones like they saw done in the bigger cities, and more efforts had been made to cultivate greenery and decoration as well. And more homes had been built for those who decided to remain and make the beautiful box canyon their home. Several more families had joined them since they settled, and of those, only a few of the families were additional witches. The original group who had traveled with them across the country were considered the elders— or founding families. They gathered together and held meetings on the regular to discuss town issues, the most recent of which had been how many non-supernaturals, or non-magical, people had moved in and how best to keep their secrets to ensure the safety of all.

"I can't believe how much has changed since we first arrived here," Rachael said, gazing around at the new growth.

"It's not only the town that is growing, but the families are as well." Marie's voice took on a wistful tone as she glanced lovingly at Rachael and Ahote's son of three. They had him shortly after they had gotten settled and married just after arriving. Marie couldn't be happier for her friend.

"Speaking of . . ." Rachael raised her eyebrows in silent question to Marie, who couldn't help the blush that crept up her neck.

"Soon. I don't know how soon, yet, but we would like to start our family now we are settled. I just feel like it's not the right time yet."

Rachael nodded. "Honor your intuition, Marie. You'll know when it's right, no matter how much I want to see you with a little one of your own." She smiled and looped her arm through Marie's just like old times, but reached for her son's hand, uniting them in the new times.

"How is Ahote adjusting?" Marie asked, knowing it had been hard with the loss of his brother, Alo, and then even harder when the other, Cetanwakuwa, left town for his own pursuits. They had never been separated since they'd been born. Then during their travels, they were attacked by Dante and his group of rogue witch hunters. The band of travelers Marie and her family traveled with included many strong witches, more than one frost dragon shifter, several members of the fae community, and other supernaturals. She was proud to be a part of their group, and even had hoped to find friendship amongst them.

Along their journey, they met the three Ahusaka brothers—men native to the lands they traveled through and gifted in their own rights. Ahusaka, they learned, meant *wings* and was fitting, as they were hawk shifters. Alo, the eldest, had fallen during the fight with Dante. His name meant *spiritual guide*, and he was the shaman and wise man of the three. Cetanwakuwa, the middle brother's name, meant *attacking hawk*, and he was the fighter. But Ahote—*restless one*, the youngest of the three—had fallen in love with Marie's best friend in the whole world.

"He's adjusting, I think. It's all very different for him to be in a structured environment and a father on top of all of it, especially without his brothers, whom he has always had around. It's been a challenge for him. But he's handling it for now. Though, as his name signifies, I sense a restlessness within him. He's like a wild animal, content and used to freely roaming the world. I know he loves me, but sometimes I'm concerned I'm keeping him here against his nature."

Marie could also see the restlessness stirring underneath Ahote's skin, but he seemed to tame it with his growing love for Rachael and their son. Marie gripped her friend's hand. "I'm always here for you. But he seems happy. He lights up whenever you or Alo enter the room."

"That little boy is his world." Rachael smiled, looking down at the child with his bright green eyes and dark curly hair. Alo looked up at her with pure adoration before jumping in a puddle from melted snow, splashing his mom with a giggle. Rachael exasperatedly looked to Marie. "Now, where do we find the tinkers?"

Marie pointed off in the direction of where the Trents' home shop was. "It's not far now. I'm excited to see if they can build what I am envisioning for Judson." Marie beamed from ear to ear, lost in her own imagination.

"Well, let's ask them. I see Charlotte entering their shop now," Rachael said, lifting her hand in a wave toward Charlotte Trent. The Trents' store was a brick facade lined with rich lumber adorned with a sign that read, *Horologist: Timepieces, Music Boxes & Gifts.*

"Hello, Charlotte," Marie called, also waving, causing Charlotte to turn and see them coming toward her.

Charlotte smiled, waved, and beckoned them to enter the shop. In her late fifties, she looked bright and full of energy. She wore her customary leather apron with pockets for her tools. Marie didn't know Charlotte or her husband Gregory well, as they hadn't been in town long, but she admired their talent with woodworking and level of expertise with their detailed timepieces. They also had done a magnificent job with the repairs on the Whisper Falls Inn's conservatory.

"Hello, ladies, won't you come inside?" said the Trents' apprentice, who also helped run the shop. Behind them, the heavy door decorated with intricate carvings and patterns Marie didn't recognize closed, followed by the welcoming sound of chimes. "What brings you to our little shop on such a lovely day?" Theodore Carver asked, as Charlotte smiled and played for a moment with little Alo in Rachael's arms before she went back to work on a project. In his late twenties, Theodore was the Trents' assistant and took orders for them as well.

"I have an idea I'm hoping to commission you and the Trents to make for me to give my Judson as a gift to celebrate the opening of the vineyard," Marie explained.

"I see. Well, that sounds wonderful. Won't you give me some more information on what you're dreaming up? If you could draw something for me, that would be most helpful as well. Gregory is not in the shop at the moment, but I'll include him in the process when he returns."

"Thank you, Theodore!" Marie clapped her hands in excitement. "This is going to be magical!" She winked at Rachael, who practically rolled her eyes at Marie's lack of subtlety. They followed him inside to the workshop and stood around a worktable, half of which was a chaotic mess filled with papers, screws, springs, and other oddities. The other half was clean, with everything in its place, and contained a stack of small boxes and trays of tiny parts.

"How's Betsy?" Marie asked. She was excited to see him beginning to settle down with the lovely young woman.

"She's well, thank you." Theodore smiled at her, then fiddled with some levers and pulls, and the table unfolded to a larger workspace. He then pulled out a piece of blank paper and handed a writing utensil to Marie.

"Marie, I should have asked, but what kind of item are you hoping we can create for you?" Theodore asked.

"A box. Similar to the famed puzzle boxes the Trents make, but a little less puzzle and a little bigger box. I'm thinking maybe something he could put some of his prized daggers or delicate metal creations inside."

Theodore nodded as if he completely understood what Marie wanted. "Could you draw the basic shape and size, or any defining characteristics you are looking for?"

Marie took the pencil and for a moment sketched some of her thoughts onto paper. "I'm not the most practiced artist, but I think this is the basic idea." She stood back and allowed Theodore to look at her drawing while she noted Rachael following Alo as he toddled around the room—trying to keep his hands out of all that looked dangerous or breakable in the space, which seemed to be a feat in itself. Marie smiled. Rachael and her son were endearingly comical to watch.

"This is doable," Theodore finally said matter-of-factly. He asked Marie a few more clarifying questions about the detail work and how many puzzle pieces she wanted. They discussed payment and all the final details, then it was time to go.

"Oh, Marie, when do you want this finished?" Theodore asked as he wrote down a few notes.

"By the opening a month from now. Which you, Betsy, Charlotte, and Gregory are, of course, invited to. I have yet to get the invitations out," Marie sheepishly explained.

"Consider it done."

"Thank you, Theodore. I can't wait to see it!" Marie and Rachael said their goodbyes to Theodore and waved at Charlotte, not wanting to disturb her while she worked, then left with the sound of the chimes echoing behind them.

Marie, Rachael, and little Alo walked through town a bit longer, then headed home before the afternoon grew too chilled for the little one to be out.

CHAPTER 4

The Court of the Sun and the Moon was the leadership of the town. The Court consisted of a representative from each of the founding families who had arrived in 1854 as part of the wagon train. The Blackstone witch hunters had always been a matriarchy, so Marie was the seat holder to attend all the meetings about the goings on of the town. Currently, they met in a home near a small park close to the entrance into the town. The home was a beautiful mansion belonging to Elsmed Fairchild and his wife, and all the members comfortably gathered in.

The Court was an eclectic mix of supernaturals—and one human—including witches, mages, moroi—which Marie had learned was a type of vampire—fae, wolf shifters, a frost dragon, and others.

"Find your seat," Anne-Marie Beaumont announced, getting everyone's attention. "Let us begin tonight. We have much to discuss." Anne-Marie was one of the leaders of the Luna Coven, along with Raffaele Augustine and Rodavan Bishop, and as such, also acted as one of the leaders of the Court as she brought them all together, revealing the need for a body of leadership to govern their small but growing town.

Marie had an uneasy feeling. She paid attention to Anne-Marie's expression while she watched everyone find their seats. Something was wrong.

"Friends, tonight we have to discuss an urgent matter that has recently come to my attention. Witches have been disappearing from our town—young witches, from those not much older than my Saundra up to those their early twenties."

A collective gasp came from everyone in the room.

"Are you sure? What if they are simply leaving?" Lawrence Mills, the frost dragon, suspiciously asked with his deep smooth voice, though by the looks on faces, everyone wondered the same.

"Family members have come forward saying their loved ones have simply vanished. No word. No mention of leaving. Just there one moment and gone the next. I can feel it in my being—the threads of the witches within my coven are no longer there. Not barely noticeable as if out of town or reach . . . simply gone," Anne-Marie explained, wringing her hands together with apparent worry.

"That is troubling indeed," Raffaele Augustine concurred.

Rodavan Bishop sat quietly to Anne-Marie's right with no expression, but looked into the eyes of everyone present until landing on Marie's, where he paused. Marie felt him, as if he attempted to seek answers from her very being. If she had any, she would gladly give them up. He then continued his perusal around the room. Marie felt affronted, as if he thought she had something to do with the disappearances.

"Does anyone have any information that could be useful?" Anne-Marie asked hopefully. "Anything strange you've noticed around town? Anything we could piece together to make sense of any of this?"

People shook their heads with nothing to offer.

"I don't think this really has anything to do with it, but I'll share just in case . . ." Marie took a deep breath. "I've had dreams of late. Dreams of issues I believe are personal, but there are moments in the dreams where the town is involved, and a darkness lurks at the edges of town and creeps closer until it morphs into the people, turning them into smoky shapes with dark tendrils." She paused to look around, and as she expected, everyone present simply stared at her, unsure what to say.

"That is definitely interesting, Marie," Anne-Marie finally said with a frown. "Far be it from me to judge how and where potential information comes from. Especially as we are supernatural beings who deal with magic and the unexpected every day. Thank you for sharing. We will continue to take it into account with all other information we gather."

Marie nodded, appreciating Anne-Marie's words. Suddenly she could feel a tension brewing in the room, a dissension stirring in the air. Some of the members openly stared at her. She even heard a few murmuring under their breaths to their neighbors. Her eyes shot toward Lawrence Mills specifically as he grumbled to Elsmed Fairchild sitting next to him. She knew Lawrence never truly liked her, and she didn't care, but to be so open about it in one of their meetings was going too far. Anger rose in Marie's chest. She had put her life on the line to save these people on the long journey they had taken together. She had fought against her own brother to stand among these people, to side with them and their beliefs for a better future side by side. How dare they!

Marie stood to her feet and shot her gaze directly at Lawrence. "I'm happy to undergo a test by Elsmed if you have a problem with me."

Lawrence raised his hands to placate her, but Rodavan unexpectedly rose. "I do not think that is necessary at this point, Marie. We all know what you have put on the line for this town, and we respect it. Do not underestimate that we will take into consideration *any* and *all* information that comes forward, no matter whom it refers to, but for now we are simply discussing it."

Marie frowned. He wasn't really standing up for her. He was simply putting aside what he believed could be the inevitable at some point. She huffed but nodded and sat back down. Perhaps she had been defensive and jumped to conclusions.

"I do not believe there is any involvement from Marie or any of the Blackstone hunters," Anne-Marie confidently stated. "But this is a very serious issue, and we need to all be watching and keeping an eye out for anything unusual in the town. We cannot allow any more witches—or anyone for that matter—to disappear. It simply seems the witches are being targeted for some unknown reason."

"We will be most diligent in our efforts," Gaby Kasun acknowledged with sincerity. She then offered Marie a slight nod and a small smile. Marie didn't know Gaby well, but she had been around since they first arrived. Rumor had it Gaby and the Kasun Pack had been around long before the wagon train arrived, keeping watch over the forest and the sleeping box canyon, waiting for the next inhabitants. Marie heard stories about a tribe who lived there long before their arrival in 1854, leaving the Kasuns and a mysterious presence to watch over and protect the area.

"Thank you, Gaby," Anne-Marie said.

"We will as well. There have been some new travelers stopping by the inn. We'll keep our eyes and ears open," Mihail Petran said in his thick Romanian accent. He and his wife opened Whisper Falls Inn at the corner of the town square. Anyone new in town would most likely visit their inn first.

"I expect nothing less from everyone. For now, be dismissed. Thank you, Elsmed, for the use of your home. We will meet here again next week. And thank you all for coming," Anne-Marie concluded.

Everyone stood to leave without so much as an exchange of pleasantries. Conversations and interactions were limited; the topic at hand seemed to weigh heavily upon all present.

As Marie gathered her leather satchel and placed it over her head and across her chest, she felt a hand on her elbow, then turned.

"I want you to know, I believe you, Marie. You have no reason to think we doubt you. Some here might, but they doubt themselves, too. I wouldn't let it bother you. But that said, if anything happens or anyone comes against you, please inform me, and I'll get involved." Anne-Marie offered her a warm smile of assurance and confidence.

"Thank you; that means a lot." And it did. Marie stood taller, more confident she was believed. She wanted nothing more than to fit in with the town and be a part of it, ensuring her legacy became an integral part of the town in the years to come. Being a witch hunter who didn't hunt witches would wear down her physical being at some point. She would still live an unusually long life, but not as long as Dante would. Marie wanted the future set for the descendants she hoped to have.

But for now, she pondered what could possibly be happening to their town as she bundled up for her chilly walk home, only to find Judson waiting for her outside. Sitting up in the horse-drawn buggy, he was wrapped with a warm blanket, wearing an even warmer smile upon his face as she ran toward him.

"I thought we could go for an evening ride," Judson said, throwing part of the blanket over Marie's lap.

"I would love that, thank you." She leaned up and kissed his cheek as he led the horse back onto the lamp-lit street.

CHAPTER 5

*J*udson pulled the horse and buggy up to a hitching post at the base of the trail to the great and mighty falls. The settling families had decided something magical resided within the water.

"It's such a beautiful but chilly night," Marie said, wrapping a wool shawl around her shoulders. Their visible breaths floated into the evening air, practically crystallizing as they spoke.

"It is," Judson agreed, as he finished tying the horse's lead to the post. "I wanted to come out and enjoy it with you." He smiled, but it didn't quite reach his eyes.

Marie frowned and raised an eyebrow. She knew him too well and for too long to think that tonight there was no more than him simply picking her up on a whim.

"Fine." He sighed. "I got wind of the topic of tonight's meeting from Anne-Marie beforehand. She was afraid some of the members might get ruffled up and wanted me in place. Just in case." He shrugged his shoulders as if there was nothing to it. "Is everything all right?"

Marie laced her hand through his. "Let's walk to our spot at the falls." She referred to the place where he proposed when they had first arrived. It happened to also be the place she discovered more of her witch hunter heritage when her family's journal revealed its hidden secrets. "There are some who doubt my sincerity . . . or possibly my trustworthiness, in the town. But I'm determined to prove them wrong and solidify my place among the townspeople and among the leaders of it."

Judson sharply nodded with a smirk. "I knew you'd bounce back just fine."

He removed his hand from hers and wrapped his arm around her shoulders as they continued their walk along the barely worn path, leading them to their spot by the small lake at the base of the falls.

Marie felt Judson hesitate when they neared the waters. She cocked her head and tried to pay attention to every small nuance of her husband. He had never reacted like that at the water's edge before—almost as if he was unnerved by it. She stopped them and turned Judson to face her, holding both his hands.

"Judson, something is bothering you. What is it?"

His expression shut down, hiding any indication that something was indeed wrong. He cleared his throat and looked out beyond her at the water. "It's really nothing, Marie. I think I've just been too immersed in working on your dagger and the stone within it—trying to understand how it truly works with the journal, what we can learn from it, and how we might best use it for our benefit. I know for certain it has magical properties, but what it can do, I have yet to ascertain."

Marie wondered if she was reading too much into his responses. Perhaps he was simply exhausted and overworked. She was about to tell him how he needed to take more breaks and ask if she could participate the next time he worked on her dagger, but she paused and whipped her head to the side. She then clutched her stomach and quietly moaned.

"There's a presence of black magic, but it's vague," she whispered.

Judson grabbed her and held her close, but Marie wriggled out of his full hold to have a hand free in case she needed to fight. As quickly as the feeling came, it left, leaving Marie more relaxed. She inhaled deeply, held it for a moment, then exhaled slowly. "It's gone."

Judson, too, relaxed minutely, though not yet sure the danger was gone.

"That was odd. Wait. Someone's nearby. I feel them watching us, but it's different than the black magic." Marie again spoke in hushed tones, so as not to be heard by any but Judson.

"I feel someone's presence too." Judson followed her gaze, then continued to look in the other direction.

They were interrupted by a sound of something rustling in the bushes a short distance behind them and away from the falls. The sounds grew louder and louder until a couple of shadows became visible in the night.

"No need for alarm, you two," a man's voice came from the shrubs as he made his way into a patch of light. Ric Kasun emerged, followed by his wife and alpha, Gaby Kasun.

"Forgive us; we did not intend to startle you," said Gaby.

"You did, but only for a moment." Judson smiled and relaxed.

"Just before you showed up, I felt something. I think it was black magic," Marie shared with a concerned expression. "But then it just disappeared, as if not there at all."

The Kasuns both nodded.

"We didn't know what we were dealing with, but we received a lead regarding something or someone sneaking through the forest right after Gaby left the meeting," Ric explained.

"So we set out to track them. I caution you to be careful and perhaps not linger too long in secluded places at night, at least until the threat is found," Gaby warned.

"Thank you, but how can we help?" Marie asked. Judson nodded his agreement as he reached for her hand.

Gaby sympathetically smiled but shook her head. "Thank you for your offer, but we are simply doing a tracking exercise tonight to see if we can find any information or leads. So far, we don't have much to go on. But thanks to you, we know we might be dealing with a witch practitioner of black magic."

"Why would a witch be taking—or worse—other witches?" Marie asked with a deep frown.

Gaby looked to Ric, and they both shrugged. "We're not sure, but we'll keep the Court apprised of anything more we find, so you'll also be informed."

Marie nodded, knowing there wasn't anything the Kasuns could allow her to help with at the present time. Perhaps if they got more information, she could be of some help. "Good luck. I hope you find something to go on."

Ric and Gaby nodded their thanks and melded back into the shadows of the shrubbery and the darkness of the night. Marie couldn't help but wonder if they had changed from, and back into, their wolves, or if they tracked as humans.

CHAPTER 6

Once back home, Marie took Judson aside before they entered the large main room where they could hear the others still up visiting with each other.

"Jud, can I see the dagger and the stone? I know you've been working on it, but I want to see how it's coming along," Marie said in a hushed tone.

Judson grabbed her hand and led her to the secret bookcase that slid sideways with the pulling out of a specific book. Before the rest of the house was finished, Judson and Marie's father, Hank, and her brother Rodney worked long and hard hours creating a secret basement. The basement was filled with various weapons Judson had created. They began stockpiling, just in case the town came upon a time when they needed a vast amount of weapons. Also in the basement was a large, long table made of a slab of metal placed upon stabilizing wooden legs. Judson had laid out several different weapons and a couple of books open with sloppy writing scrawled across the paper and various rough drawings.

"What have you been doing? It looks like you're conducting experiments," Marie noted as she ran her hand across the metal top and along some of the journals.

Judson lowered his head. "I am. I didn't want to tell you until I had something more concrete to go on."

Marie frowned. "I could help. Why didn't you tell me?"

"I was so close to figuring something out. It started as a surprise, then it became an obsession."

"So explain what you're doing."

"I think the stone in your dagger, coupled with the aether in the water from the falls, will infuse metals with magical properties," Judson started to explain. "The metal speaks to me. Your dagger gave me the inspiration when I held it, and it showed me how to use magic to reproduce it."

"Okaaaay," Marie held out the word as she tried to understand where he was going with his line of thought.

"Don't you see? If we can infuse the metals with magic, the weapons we create could be designed to fight specific species or be used against certain kinds of magic, whereas a regular sword might fail."

"Oh . . ." She paused, understanding dawning upon her mind. "Oh! That's amazing, Judson! However did you realize this?" She grabbed one of the journals and leafed through Judson's scribblings, taking it all in.

"When I was tinkering with your dagger and the stone, I added some more of the water and was able to dissect the smallest portion—"

"You destroyed the stone?" Marie's eyes widened in horror, and she watched him retract his words.

"No, it's amazing! I sliced off the smallest bit using a magnifying glass and then it regenerated itself. It regenerated itself! I've never seen that. I think I've discovered some elements involved that make this a renewable source for the making of weapons. I'm not an alchemist, so I don't understand what everything I've discovered is, but I think we could talk to someone if you want. I think it should stay within the family for now, however. At least, until we know more . . ." Judson trailed off, realizing he had gone off topic.

"Wow, I don't even know what to say. This is what they meant in the journal, though! My journal is in the safety box in the wall. Can you hand it to me?" she asked, her eyes glossing over with thoughts of the possibilities. Judson handed her the journal, and Marie began to thumb through it, but then looked up and smiled. "I forgot. I need the stone to connect with it to make the hidden parts come forth. Such a brilliant maneuver by the witch who helped my family to create it."

"Agreed," Judson said with a smile. He reached for the dagger and gently placed the hilt in Marie's hand.

She examined the stone set within the delicate metalwork, and sure enough, the stone was complete and whole, not a scratch on it. Amazing. Marie positioned the journal just beneath the dagger. The metalwork on the cover was in the complete reverse from the design on the dagger, each resembling the shape of an elaborate butterfly, but truly it was the stars that made up the mark only witch hunters were born with. Both sides of the metalwork fit nicely together, like puzzle pieces locking into place. And when the lock clicked, Judson carefully placed a dropper of aether water on the stone, and it began to glow.

This time, however, Marie noted that Judson pulled his hand back extremely fast, trying his best not to get any of the water on his skin. But a drop of the water did land on his skin, and a spark flew out from his hand.

"Judson! What is happening to you?" Marie shouted.

"I . . . I don't know. I didn't want to scare you. I think it's something to do with the magic in the water. It's reactive on my skin. I've been trying not to touch it." Judson's face had gone pale, and an element of fear passed across his eyes.

"Scare me? Are you kidding? Do you know who we are and who our families are?" She laughed. "That's an absurd thought. But I can appreciate that you were unnerved by it and wanted to understand it for yourself before telling me." She frowned but continued with understanding. "It sounds like something I would have done to you."

"You're not mad?"

"Why would I be mad?" She pushed away his worries with a flick of her hand. "We'll figure this out together. But no more secrets, okay?"

"Agreed." Judson had the audacity to look sheepish before his next confession. "I have one more secret, but you can't know until the vineyard party. I'm sorry."

She laughed. "Fair enough. I have one of my own in that regard as well."

Marie winked at him, then examined his hand within her own. But what she felt was more than she had expected. Perhaps the aether in the water did more than simply react to his skin. She frowned but would have to see how it played out. For now, they needed to understand the great mystery of the magic-infused stone.

"Oh, look at this bit." Marie's words filled with fearful anticipation. "Of course, the first page I land on to read mentions the hunter's ability to suck out the magical souls of a witch once they are dead. That's creepy and definitely not what will win me points with the Court." She skipped a few more pages to see what else she might land on. "I wonder if there is anything in this about why my senses seem to be coming and going at random times." Her eyes scanned the pages furiously. "The Court is going to find this weapon information fascinating," Marie redirected their conversation to get them back on track. "The possibilities are endless."

"True. It also means we have within our midst a powerful artifact that, in the wrong hands, could be used against us or the town. So for now, we need to be careful with our information."

Marie nodded and ran her hand up to Judson's shoulder, where she rested it while they continued to examine the evidence before them. Judson told her of all his experiments and the outcomes he discovered.

"The truth in the outcome can't be completely verified unless used on a particular species, but there might be ways to test it in a minute manner without hurting anyone," Judson explained.

"I can't wait to hear how that's going to go over," Marie laughed.

CHAPTER 7

$\mathcal{T}$he next day, Marie, Rachael, and—upon Judson's insistence for backup—Ahote traveled into the square with little Alo to get some sweets.

"Oh, Marie! Rachael!" a woman called from behind them. When Marie turned, she was pleasantly surprised to see Priscilla Augustine approaching her. Priscilla and her husband, Raffaele, as well as some of her husband's family, traveled among them on the wagon train, and Marie became quite fond of her over the time. Priscilla was young, in her early thirties, and a spitfire of a witch. Raffaele was a strong and powerful witch and sat on the Court with Marie.

"Hello, Priscilla!"

"Good afternoon, Priscilla," Rachael added as she handed Alo into Ahote's arms. "We were coming into town for a well-deserved treat. How is your day?"

"Very well, thank you, Rachael." Priscilla smiled at the little guy and tickled his hand as he reached out to touch their new visitor. "Marie, Raffaele shared your dream with me. I want you to know I find it very interesting. I believe in the power dreams have. It's a message . . . a warning even, for us. Could you please keep me apprised of any new developments? I'd like to try to help you sort through it if possible. Powerful dreams, along with the essence of a seer, run in my family, and I have a significant amount of experience with them."

Marie was a bit shocked Priscilla was being so forward about such things, but she glanced quickly around and found no one close enough to hear them.

"Thank you, Priscilla. It means the world to me you are taking it seriously. I'm sure most in that room last night did not." She put her hands on her waist in a subtle show of annoyance.

"Actually, I think you'd find more of them took it to heart than they let on. In our world, dreams can be significant portents of things to come," Priscilla explained with an air of gravity.

"Dreams are very important in my family also," Ahote said, surprisingly. He was often quiet when other people were around. But Marie knew he had found ease with Priscilla and her husband during their travels. "We must heed the warnings, but it is difficult when we do not yet understand them."

"Very true point, Ahote," Priscilla agreed. "So we must try to understand the best we can."

"I'll keep you informed if anything new should present itself to me," Marie said, acutely aware that several people had slowed down near them. Not close enough to listen, but close enough that it was unmistakable who they were watching. She felt a chill of unease slide up her back.

"I think it's time we get our treat and head home," Rachael said, also picking up on the attention they seemed to be drawing.

"Why are they staring at you like that, Marie?" Ahote asked quietly.

"Because they think I have something to do with the disappearances of late," Marie grimly replied. But then she got mad. Marie stood tall and faced the handful of people staring at her with a determined look on her face.

"Oh, Marie, this might not be the time," Priscilla warned under her breath. "I will stand with you, but you must be careful not to make a scene."

Marie gave her a curt nod. "I'll just go speak peacefully with them then."

She took two steps in the direction of the witches who stared at her as if she were guilty.

Before she could even open her mouth, a youngish girl—a witch—stumbled out from the alleyway between the buildings. Her hair was a matted mess, but everything else about her appearance was presentable, nothing torn or tattered. Her complexion, however, was pale and her face gaunt. Perhaps she hadn't been attacked. Perhaps this had nothing to do with the other witches. Perhaps . . .

"Help," she spoke with a gravelly tone, as if her words were raked across jagged rocks. She practically fell on top of Marie, who caught her before she hit the ground. Everyone gasped in surprise.

"Are you all right?" Marie asked in panic. "Who did this to you?" she rushed out, sensing the girl's wherewithal would expire soon.

"Vampire," she uttered before passing out.

"Did she say vampire?" Priscilla asked with a whisper, kneeling down to place her hand on the girl's forehead.

Marie nodded, unsure even what to say.

"Could that be?" Rachael asked, kneeling down on the opposite side and placing her hand on the girl's wrist. Both witches felt for the girl's life force.

Priscilla frowned and said, "I suppose anything is possible."

"Is she . . . ?" Ahote hedged his words, sensing the growing crowd.

"No, but her essence—you know the one of which I speak—is almost fully drained. She will never practice . . . or I should say, she'll never use those talents again." Priscilla shook her head in dismay, still fully aware that those beginning to surround them were not all supernatural members of the community.

Marie stood and addressed the crowd. "Someone go get the doctor! This girl has passed out from malnourishment. She needs medical attention right away."

Several people scattered to retrieve the necessary help.

"Good thing the doctor is a member of the coven," Priscilla whispered.

"Indeed." Marie held the limp girl in her arms and carefully looked over her face. "Not a scratch on her. But why is her hair in such disarray? She had to have fought off something. It doesn't make sense her attacker was a vampire if her blood is still intact."

"Energy parasite," Ahote supplied. "Like a vampire but steals energy. I have heard stories of such a thing long ago. A type of demon."

"An energy vampire?" Rachael's face scrunched up quizzically. Ahote nodded and watched those around them carefully as he held their son close in his arms.

Marie noted the fear in his eyes. "Ahote, why don't you take Rachael and Alo home. I'll wait to speak with Anne-Marie and then be shortly behind you."

A look of understanding passed between Marie and Ahote. Whoever was taking the witches most likely was draining them for their energy, and she didn't want Rachael or their little one in the line of fire, so to speak. And neither did he. About to protest, Rachael saw the look her husband gave her as he motioned toward their little one, which she, of course, could not argue with. Rachael would do anything to protect their young one.

Two women with long work dresses held up their hems, rushed up, and lowered themselves to the ground next to Marie. Anne-Marie Beaumont and another member of the Luna Coven performed their own quick assessments of the girl while Marie and Priscilla moved gently out from under the girl.

"Come, let's get her into the wagon the doctor brought," Anne-Marie directed, pointing to a horse-drawn wagon ready to go. Marie hadn't even heard the hooves or the wheels of the wagon pull up next to them in her focus on the girl. She barely even felt the girl's witch essence; hardly any remained in her system.

The doctor bent down and scooped the frail girl into his arms, careful not to jostle her too much. He then laid her in the flatbed of the wagon on top of a pile of blankets, and the witches climbed in after to surround her with love, protection, and whatever healing energy they could sustain her with until they took her away.

"Come, Marie and Priscilla," Anne-Marie called. "I need to know all you saw and anything she might have said."

Marie and Priscilla climbed up into the bench seat of the wagon next to the good doctor, followed by Anne-Marie. And as quickly as they arrived, they dashed away to Anne-Marie's home.

CHAPTER 8

Inside the beautiful home, the witches laid the girl—in her late teenage years—on the dining room table and gathered around her. Marie stood back to give the witches room but also for herself, as her witch hunter senses tingled all up and down her arms almost to the point where it was too much to bear and she would need to leave the room. But thankfully, the witches chanted a few spells and then it was over. She relaxed for just a moment with the release of their power, but their presence alone still had a large effect on her being. Marie didn't recognize the girl, so she watched each of the women there to determine who her mother was.

"She is stable for now," one of the witches declared, "but I am afraid the part of her that makes her witch is now greatly diminished, to the point she may not be able to ever practice magic again."

A woman she recognized as a member of the Luna Coven, but whose name she didn't know, ran up to the girl, sobbing, and threw herself over the girl's chest. Marie instantly could see this was the girl's mother. It made her heart relieved to know the girl would feel her comfort.

"This is unacceptable," another woman spat. "Something must be done to stop it." She had the audacity to turn and glare at Marie.

She practically felt the force of the energy behind the witch's stare hit her, causing her to gasp.

"Now, just a minute." Priscilla physically stepped in front of Marie. "I was there. I saw the entire thing, and even if I hadn't been, Marie has no part in whatever is happening. She and her family have lived peacefully among us for these past several years, and we got to know them even before that. Her heart is good and pure."

Marie stepped up beside Priscilla, placing her hand on her arm, grateful to have a friend stand up for her and her family, but she was not willing to let someone else be her shield. She would stand up for herself as well. The tension in the room grew. Some deflated, hearing the truth in Priscilla's words, while the others needed someone to blame. Marie understood that.

Clearing her throat and redirecting the room, Anne-Marie asked, "Marie and Priscilla, could you share what transpired right before she collapsed?"

Marie nodded. "Of course. We were standing in front of the sweets shop talking with Priscilla, who had just joined us—us being Rachael, Ahote, their son, and myself—and we were about to find a treat for the little one. From the alley behind us, this girl"—Marie pointed toward the table—"stumbled out, barely conscious, with the look of death knocking on her door, and I caught her as she fell onto me."

"She had called for help just before she fell," Priscilla added, "and then Marie asked her who had done this to her, and she said 'vampire.' But upon our inspection of her, there were no puncture wounds and her blood flow seemed strong to me. Rachael and I both checked her witch essence, noting how drained she was, and that's when we called for someone to get the doctor and you." Priscilla nodded toward Anne-Marie.

"We discussed the possibility—along with Ahote, who concurred he had heard stories from his people of such a creature— of someone who could steal energy rather than blood. So perhaps not an actual vampire. Just a thought we discussed," Marie offered.

"Very interesting indeed." Anne-Marie pursed her lips in deep thought as she glanced at each person in the room. "I'm not aware of any in town with the capacity to do such a thing. Could it be someone already here with a power they hid from us?"

No one had an answer for her.

"In my dreams, the waterfall calls to us. But not only us," Priscilla started to say in a wistful tone, almost a semi-trance state. Marie wondered if she was channeling her seer gift at that very moment. "Others will follow the path to the water. Others will be drawn by the power of the falls. Many will be invited to remain, and many we do not wish to stay." Priscilla shook her head, and her eyes cleared. She looked directly at Anne-Marie. "More needs to be done to strengthen the wards. This is a warning to us all."

Marie stared in awe at her friend. She had never seen her access that part of her witch gifts. Her skin felt the bumping effects of a chill that ran up her spine. But Priscilla was right. They needed stronger wards around the town.

"Is there still a possibility it could be a witch hunter? Unrelated, of course, Marie," a witch named Martha Daryn asked with a snide and accusatory tone.

Marie hadn't cared for her much before she spoke, now even less so. "No, it's not a witch hunter's power to siphon energy from a witch. Only when a witch hunter kills a witch do they absorb their magical essence as a life-sustaining substance . . . unless . . ." Marie paused, suddenly unsure. "Well, I suppose it could be possible if they had an outside power source assisting, but I've never heard of one."

For the first time since arriving in the small town, Marie felt like an outsider, like she didn't belong. By her own words, she fed the suspicion the doubters had already been nurturing. She thought of her family. Not only was it a tragedy and dangerous for the witches, but she hadn't thought of how it could turn to a danger for her own family.

"Thank you for your transparency, Marie," Anne-Marie said, sensing the sudden shift of tensions in the room. "You have always been such a support and a leader in guiding your family to merging into the community we have all built here together."

Marie could tell she was attempting to shine a positive light on the resident witch hunters, but she had her own doubts it would work.

"For now, our work here is done. The girl will recover, but sadly her magic will not. We will keep a twenty-four-hour watch on her along with her parents and hope when she wakes up she can tell us what happened and who did this to her. Until then, everyone return to your homes and your families. Keep everyone safe, keep your eyes open, be diligent, and no one go anywhere alone. Blessed be," Anne-Marie concluded with a bowed head.

"Blessed be," came the collective response.

"Blessed be," Marie said under her breath, unsure if she should say it with the rest of them or not. Marie ducked out of the home before anyone could speak to her. She needed to get home. She needed to think, and she needed to speak to Judson. The situation had become more dire than she had ever ventured to guess it could. Her family needed to be ready for anything.

CHAPTER 9

*M*arie was very disturbed by the turn of events and the conversations brought up over the last couple of days. She went to bed after having a painfully honest discussion with her family about their options if the town turned against them. Disturbed as she was, she shouldn't have been surprised she was visited by another dream.

In her dream, Marie ran down the aisle of the vineyard once again, but this time the people disappeared one by one. She noted, however, the only ones disappearing were witches. And not only did they disappear, but they turned into shadowy shapes sucked out of their places and into the forest of dark trees behind them. As they added their mass to the darkness within the forest, it grew and grew, taking on a giant, towering humanoid shape looming over the town until it was shrouded in darkness except for the lightning striking all around it.

"Marie . . . Marie . . . Judson, wake up!" Marie vaguely heard Rachael's voice in the backdrop of her dream, but it was enough to pull her out of the despair she had begun to feel and wake her up.

"Ahote says there is evil outside. Get your weapons, and let's go!" Rachael said, with a hint of fear but also the slightest hint of the thrill of the chase. She wasn't one to give up easily or back down from a fight, and they'd had a few trying to get where they were presently.

Judson jumped up at her words, grabbing his bedside gun before even pulling on his trousers and boots. Marie, too, threw on a wrap and her boots, grabbed her dagger and a pistol from the vanity, and followed him out of the room. Her breath was uneasy, as she still recovered from her dream.

"You all right?" Judson quietly asked, sparing a quick glance back at her.

She waved him off. "Yes, yes, I'm fine. Just another dream is all. Mainly the same, but . . ." She trailed off.

"But what?"

"The darkness grew as it sucked away the witches until it covered the entire town," she said with a shake of her shoulders, as an icy chill spread down her spine.

"Well, that's not good," Judson stated plainly.

"No, Judson, it's not." She was sure he would have said more or asked more questions if they hadn't been so quickly awoken in the middle of the night.

They met up with Ahote, Rachael, Hank, and Rodney, each carrying guns, at the front door.

"Do we know what's out there?" questioned Rodney, wiping the sleep from his eyes and barely getting the front of his nightshirt tucked into his trousers.

"No. Ahote woke up and said he felt the evil. I felt something trying to tamper with the wards I placed around the house, but whoever it was wasn't able to cross them," Rachael proudly said.

"Possible evil wanting to send us to our untimely graves. Got it," Rodney sarcastically stated as he prepared his gun.

"Who is with Alo?" Marie asked, needing to know everyone was taken care of.

"Caroline and Michael are with him," Rachael assured her.

"Let's go before it's too late and whoever is out there is gone," Judson harshly whispered. Marie knew he didn't mean anything by his tone; he was nervous for his family and his home in case the worst should happen.

They snuck out the front door with great caution, knowing they had several feet until they reached the boundary of the protective wards Rachael had set. Each with their weapons extended, they searched the property for any sign of disturbance, any sign of movement.

"I don't see anything. Marie, do you feel anything witchy or otherwise?" Rachael asked.

Marie took a moment and closed her eyes to send her power out into the darkness of the night. Breathing in slowly, she focused on the stillness of the night, the lack of sound from nocturnal critters, and simply reached out her senses and felt.

"It's there, but it's faint," she finally said, opening her eyes. "The feeling is confusing because I feel it stronger one second then less another second, as if it's fluctuating. Which is highly unusual, as far as I've experienced." Marie frowned. She peered into the back area of the home but didn't see anything.

"I feel it again! It's moving that direction," Marie abruptly said, pointing out behind their property heading into the vast expanse of land that led up the mountain. "Whoever it is, is now moving fast."

"Ahote, can you track it?" Judson quickly asked.

Ahote nodded, unabashedly dropped his clothes and weapons, shifted right on the spot into a large hawk, and took to the sky with no hesitation or words.

"I sure wish I could do that," Marie said wistfully. "Not the losing my clothes part, but the flying part." She snickered.

Rachael laughed. "You're afraid of heights. You'd be like a bird that flapped from one low tree branch to another, never taking to the skies."

Marie huffed. "Don't shatter my dreams. Maybe being a bird would take away that fear. You never know."

"Well, if the person wasn't already gone, you two would definitely scare them away with your talking alone," Hank grumbled, putting his gun down.

"Sorry, Dad. I already felt them go . . ." Marie stopped mid-sentence with a realization. "Actually, I didn't feel them *go*. I felt them simply disappear. The feeling was there and then just gone. That's not how it works. Usually it trails off as the witch gets farther away. My senses really seem to be off lately." Marie flexed her hands, examining them as if she could see something wrong.

At that moment, Ahote came back, walking as a man, from around the other side of the house, shaking his head and buttoning his shirt. "It is most unusual, but I lost them."

"Ahote, if you don't mind my asking, how do you track?" Hank asked.

"I, too, can track dark magic, similar to Marie, but only when in my bird form, and it is not the same every time. It is an unusual gift to me." He picked up his weapons, then twisted his hands around the edge of the dagger he held between his hands.

Marie turned to go inside.

"Where are you going?" Rodney asked.

Concern etched across her face, Marie faced them all straight on. "I . . . I need a moment to myself to think this over."

Marie didn't return to her room, but instead went into the room they referred to as the library, which was truly just a small room with a fireplace and a hand-built wood bookshelf with a few of their mementos, trinkets, and books they brought with them from their homes back east and things they had gathered since. She stoked the fire and curled up on the floor in front of it with an additional blanket until the fire heated the room. A feeling she hadn't felt in quite some time crept into her mind and being. Doubt. Marie hadn't doubted her ability or her senses until the meeting last night, when others looked upon her with suspicion and distrust.

"Why now? Why are my abilities having trouble now? Is it because I don't actively hunt witches?" she asked herself aloud, ashamed to even have to think the thoughts, but there they were, right at the forefront of her mind. Marie struggled to wrap her mind around what could be going on in the town and what her place in it all was. Clearly she was involved somehow; she just wasn't sure what that reason could be.

Sighing, Marie fixed her gaze on the flames growing tall and fierce. The heat radiated outward to wash over her in wave after wave of warmth. Gradually she let down the last blanket she had piled on top of her. She knew Judson would be worrying for her, but she needed some clarity.

Even though she had nothing to do with the dark events happening to the witches of late, she felt responsible. What if the townspeople didn't believe her or the ones who had previously stood up for her and her family? If something didn't resolve soon, would they force the Blackstones to leave their new home and the town they helped build? And if they left, what about her brother and rogue witch hunter, Dante, who would stop at nothing to find them and try to "rehabilitate" them toward his way of life or extinguish them from theirs? It would all be for nothing—leaving Virginia, the cross-country travels by wagon train, those they had lost along the way, and all they had gone through for the new way of life they had acquired.

Furious at her current situation, Marie stood, wrapped her shawl tight around her shoulders, and paced in front of the fire.

"No, this can't be. I won't let it be the end. I trust my abilities and what I sense. I will do all I can to resolve the situation and find out what is going on in this town," Marie chanted, over and over like a mantra, until she believed it and felt strong and sure of herself once more. She needed to rise out of her downward mental spiral. She stopped in her tracks and gave herself a sharp nod. Newly determined, she left the den and promised herself she would pursue the source in the morning.

CHAPTER 10

$\mathcal{T}$he next day Marie woke with a renewed sense of purpose fueled by her resolve from the night before. She kept some of her plan to herself because she knew Judson wouldn't let her go out on her own, especially after Anne-Marie had told them not to at their Court meeting. She did feel bad about not abiding by Anne-Marie's request to stay with others, but she knew in her gut she had to seek out the threat, and she couldn't endanger anyone else.

Marie spotted Ric and Gaby Kasun near the Haven Saloon and altered her direction straight for them. She had an idea and wanted to ask them their opinion. Of course, by speaking to Gaby—who sat in on the meetings with the Court as a representative of the shifters even though the Kasuns hadn't traveled with them in the caravan—she would be divulging her plan and putting herself at risk to be stopped. Or perhaps she could get Gaby on her side.

"Good afternoon, Ric and Gaby," she said with a smile, like it was any other day.

"Hello, Marie. Nice to see you today," Gaby replied for them both.

"I'm glad I ran into you. I was actually hoping to ask you a few questions, if you have a moment?" Marie asked.

"Of course, Marie, go ahead." Ric inclined his head, suggesting she proceed.

"Thank you. First, I am wondering if you can tell me any information from your tracking the other night," she said quietly, in case anyone nearby could hear.

Ric and Gaby's gazes quickly shot to each other then back to her. "Marie, why do you ask?" Ric asked.

"We ran into you that night, and I admit I'm curious if you found anything."

"No, we didn't find much, to be honest. But the Luna Coven has asked us to keep things we find to ourselves—outside of informing them first—so as not to stir up any fear in the town," Ric explained.

"Even from those of us on the Court?" Marie was now skeptical.

"I don't agree, but for now, we tell them first," Gaby offered.

"No, that doesn't sound right to me at all." Marie frowned.

"To be fair, I think it is to keep the focus off you and your family. There were members of the Court who were quite suspicious of you. And while we believe you and your family are innocent, we are trying to keep the collateral damage to a minimum."

"I hear that, Ric. And while I appreciate the thought to protect us, I mean to solve this mystery and remove the suspicion on my family all together," Marie said, a little more adamantly than she intended. After all, the Kasuns were simply doing as they were asked, as protectors of the town.

"I caution you to not get too close. If you are in the wrong location at the wrong time, you will be implicated, and the town would be further on edge. People do crazy things when they are afraid and unsure. They fear what they do not understand and will jump to conclusions based on anything just to have someone to blame, even if they are innocent," Gaby warned.

"I promise to be careful, Gaby. Thank you for your concern, but I can't let this go. It is in my soul, in my very being, to pursue this to the end." Marie pressed her hand to her chest as she spoke. "With all the dreams I've been having, I feel I'm involved one way or another, so I'd rather be a part of the solution than sit by and let more bad things continue to happen to the witches of this town and anyone else it might involve."

Marie didn't know how else to end their conversation, as they wouldn't be agreeing, so she turned on her heels and began to walk away.

"Marie," Gaby said with a hushed tone as she came up alongside her. "I will do what I can to back you up in any way if I am able and free to do so. I would do the same in your situation. Your actions are admirable and should be assisted, not shut out to keep you safe."

Marie reacted without thinking, flinging her arms around Gaby's neck and giving her a hug. "Thank you," she whispered, then left without further words.

Marie continued her quest for information around the town to see if anyone had heard of anything strange or out of the ordinary. She assumed she probably stirred up some kind of trouble with the Court by asking questions, but she needed the info. She couldn't explain why, but in her soul she felt time was running out. The feeling was an annoyance that wouldn't leave her alone. It pressed upon her heart that if she didn't find out something soon, another witch would be endangered, and they could be more than simply drained this time. That thought caused Marie to wonder why the girl they came across the day before near the alley was left alive and not taken. She was grateful, but wondered about the cause. Had whoever captured the girl been interrupted? Did they not actually need the energy? How did they consume it? What were they doing with it?

Marie found herself in front of the temporary setup on the west side of the town square. The small wood shop was used by the Lancasters. The Lancasters were a family of witches, newer to town, invited by the Augustines. The Lancasters made potions, candles, and various soaps and scents and sold them from the wood shop that resembled more of a shack. Mr. Lancaster—Rufus, Marie thought his name was—worked on their more permanent shop residence nearby in his spare time. Even if she didn't already know he was a witch, the magical essence she sensed from him in the form of tingles shooting up her arms would have told her the truth.

"Mr. Lancaster?" she called to him as she approached cautiously in case he was unnerved by her presence. Marie hated that she suddenly felt on the defense, like she was indeed guilty of something. She stood taller and inhaled sharply through her nose. She would not be intimidated by even the imaginary feelings that plagued her mind because of the uncertainty she entertained.

He smiled at her approach, which relaxed her into a returning smile.

"Hello, Marie. What can I do for you today? Are you looking for a particular scent or tincture? We have a new batch the missus just whipped up." He gave her a toothy grin and with the gesture of a hand, invited her into his lean-to shop reinforced with magic to keep it standing.

"Thank you, Mr. Lancaster. I've only come to ask you a question or two, if you're not in the middle of anything," Marie clarified.

"Shoot, little lady," Rufus encouraged. He was a kind older gentleman who had been around town only a short time. It was becoming harder to keep track of all the new people coming into the town. She thought she might mention to Anne-Marie that they come up with a way to do so. Perhaps they could use amulets or something with a magical brand of sorts.

Marie smiled and nodded. "Mr. Lancaster, I'm sure you've heard reference to the young girl we found yesterday and the other missing wi—um, people recently." She paused and gauged his reaction to ensure he had indeed heard the news. Since his family were witches, he should have been notified to be on the lookout. He slowly nodded. "I'm helping find who is behind it all, and I'm wondering if you have any information that could be relevant. Has anything strange gone on with you or your family? Have you heard or even sensed anything out of the ordinary?"

"Now, Ms. Beaumont has already come by and asked questions of a similar nature, and I didn't have anything to tell her then. But earlier this morning, we had a disturbance of the wards on our barn. The ones around our home are solid as a rock, but mind you, we didn't think to make the ones around the property as strong. So the wards alerted us of an intruder, but we didn't find anyone. It was like a ghost came to pay us a visit. Now, Mrs. Lancaster doesn't think that's the case, but I didn't find anyone or anything disturbed. I think they might have just been testing the wards to see how close they could get." He frowned, then looked to Marie. "Do you think they were after our girls?"

Marie's expression soured. "I think it's possible, but we don't know what exactly this person—or people—want, let alone why they are targeting those they have. I'm sorry, Mr. Lancaster, but I suggest you strengthen your wards as soon as you can."

"Already done, Miss Marie. No one is getting onto my property without a major problem hitting them in the face." Mr. Lancaster chuckled to himself. Marie could only guess what kind of ward he set; it probably included some kind of hex to their physical person to point them out.

"I'm glad for you. Thank you for your time, Mr. Lancaster. Please let me or the Court know if you have any other situations or hear of anything that could be helpful."

He agreed and waved Marie on her way down the dirt and cobblestone street, but before she got too far, a group of young witches and mages, appearing unruly and angered, emerged from behind a structure.

CHAPTER 11

$\mathcal{M}$arie stopped and smiled as the group emerged from the area between two structures, where they had apparently been waiting for her. Her heart rate accelerated, but she refused to let them see her fear. Some of them were teenagers she knew, and she knew the parents of others. For some reason, they thought to take it upon themselves to confront her. What would they do to her? Possibly scare her, sure. But there in broad daylight, in front of several townspeople nearby—all she had to do was shout or scream and someone would surely come to help. But Marie would not be threatened.

"Hello! It's a fine day to be enjoying the outdoors, wouldn't you say, Jon? I had a nice chat with your parents just the other night."

Marie caught them off guard. Some of them faltered in their steps toward her and pretended to casually be hanging around. But others decided they'd rather have a confrontation.

"You need to stay away from us and the others in our group," a young man spat. Marie noted his choice of words, thankfully keeping the public in the dark about the witches and their coven.

"You need to show some respect, Denny. You don't know what you're talking about," Rachael said, charging up with Ahote hot on her trail as they came to stand with Marie. Denny reared his head back as if he'd been slapped, seeing that another witch would stand against him and side with a lowly witch hunter. Denny was a member of the Green Coven, and Marie didn't know him other than by face, but she had a feeling Martha Daryn's attitude ran rampant in that group.

Marie placed her hand on Rachael's arm, letting her know she didn't think the confrontation was worth the spectacle they were about to create. Marie turned her head to smile at Ahote and noticed a few others had joined to stand behind her, including Mr. Lancaster and his wife. Also among them was a young woman in her early twenties, whom Marie didn't recognize, but based on the low-level vibe she received, the woman was half witch. Marie appreciated her stance with her and smiled at her even though she didn't know who she was. Marie glanced at her face quickly to reassure herself that the girl was indeed already half witch—not that she'd been drained like the other girl who hadn't been quite so lucky to still be half witch. Marie chose to trust her hunter gifts, but still she hoped for a chance to speak with the girl once the group confrontation subsided.

Thankfully, at that moment, Sheriff Ric Kasun and a few other members of the Kasun pack stepped out of the saloon and moved in her direction to be a strong presence in case the situation got out of hand. The group's eyes widened upon seeing them, and several stepped away almost instantly.

"I guess they don't want to stand up to the sheriff . . . or maybe it was the idea of a snarling pack of wolves on their tails," Marie whispered to Rachael, who stood so close she would hear her.

"I think they'd rather not have their parents get wind of their involvement," she said with a chuckle.

"That too." Marie snickered.

"I hope there was no trouble here," Ric Kasun said as he walked up to Marie.

"No, at least not yet. I think they were trying to scare me, though," she admitted.

"I'm sorry, Marie. You and your family don't deserve that. We need to catch the culprit soon or I'm afraid the town is going to lose all sense of its values and camaraderie.

"I agree."

Sheriff Kasun signaled for his guys to head out, leaving Marie and those with her standing in the road. She turned to thank those who came to support her. She felt drawn to the girl she saw and wanted a chance to talk to her. But when she looked for her, she was gone.

"Thank you for being here with us, Mr. And Mrs. Lancaster." She turned to Rachael and Ahote. "Thanks, your timing was perfect." Marie took a deep breath.

"Of course, dear. We know you have nothing to do with any of those disappearances," Mrs. Lancaster said with a sweet smile.

"Thank you. Did by chance any of you see the young woman with you—slender build, pale with red hair?" Marie asked. "I'm not sure who she was, but she's gone now. I was hoping to talk with her."

Rachael and Ahote both shook their heads.

"Are you seeing ghosts now?" Rachael teased, and looped her arm with Marie's.

She laughed. "I don't think so. No, wait, I felt her. She was either drained or she had to have been half witch."

"Let me know if you see her again, and I can find out who she is. Maybe she's a part of the Green Coven or new to town," Rachael mentioned.

The Lancasters returned to their shop and took the vibrant essence of their magical energy with them, relieving Marie of most of the tingles shooting up and down her arms. She had been around Rachael so long, the usual sensations she felt from having her around were normal by this point. More often than not, it was unusual to not have any feelings at all when she was away from Rachael.

"Oh, Marie! There's Mrs. Brouchard just over there. She's one of the friendlier witches in the Green Coven. Maybe she knows your mystery girl," Rachael excitedly said.

"Lead the way. You might be more welcome to ask questions than I would at this stage," Marie admitted sadly.

"Cheer up. We'll get this figured out in no time. And then they'll all be sorry and owe you lots of gifts," Rachael said with a wink.

Marie laughed, which she knew was Rachael's intent. "I'd like that," Marie teasingly returned. "They should bring gifts."

"Why would they bring gifts?" Ahote asked, confused, making the girls laugh even more.

CHAPTER 12

*W*alking past the saloon, Marie let Rachael approach Mrs. Brouchard while she and Ahote stood slightly back to give them space. But then a lovely surprise happened.

"Marie, Ahote, come join us. You don't need to be shy," Mrs. Brouchard said, waving them forward. Marie's shoulders relaxed. She hadn't realized how tense she was, ready for someone else to doubt her and judge her without proof. It was one thing for someone to come against her for something she believed in. She was used to that from her siblings who chose to go rogue with her brother Dante. But for someone to affront her just for being who and what she was, was a hit on the lowest level. She vowed never to do that to anyone going forward.

Marie smiled and casually waved as she approached. "It's so good to see you, Mrs. Brouchard."

"It's good to see you as well." The woman smiled. She was older than Marie and Rachael, probably in her fifties, but with the witches, one could never truly tell. "Rachael was just telling me you had a question regarding one of the members of our coven. Is that right?"

"Yes. Earlier a girl—maybe in her early twenties—joined our group to stand up to some annoyances, and I wanted to thank her, but she took off before I could say anything. I'm wondering if you might know who she is. She was slender with shoulder-length red hair and fair skin. I believe she is half witch. Might you know whom I am referring to?" Marie asked.

The woman considered for a moment before her eyes widened. "Oh dear, how could I forget? Yes, you must be speaking of Cynthia Walvern. She was always an interesting girl in her youth. I'd imagine she is about twenty-one or twenty-two now."

"That seems about right," Marie agreed. "Do you know anything else about her?"

"All I know is that she was very smart and wanted to learn skills in the medical field. She was only half witch, and her powers didn't do much for her, if I remember right. Her mom had mentioned something of the sort, in confidence of course."

"Of course," Rachael encouraged, though Marie knew her response was sarcastic.

"So she left not long after they had arrived. They had only been in town a short time. I think she was having trouble with some of the other younger witches, since she wasn't a very competent witch herself and couldn't compete with them."

"Wait just a minute," Rachael interrupted. "Just because she is half witch doesn't mean she is a lesser person. Maybe she needed proper tutelage or a differing perspective. And perhaps your other more *competent* youths were bullying and crushing her spirit. I don't blame her for leaving if that's why."

The woman looked affronted, as Marie knew she would. "Well, I—that seems to be a bit of an overreaction!" Mrs. Brouchard hissed. "Just because you *could have* been a coven leader had your mother not died does not mean you *should have!*" Rachael reared back as if slapped in the face. "Oh, yes, I know about you and your unruly magic. What's left of your coven is better off working with the more established ones in this town."

"How dare you! My mother was killed. Not that it's your business, but I have mastered my magic! And at least I'm not a pompous arse of a woman!" Rachael yelled back.

The woman had no words. She turned and marched away with a swish of her bustled dress and threw her sash around her shoulders with her head held too high as she went to meet friends down the road.

"That went well. You really are coming along with your people skills, Rach," Marie said with unbridled sarcasm.

Fuming, Rachael growled under her breath and placed her hands on her hips.

"Breathe, my little fighter," Ahote soothed, stroking her arm, and she began to calm.

"Excuse me," a small feminine voice called from behind the side wall of the saloon. They all turned to see the very girl they sought peering around the corner. Her green eyes were wide with surprise, set against a creamy yet speckled complexion; her eyes reflected having seen too much in her short lifespan, but she still held a glimmer of hope. Her wavy red locks were cut abruptly at her shoulders, and she appeared much too thin. "I couldn't help but overhear what you said on my behalf. Thank you. No one has ever stood up for me before."

Rachael quickly moved forward, and Marie was right behind her. "She was out of line," Rachael said, then continued, "I'm Rachael Stronghold, and this is Marie Blackstone. Who are you?"

The girl gave them each a small smile. "Cynthia."

"Thank you for standing with me earlier, Cynthia. You don't even know me, but I appreciated it," Marie added.

"No one should be pushed around, but especially by that lot. They are babied brats and deserve whatever they get," she said with unexpected vehemence. At seeing their surprise, Cynthia shrugged her shoulders and admitted, "They bullied me when I used to live here. I don't have any kind feelings for them."

"I understand that," Rachael offered, to put the girl at ease.

They chatted for a little bit and introduced her to Ahote before they decided to continue their walk through the rest of town.

"I heard you asking some questions, trying to find out who is behind those witches being taken," Cynthia admitted. "I would like to help you find the bad guy. No one should be picked on, and I want to have a chance to be the heroine in this story."

Marie paused. She felt a little strange to hear the girl had been essentially following them to know she'd been asking questions. But if she had gone through what Cynthia had, perhaps she'd want to be careful about who she talked to and want to find out information about them beforehand too.

Marie glanced around them to ensure no one was close enough to listen. "I feel I should tell you: I've been warned to not pursue this. I can't stop you, but you need to know what you're getting into and the possible dangers."

"I'm well aware there could be danger, but I think I can cover myself enough, even only being a half witch. I want to help."

"I also feel I should tell you I am a non-practicing witch hunter. I can guarantee your safety from me, but that's about it," Marie said honestly, then quickly looked away as if suddenly the girl's reaction mattered to her.

"I know who you are, Marie," was all she said in reply, as if it didn't matter to her. Marie smiled as an invisible weight left her shoulders.

"Okay then, let's see if we can find any clues to solve our mystery," Rachael declared, patting Marie on the back.

"I think we have investigated almost every area around the main part of the town here. Perhaps it's time to expand the search a little farther out." Marie pointed in the direction of the closest wooded area.

"The forest?" Cynthia asked. Her footing became unstable and she almost tripped, but Marie caught her elbow to help steady her. "Thank you," she breathed with a sigh of relief.

Marie received the familiar yet weakened sensation from a witch she normally did, but something caught her off guard—a feeling of nothingness, a void within the girl's being. Marie caught herself before she gave some kind of telling reaction. She didn't want to make Cynthia feel uneasy, but she wanted to know what the other half of her being was. Marie had assumed half witch, half human.

But currently, she had to guess she was something other than human. But what?

"It's not far, and we won't even go inside the forest, since it's starting to get dark. But we can walk the perimeter and see if there are any clues."

"What kind of clues are we looking for?" she asked Rachael.

"Anything, really," Marie supplied instead. "Anything that strikes you as odd or out of place. I know Sheriff Kasun and his patrol are searching the woods, and they'd know for sure if anything was out there, but I just have a feeling I'm supposed to."

"Let's do it, then," Cynthia said enthusiastically, complete with arm gestures.

"What do you think, Ahote? You've been quiet," Rachael said, reaching for her husband's hand.

"I think it is a good idea. I think there is danger afoot. Keep our eyes open," he said.

The four of them remained silent as they walked the edge along the treed area south of town, listening and watching their surroundings. Marie cast out her senses often but came back with nothing in the realm of any other witches in the vicinity or any kind of black or dark magic, at least in the area they covered.

"There's nothing here," she finally admitted.

"Let's go back and come up with a new plan," Rachael offered, trying to keep Marie's hopes up.

"No, that's enough for today I think—" Marie whipped her head in the opposite direction. "Wait . . ." She stopped and narrowed her eyes, looking deep into the woods. She closed her eyes and let her senses stretch out. "I feel something, something dark, but it's faint." Marie gripped her stomach with one hand and rubbed her forearm with the other. Suddenly, she cursed a word she hardly used and stood straight. "It's gone already. What is going on with my senses?"

"It's okay, Marie. You'll find it again," Cynthia said with reassuring confidence, reaching out to touch Marie's arm, but it hung in the air momentarily as she changed her mind and let her hand drop.

"Thanks, Cyn, I hope so—can I call you Cyn?" she asked, unsure.

"Actually, I prefer Cynthia." Cynthia slowly backed away. "I need to go. I'm sorry. I just remembered I told my mom I would be back by now. She worries. Thank you for letting me hunt with you for a bit. Can I join you another time?" She kept backing away.

"Of course," Marie said, watching her leave with confusion. Just before Cynthia turned, Marie caught a flash in her eyes. Marie blinked. She could've sworn she saw her eyes change color, or grow darker at least. Weird. Now she really wanted to know what her other half could be.

"That was oddly abrupt," Rachael said, and Marie nodded.

Not even a few minutes later, they were stopped by a woman in a housedress tying her bonnet around her head and under her chin as she ran out to meet them.

"Marie Blackstone?" she asked.

Marie nodded. "Yes, I am she. What is going on?"

The woman panted, slightly out of breath, but quickly recovered. She also was a witch. "Anne-Marie asked me to collect you. The young girl"—she quickly assessed who was with Marie and if she should be transparent or not—"who passed out the other day has awakened. She thought you might want to meet her and sit in on the questioning."

Marie's face lit up. "It's such good news she woke up! And yes, please, I would very much like to be present for that." Turning to Rachael and Ahote, she asked, "Would you mind terribly if I caught up with you later or at home?"

"Of course not. We will see you at home unless it's past dark; then I'll send Judson for you."

CHAPTER 13

*M*arie hadn't received one clue or found a piece of evidence since they had gone into the main part of town a couple days ago. The inaction and the unknown was driving her crazy. The meeting with the girl who returned to consciousness was a failure—other than her waking up. Marie was so grateful for her state of being, but unfortunately, the girl couldn't remember anything but black eyes and the feeling of being sucked into a small hole. She was still so weak and frail. That information really wasn't much to go on, but did confirm the energy parasite they had previously discussed.

Something was building. Something was coming. She could feel it. Her dreams had gone silent. The witches hadn't reported anyone else being abducted. Whoever had been taking them was biding their time —or they had left town, but Marie didn't think so. But why? If, as she suspected, the creature needed a witch's essence to sustain itself or survive, then it was only a matter of time. But if the being needed the magic for a specific purpose, then perhaps the project had been completed and it no longer needed their energy. She attempted to make a list of the creatures that could need that magic, but unfortunately it was a small list—what does one even call an energy vampire?

Marie made her way into the kitchen to make her and Judson lunch. Their kitchen was beyond anything they had in the past. The black cast iron wood stove made her smile as well as heated the room. Having a witch in the house was an added bonus, as she could help remove the soot from the draperies and the walls with a simple spell.

Rachael was bent over at the fireplace, stirring soup in the large black cauldron positioned above the flames. "Rachael, have you seen Judson?"

Rachael straightened up and glanced over at Marie. She paused for a moment. "I think he said he was going to be at the forge working on something."

"My dagger, probably. Some of the metal detail work was wearing thin. He's fixing it—again," Marie explained with a smile, but then her hand flew to her chest, and she sharply inhaled. "Judson," she whispered, and ran out the front door.

Something was wrong, but she wasn't sure what. What she felt wasn't because of her witch hunter abilities, but more a gut reaction from her connection to Judson. She ran across the expanse of the back of their property, and out of the corner of her eye, she spotted Cynthia awkwardly pacing outside their land. Marie did a double take to ensure she truly saw her.

"Cynthia! I don't have time to stop. Come with me!" Marie shouted and waved Cynthia to follow her. Marie was first to burst through the doors of the temporary blacksmith shop. Her eyes scanned the room and quickly found Judson at work on her dagger by the fire pit, sticking it into the bucket of water to cool the work he had just accomplished.

"Judson? Is everything okay?" Marie asked, her chest heaving as she sucked air into her lungs once more while her heart beat out of control.

Judson's expression suggested he had no idea what she spoke of. "I believe so. Are you okay, Marie?"

He set the dagger down and rushed to her, placing both hands around her upper arms, seeking out what could possibly be wrong with her.

"I had a feeling. Something wasn't right, and I had to come check."

Judson cocked his head. "Unless you had a premonition and something was about to go wrong with the fire and you stopped me before it happened, nothing was out of the usual out here."

Marie frowned. "So weird. My instincts have been all over the place. Maybe you're right. Perhaps we prevented something."

Judson glanced over her shoulder as the door clicked shut. "Hello," he said awkwardly with a confused smile. "Can we help you?"

"Oh, Judson, this is Cynthia. The girl I mentioned we ran into the other day in town. I found her outside on my way here." Marie turned to Cynthia and waved her forward. "Cynthia, this is my husband Judson. He does the best iron work in town, if you ever need anything made."

Cynthia smiled. "I'll remember that. It's nice to meet you, sir."

"Likewise," Judson responded. "I'd shake your hand, but I'm a bit of a mess." Judson raised up his hands, palms out, to display his grime from the morning's work.

"I'll take Cynthia with me to fetch some lunch for you. Carry on with your work." Marie shooed him away.

"Can I watch for a moment? I've never seen metalwork in progress." Cynthia's eyes were wide with curiosity.

"It is quite fascinating," Marie admitted with a wide smile. "Sure. We'll stay quiet, Judson, just for a bit, then we'll let you work."

Judson went back to the fire pit and picked up the dagger.

"Soot yourself." He chuckled to himself.

"Wow, he gets a new audience and is already trying to be funny." Marie waved him off and rolled her eyes for Cynthia's benefit, to which the young woman giggled.

"I like you two. Most married couples your age end up being too serious too soon and then they just grow old."

"I think the struggle is that life gets serious out here in the wild, and people have to grow up fast. We've been blessed to truly enjoy each other's company and our life together, even when it's been hard."

Judson heated the next piece he needed to work on: a long sword that had a chip in the blade. He stuck the sword into the fire to heat and soften the metal. When he pulled it out, he lifted his hammer and began to work. The sounds of metal striking metal echoed through the shed. Sparks of red and orange flew through the air at the contact.

Marie glanced over at Cynthia. Her wide eyes reflected the dancing of the flames, which quickly turned to something more awkward. Marie watched Judson again, trying to see him through the eyes of someone younger who didn't know him. He wore an old work shirt he had ripped the sleeves off of for better arm movement, which also exposed his defined and muscular arms. He also wore a full leather apron that hugged his body. His tanned skin was slick and dirty with the heat and grime of the room. She and Judson had known each other since they were young, but suddenly Marie fell for him all over again. When she observed Cynthia watching her husband once more, she felt pride that her man was quite the specimen to look at, but at the same time a pang of jealousy. She didn't know Cynthia yet, but she didn't think the girl would disrespect her right in front of her. Either way, it was time to leave.

Marie cleared her throat, and Cynthia had the grace to blush. "It's okay. He is quite fascinating. Look but don't touch," Marie offered a friendly warning and wink. Cynthia giggled but nodded her understanding.

A clatter sounded behind them, and both turned quickly to see what had happened. Judson had knocked off a couple tools next to him on the ridge of the fire pit. Looking at Judson's face, he seemed confused by what had happened.

Cynthia made a strangled sound from her throat, like she was choking.

"Cynthia, are you all right?" Marie asked, so confused about what was going on.

"I have to go. I'm sorry." Cynthia's eyes flashed from vibrant green to a dark dulled color, almost black, then she swiftly ran out the door without another word.

Marie didn't have time to think more on it as she turned back to Judson, shock on her face when she saw him.

"Judson," she whispered with awe. Not only were there sparks from the fire as he continued to strike the metal, but blue and green sparks came from his hands, blending into the montage of the sparks flying. Marie felt it then again.

Magic. But also a debilitating sense of black magic.

"Judson? What's happening?" she said louder, barely able to get the words out, clutching her stomach.

Judson came out of whatever trance he had been in while diving into the rhythm of his work. His eyes grew wide with shock. He apparently had no idea he was doing it. Unintentional magic emanated from him.

But how? He wasn't a witch—at least not that they had known.

"Marie? What am I doing? How is this happening?" he asked, panic lacing his words. "I thought it was from the aether in the water from the falls."

"Judson, I *felt* you." Her words held as much shock as her face.

He looked at her inquisitively.

"I mean, I felt you as I feel *witches*."

Neither of them spoke for a few moments. The weight of the situation grew heavier and heavier the longer they stared into each other's eyes. No one moved.

"I'm not a witch," Judson finally said.

"I think that may not be true. Perhaps we need to talk to the Luna Coven. I think they have ways of testing this sort of thing, don't they? Didn't your mom's coven?"

Judson slowly nodded, his face pale and his gaze distant. He appeared to be in shock. He still held his hammer with a white-knuckled grip until he realized it and let it slip to the ground.

Marie vaguely wondered if Cynthia had seen Judson's sparks and it caught her off guard. Being a witch herself, it shouldn't have scared her, but maybe she, too, felt the dark magic Marie had. But that was something she couldn't comprehend at the moment.

CHAPTER 14

*M*arie, Judson, and Rachael rode into town on their horse and buggy to arrive faster. Rachael had spelled a bird to deliver a message to Anne-Marie to inform her of their arrival and ask to have the high council of the Luna Coven with her. Ahote would stay with their little one while Hank, Rodney, Michael, and Caroline worked the vines, preparing them for winter in the Blackstones' vineyard for the new winery they were about to open. The first run of wines in a variety of reds and whites was in the process of being tested. Life had to carry on, and Judson ensured them they wouldn't be gone long.

Pulling up to the mansion where the Court held their meetings, Judson got out and shakily tied the horse to the post. The three of them walked up the front steps. Priscilla Augustine opened the front door and welcomed them with an understanding smile and showed them inside. No one seemed to know what to say while they awaited Anne-Marie.

Not even a minute after they sat, Anne-Marie entered the house.

"Marie, Judson, what seems to be happening? Rachael was vague with her missive, which I understand. The birds tend to confuse information if too many details are given." She winked at Rachael, attempting to alleviate some of the tension in the room.

Marie took a deep breath and began on her husband's behalf. "For some time now, I've noticed Judson struggling with something personal, but when we finally addressed it, he believed it had something to do with working with the aether from the falls and my family's stone in the dagger. It made sense to me at the time, but then I started *feeling* him as I do with you all." She glanced around the room at all the witches present—the Augustines, both Raffaele and Priscilla; Rodavan Bishop; Rachael, of course; and a few others. She also noted Elsmed Fairchild's presence because, of course, the mansion was his home.

"Judson, can you share your experience with this?" Raffaele asked.

Judson nodded. He wrung his hands, then wiped them on his pants before standing up, clearly uncomfortable. "As you know, I grew up in the Stronghold coven back east in Virginia. My mother was a witch, but I was adopted into her family. Or so I was told. I have never had any magic to speak of. When we arrived here and I started using the water from the falls, I began to have some strange things happen. Sparks would fly when I was intently working on something. I assumed it was the water having some kind of strange effect on me as I worked. I began to feel other sensations that were new, but they were very subtle and didn't go very far. I couldn't make anything happen. I remembered some spells from my youth and even went as far as to try some, but nothing happened. In fact, I gained pains in my head instead. Today, I worked in the forge almost as if in a trance, then I awoke to blue and green sparks coming from my hands, and I hadn't been working with the aether." He looked at his hands, then to each of them for an answer. "Can any of you explain what's happening?"

Anne-Marie offered him a small knowing smile. "Judson, we have a test we can perform to check your heritage—whether you have witch blood or not. I'm certain, however, your coven back home would have had this same test. I also asked Elsmed to be here.

He has a gift to ensure the honesty and validity of our thoughts and memories. If you let him, he can perform his own sort of test to see if we can determine what happened in your past based on suppressed memories you may have."

"Yes, to both!" Judson said enthusiastically. "Any information we can gain would be helpful, thank you."

Marie grabbed his hand and squeezed him tight in support.

Anne-Marie nodded and gestured for the witches to stand. In her hands she held a small bowl. "Judson, please stand in the middle. If you could give me a strand of your hair from your head and a drop of your blood, I will mix it with a special revealing powder I created. As we surround you, I will say a spell."

Without hesitation, Judson yanked a hair from his head and gave it to her. Then he pulled out a small knife from his pocket, but Rodavan stopped him with his hand outstretched and an exasperated look.

"Please use this." He handed him an athame—a knife used in rituals, most likely cleansed and purified to use in such a situation. Judson accepted it with an appreciative look. He didn't even flinch when he poked the tip of his thumb.

Anne-Marie held out her mortar for him to allow several drops to fall in. She then added her powder, blended it all together with the pestle, and the witches began to chant. Judson held still in the center of the circle.

Marie watched with a hint of nervousness for her husband. One way or another, they would find something, and she hoped it wasn't more than her loving Judson could handle.

A moment later, the chant ceased. Anne-Marie stepped in front of Judson and smeared the paste she created of powder and Judson's hair and blood onto his forehead. The blood sizzled and popped the moment it touched his skin, and he flinched.

"Be calm, Judson," she reprimanded. "Elsmed, please step forward and conduct your test."

Elsmed, with his stoic, unreadable expression, took his place in front of Judson. Marie always felt uncomfortable around Elsmed, although he had never given her reason to feel that way. She had always felt he was looking into her soul and could read her life story without her permission—she supposed he actually could, but she didn't like not knowing what he saw. She'd rather he simply asked her to share it. But now she wondered more than ever if Judson had a history hidden from him.

"Open your eyes, Judson. I need to read your soul," Elsmed instructed with a flat tone. Judson did as he said and allowed Elsmed to truly look into his history. Marie admired her husband's bravery.

Only a moment later did Elsmed blink and take a step back, indicating he was finished. Everyone looked to him for his response, but he looked to Anne-Marie first.

She nodded. "Judson, based on my test of magic, yes, you have witch blood. And always have." She looked at Elsmed.

He also nodded but added, "Based on my findings, I agree you have always had witch blood. The woman you knew as your mother was actually your aunt, caring for you when your mother died in childbirth. They didn't want you to carry the weight of feeling it was your fault she died. Your father was also a witch—a powerful one, based on what I saw. I do not know who he is, but he was not present. Feuding covens, I believe."

"Why didn't he have power until now?" Marie interrupted.

Elsmed gave her a look suggesting he was about to get there. "There is a spell on him to lock down his magic lest he ask questions they had no answers for. They thought they were doing what would be best for him. If the father knew he existed and had the power he does, the other coven would come for him and claim him for their own. Your aunt couldn't have handled that loss as well. She did her best to teach you all you would need to know without teaching it to you as a witch. Everything you need and are is within you. Anne-Marie and the coven simply need to unlock your magic."

"Thank you, sir," Judson said with an inclined head.

Elsmed took a step back, as if his job was done, and then he left the room.

"I believe your contact with the aether in the water was simply a catalyst to ignite your suppressed ancestry," Anne-Marie added.

Judson's face was a kaleidoscope of emotions. Marie came alongside him and held his hand in both of hers. She wanted him to feel all the love she had always had for him, plus even more.

"Are you ready to unlock your magic, Judson Carter Blackstone?" Raffaele stepped forward as he asked the question. Priscilla joined him and held his hand. Rachael, then Rodavan, did the same, and the others as well as Anne-Marie completed the circle around them both. Marie slowly inhaled, willing her body to remain in check with all the witches so close. Tingles shot up and down her arms, but she had control. After all, this moment was for Judson, and she wouldn't miss it for all the discomfort in the world.

"Yes, please unlock my past into my present as I become my future," Judson profoundly said into the silence of the room.

The room chanted as one, over and over. Their voices grew in strength and power until something in the atmosphere snapped and a bright light exploded before their eyes. Simple as that, Judson Blackstone became the first witch married to a witch hunter.

CHAPTER 15

*J*ust before they left, Raffaele encouraged them to take some time for themselves and go for a walk to enjoy and absorb the magic of nature, especially for the new witch. It would give Judson some time to let the news and magic settle. So they did. Rachael accompanied them because they thought of her as family, and Judson had many witchy questions for her.

"Do you always feel this much energy constantly flowing through your system?" he asked first, as they entered into a wooded area past the mansion.

"No, I don't think so. Having always had my magic, I'm not sure what you're going through, Judson. I'm sorry. I believe what is happening is akin to an awakening, where everything is alive and surging with an incredible force but will settle as it merges with your body, mind, and spirit."

"What does it feel like, Jud?" Marie asked, curious as to all the new things her husband was experiencing.

He thought about it for a moment. "It feels like the adrenaline rush I get when I'm in a forging state, creating something beautiful from a piece of metal piping, but much more."

Marie squinted in his direction, attempting to understand that feeling.

"Maybe more like when you can sense a witch's magic, Marie, and it's very powerful, but instead of in your arms, it is all over your entire body," Rachael tried to help out.

"Good one, Rachael. Thanks. Yes, Marie, I think it might be like what you've described to me," Judson offered.

"That makes sense." She reached for his hand, and a twinkle lit her eyes. "Do you want to try some?"

Judson stopped. "Some what?"

"Magic, silly." Marie laughed. "Rachael's here. She could help guide you."

Judson's eyes lit up like a little boy at Christmas. Marie knew it had always been hard on him being the only one in the coven who couldn't do magic and always wanting to. Her heart melted at his unbridled excitement at finally being able to make a dream come true.

He turned to Rachael. "Would you help me?"

"Of course," Rachael said. Her smile reached from ear to ear. They stopped walking, and Rachael looked for and found a pine cone on the ground. She held it out in front of him. "Now, pretend this is a candle. Visualize it as a candle. Visualize your magic welling up within you, then traveling out from you to light the tip of this candle. Watch me first, then you try."

Judson nodded and stared at Rachael intently. Marie watched closely, silently cheering Judson on and wishing there was something she could do to help him. Rachael lit the pine cone candle with practiced ease, then extinguished the flame and turned to Judson. He took the candle and handed it to Marie, who smiled, grateful to have something to assist with.

"Focus, Jud. I know you can do this," Marie encouraged.

Judson's eyes narrowed, and his face scrunched up tight, but nothing happened. He blew out a frustrated breath and looked to the sky. "It's not working."

"No, of course not. You looked like you were constipated."

Rachael and Marie both laughed. Judson also laughed and relaxed. "Now this time, relax. Magic is a part of who you are. Even if you are just realizing it. It's always been there. You are learning to connect with it. Try this: Visualize a box in the center of your being. In that box is all the power that is yours by birthright. Now mentally take your hand and open the box; reach inside and grasp the power. You don't need to rip it out. Just hold it in your hand. Claim it and allow it to travel throughout your body until it is ready to be used."

"It sounds like you personify your magic," Judson stated.

"I guess I do. It helps me to be one with my magic and gives me grace when it's not performing as I need it to." Rachael shrugged. "Okay, now try again. Remember to relax."

He nodded sharply and inhaled a deep, slow breath, then held it and peacefully released it. He gently focused on the pine cone candle, and a moment later, it sparked and sputtered until the flame caught. Judson whooped with excitement, and Marie allowed tears of happiness to stream down her face. Rachael beamed with pride.

Instantly, Marie doubled over, holding her stomach.

"Black magic," she rushed out, before she was debilitated. Rachael and Judson came around Marie, and the three of them were on guard.

"Where? Can you tell?" Rachael asked.

Marie nodded and tried to point straight ahead, but her hand shook with tremors.

"Of course she can tell," a feminine voice called haughtily from behind some bushes. A moment later, Cynthia sashayed confidently through the foliage. "She's been able to tell every time I show up. Lucky for me, she's so insecure, she doubted herself and her powers. As soon as she sensed me, I disappeared to encourage that doubt." Cynthia laughed, but it didn't sound like the young woman they had spent time with.

"Cynthia?" Rachael was confused. Cynthia shot a look at Rachael, but instead of bright green, her eyes were shiny black orbs.

"I'm not Cynthia, not really," the woman who looked like

Cynthia explained. "You see, I'm half Cynthia, but I'm also Cynder, her other half."

"Her other half?" Judson asked. "What do you mean?"

Marie had a brief moment of realization at why her other half felt like a void. It was full of darkness.

Cynthia—or Cynder—moved closer, her red shoulder-length wavy hair swaying with the movement. Cynthia had been more timid and didn't walk with such attitude. The sight was strangely comical. As soon as she realized she had done it, her power ebbed, and the beacon of dark magic that had shot out from her toned down. Marie could stand up straight and breathe more normally now.

"Apparently, I'm relegated to explaining everything in this life," Cynder said with annoyance, under her breath.

"This life? Who are you?" Rachael asked, more skeptical.

"I told you. I am Cynder, an alchemist from another land, but I am also so much more. I made great discoveries and found a way to preserve my life and put magic to good use."

"The magic is your energy source," Marie stated as understanding began to dawn on her.

"Very good, hunter. You and I have more in common than you would like to let on." Cynder lifted a corner of her lips and sneered at Marie.

"My brother maybe, but not me." Marie rushed out the question she'd been seeking the answer to. "What about the others? The witches . . . the ones you stole magical energy from—where are they?"

"I had no further use for them. If any of them are still alive . . . well, you'll never find them, so they might as well be dead."

Hope soared in Marie's chest that the witches might still be alive, if only drained of their magical energy. She also knew that to a witch, many would feel they would have rather been dead than have to live without their magic. Still, she would find them and see them back with their parents one way or another.

"How did you become half a person?" Judson asked curiously, not fully understanding what was happening.

"Half? Half a person?" Cynder shouted, anger rising to the surface and making her seem to grow taller. "We are a full person—we are more than a full person, with twice the abilities and powers."

"Calm down, Cynth—Cynder, please," Rachael pleaded with her. "We're trying to understand. Please tell us your story." Marie recognized she was buying them time, hopefully for help to arrive.

Cynder seemed to visibly shrink back down to her original size. "Rachael, you can be sensible when you want to. I *would* like to tell my story. No one ever wants to hear it. It began when this young and foolish girl came looking for the famed alchemist to assist her in her medical studies. I had already killed the alchemist and possessed his body at this point; she got in too deep and didn't realize what she was playing at when she released me. It was all too easy to possess her after that."

"And who were you before you assumed the role of the alchemist?" Marie asked.

"Apophis, a demon of chaos. But I had found it troubling to sustain myself in this life cycle on this world, until I met the alchemist. She was already doing advanced work, but no one would believe her or give her the time of day, especially being a woman. But now I have all her knowledge. However, her body held no strength as a human and began to wear out over time. This body, though . . ." Cynder gestured her hands awkwardly down her sides. "Cynthia's body is stronger, having witch blood. Though, I admit, I grow tired of her weariness. Had I known she was only half witch, I might not have bothered with her, but my prospects where we lived were meager. Now, I seek a stronger vessel to abide in." Cynder—Apophis—Cynthia—whoever it was looked directly and hungrily at Judson.

"Oh, no, you don't." Marie stepped in front of him. "You don't get to come here and just take what or whomever you want."

"I think I do."

Marie gasped. "Look!"

She almost missed it. But Cynder's body blurred momentarily. And the green eyes of Cynthia suddenly showed through.

"Help!" she cried. "I'm so sorry. I don't have much time. I can't hold her off. I didn't realize the deal I was making. The alchemist promised me she had a way to restore me to full witch status if I assisted her in a project. I didn't realize I was the project. I know where they are . . ." Cynthia gasped for breath as if going under water, and her head shook repetitively before her body blurred again and the black eyes of Cynder returned.

"Cynthia is still in there," Rachael whispered. "We have to find a way to save her."

"Agreed," Marie rushed out.

Cynder stalked forward, her eyes locked on Judson. "Cynthia will never get out. She made her bed."

"Why . . . why do you want him and not me?" Rachael stammered, changing the subject.

Cynder flashed her eyes in Rachael's direction. "Because, you foolish woman, he is a newborn witch. His power is at its strongest and most unruly. His magic calls to me." She physically licked her lips. Hunger sparked in her eyes—hunger for his raw magic.

"Just let her try," Judson said, taking a fighter's stance and holding up his fists in defense.

"Judson! Don't antagonize her," Marie whisper-shouted. "I can't help if the darkness takes over." Fear ran down Marie's spine as she thought of her dream.

"The darkness will ultimately take this whole town, then move on to the next one," Cynder said with an evil laugh.

"No, it won't. We will stop you." Marie faced off with the two-part being, but it only continued to laugh, seeming more evil as it did. As a demonstration of Cynder's growing power, she shot a stream of lightning out from her hand and into a nearby tree, splitting it in half lengthwise. Everyone ducked.

"What do we do?" Rachael whispered fast, while the noise of the tree splintering covered their voices.

"Distract her. I sense witches coming," Marie said. Marie didn't actually sense the witches coming yet. She hoped they would, but she didn't know what they were going to do or how to get out of it all safe and sound. So she improvised to give Judson and Rachael courage. They were a ragtag crew: a hunter with no physical powers, a witch whose magic didn't always cooperate, and a new witch with no idea yet what he was doing. But Marie couldn't let them know she feared for them. She suddenly had renewed faith in her own abilities, realizing that they never were on the outs, but were being manipulated by Cynder's darkness.

"How do you harness control of both your powers and Cynthia's witch powers at the same time?" Judson asked, trying to get her talking so she wouldn't blow anything else up.

"Cynthia is puny. I have no trouble controlling her measly powers. She was weak. That was how I was able to so easily convince her to help me. However, her witch ability with lightning is a handy trick." She stalked forward. "But you, Judson—I can sense the strength of your magic from here. It wafts to me and smells so delicious. You and me, we could do terrible things together." She licked her lips once more.

The action was so reprehensible, Marie wanted to throw up.

"She is not puny, and she is not weak!" Rachael stepped in front of Judson and waved her hands around. She threw out a spell, and a rope appeared and wrapped itself around Cynder. Rachael tried to restrain her, but Cynder used the power Cynthia had with the elements and set fire to the rope, which quickly burned.

"You dare to restrain me?" Cynder yelled.

"Cynthia, I know you're still in there," Rachael shouted at the top of her lungs. "If you can hear me, I need you to try to take control again. We need you to fight back. Take control of your power and your life. Fight with us. We can help you!" A single tear slowly traced the contour of Rachael's cheek on its way to the tip of her chin, then down to the ground. Marie knew Rachael wanted to save the young witch, but she didn't see how it was possible at this juncture. "We can free you from this monster!"

Suddenly Marie had an idea—something she had read in her

family's journal, something she never thought she would need to know.

Cynder swiped her hand violently to the side, sending a gust of wind toward Rachael. The wind picked her up and threw her hard against the trunk of a tree. She fell to the ground with a loud thud. She lay there unmoving, barely breathing.

"NO!" screamed Marie. She ran to her best friend—her sister— and fell down beside her.

A moment later, the cavalry came through the woods behind them, in the form of the Luna Coven and some of the most powerful witches the town had, along with a few others of immense power.

CHAPTER 16

*S*eeing Rachael lying on the ground devastated Marie at the deepest part of her. She placed her fingers at the pulse of her neck; it was weak but still there.

"Hang in there, Rachael. You're strong. You've got little Alo waiting for you at home. Just keep breathing." Marie ripped a piece of fabric from the hem of her skirt and wrapped it around the gash in Rachael's head to stanch the bleeding, praying to anyone who would listen to save her friend. Judson ran to where they were on the ground and took a position in front of Marie and Rachael to protect them.

"Cynthia Walvern," Anne-Marie said, the authority in her voice carrying over all the noise as if she had shouted.

"Cynthia is not in control. I am Cynder. Get it right! You wouldn't train Cynthia in her craft or treat her with the respect she deserved, so she came to me, and I am the one who trained her and developed her power, even as weak as it was. But when we joined together, we both became more powerful. I. Am. *Cynder.*"

Anne-Marie didn't even flinch or back down at anything Cynder said, whether it was true or not. She kept her expression neutral, her tone flat and in control. Roman Bishop as well as his father Rodavan came to stand on either side of her. Priscilla and

Raffaele Augustine stood behind them, along with other Court members Lawrence Mills and Elsmed Fairchild. Marie couldn't figure out how they all knew where to find them. Marie figured it couldn't hurt to have a frost dragon and fae to assist just in case. No one knew what Cynder was capable of.

"I'm flattered you believed you could stop me with so few of you. Your collective power is still not enough." She laughed, unconcerned by their limited abilities.

"It is not just them." Marie stood with dirt-stained tear tracks on her face and blood smeared on her skirt. "Rachael fought for you, Cynthia. I know you can hear me. When I tell you, you fight with everything you have for control."

Cynder only laughed, although her image blurred in and out, which told Marie Cynthia had heard her. Cynder swayed on her feet, but she seemed unfazed by it. "It's only a matter of time. I just need a little more power to take over completely, and I will have it!" She moved toward Rachael and Judson, the closest of the witch magic. But Rachael, being weak and debilitated—on the brink of life—was an easy target.

Not on Marie's watch.

She jumped in front of both Rachael and Judson. Hearing his grumbled complaint behind her, she allowed her husband to move beside her.

"My dagger, Judson." She held out her hand expectantly. She knew he had it on him when they left. She remembered him using it in her dream—that couldn't have been a coincidence. He kept it hidden in the waistband at the back of his pants. He looked at her, confused.

"Marie? Don't do something stupid." He handed her the dagger.

"You know me better than that." She winked at him and took the dagger.

"That's what I'm afraid of," he whispered under his breath. "At least let me help."

She nodded. He was to be a part of it as well. "I read about it in the journal but didn't understand what it could mean until now. It's time for this witch hunter to rise up and take my place on behalf of all my family to come after me." She held the dagger out, but it was so small, Cynder laughed even harder.

Marie had to admit it didn't look good from the outside. She glanced to the others, who looked on with their own skepticism, except for Anne-Marie and Priscilla. The Bishops actually looked bored, and Lawrence looked mad. Elsmed—she couldn't tell what Elsmed was thinking, but if he could truly read minds, perhaps he already knew her plan. Unexpectedly, he crossed his arms and winked at her. Marie's heart soared. Anne-Marie and Priscilla both looked at her with faith and strength. Anne-Marie gave her a subtle nod. They would have her back.

"Cynder, this is your warning. Give up Cynthia and go back to where you came from!" Marie shouted.

"No. I earned my place with her. She gave up part of herself for me. Unless you're offering Judson, then I'll stay right where I am until I get something better!" she spat out. Her body jerked and moved at odd angles. She frowned and reared back as if surprised.

"So the little witch wants to play. You ungrateful wretch!" Cynder opened her hands and called lightning from the sky. She tossed it back and forth in her palms, gathering her strength and weakening whatever power Cynthia had left.

"Now, Marie," Anne-Marie quickly but quietly encouraged.

Marie stepped right in front of Cynder, took her dagger, and sliced her own hand, releasing a flow of blood.

"You didn't even try to stab me!" Cynder mocked, and cackled with sarcasm. "Is that it?"

"No. This is." Marie smeared her blood on the stone encased in the hilt of her dagger. The stone glowed, growing brighter and brighter. She held it in front of Cynder.

Everyone waited in anticipation for what would happen. If anything.

Marie closed her eyes and focused on the ability within her that was unique to her as a witch hunter. She found the spark of magic within Cynder she knew to be Cynthia's witch essence and pulled it toward her. As a witch hunter, she could pull the magical essence out of a witch and absorb it within herself—usually only if they were dead. That was how her brother Dante and the rest of the rogue witch hunters she left behind did what they did. But she had magic and her family's dagger on her side. Marie still felt guilt over what she was doing. After all, she chose to leave that way of life behind in order to have the life they now enjoyed. She may very well be asked to leave afterward, but she also knew it might be Cynthia's only chance. And for Rachael, she had to try.

"Nothing's happening! You're so foolish," Cynder chanted over and over. "Such a letdown." She shrugged her shoulders. "Oh well, no more playing. You're wasting my time." She released a shot of lightning toward Roman Bishop, but he quickly deflected it overhead into nearby trees with his own magic. Trees and branches fell around them.

Marie felt a surge of witch magic envelop them and wondered if one of the witches put a shield of protection around them. She barely had time to notice. She had to focus on what she was doing so she didn't damage Cynthia's soul and pull her essence too hard. Judson placed his hand over hers on the dagger, and she felt him release whatever magic he knew how to give.

"Witches, now! Cynthia, now!" Marie shouted under the strain of what she was doing. She felt the witches come together and share their magic, then direct it toward Cynder. She hoped that while she pulled on Cynthia, it gave the witches enough room to bind the demon with their magic and pull Cynder out. Her hope was that Cynthia would fight with everything she was to take control of her body, and while Marie pulled on her, she could push Cynder out from within. She had to find the perfect balance of pull and give to not pull Cynthia's soul completely out. She had never done it before, so she carefully teetered on the line, afraid of pulling too hard.

Marie could feel the tug-of-war within Cynthia. Tension grew and grew. Sweat beaded on Marie's forehead, then trickled down the sides of her face. A bundle of nerves grew tighter and tighter within her stomach.

A hand rested on her shoulder. She had the awareness Elsmed had come behind her. She didn't know what all his power was as a fae, but she felt strength and energy pour into her. He was lending her what he could.

"It's working. Keep going. She's almost free. I can sense it," he said in a low tone behind her.

And so she did. Finally, something snapped! A bright light shot out from her dagger. Cynthia fell to the ground unconscious. Marie flew back. Had Elsmed not been behind her, she would have landed on her backside. Judson reached for her hand to steady her. They ran to Cynthia lying on the ground. Elsmed placed his hand on her forehead and gave Marie a small smile and a reassuring nod. Marie was relieved, but she needed to see her eyes.

A scuffle sounded behind them. When Marie turned, she was surprised to find all the witches extending their hands toward a mass of darkness that grew larger than she thought was possible to hide within a young woman's body. They had Cynder—or the demon—bound and contained by their magic.

"Lawrence, the container!" Anne-Marie shouted.

Lawrence Mills came forward with a handmade box and opened the lid, placing it on the ground below the center of the dark mass. The witches chanted a spell while Anne-Marie guided the demon at the epicenter down into the box. By some magic, a void opened inside the box and sucked the darkness into it. An audible pop sounded when it was complete, taking the tension of the moment with it. Lawrence quickly shut the lid and locked it. Rodavan Bishop knelt down in front of the box and whispered a spell of his own that sealed the box.

"Rodavan, Roman, and Raffaele, please have a hellhound escort it back to where it belongs—in Hell," Anne-Marie directed.

Everyone breathed easier. Cynthia opened her emerald green eyes and cried. "She's gone. I don't feel the darkness anymore."

"No, you're free," Judson said, while Marie ran back to Rachael on the ground to tell her.

"We did it, Rach! Cynthia's free. You fought for her, and she's free," Marie said with tears and laughter. She stroked Rachael's head when she tried to open her eyes and smile.

"Thank you. She deserved to be free." Her breathing was shallow, but she had words to get out. "Take care of them for me. Promise me, Marie."

Marie lost all color in her face. "What? No, you take care of them. You're going to be fine."

"Promise me, Marie. You're my family. Raise Alo as your own. Promise."

Marie choked on her emotion, but said, "I promise."

"Love you, Marie."

"Love you too, Rach." Her eyelids fluttered closed, never to be opened again. Marie collapsed and sobbed.

EPILOGUE

*M*onths after Rachael had passed on, Marie finally had the strength of heart and mind to not only leave their house but to officially open the Blackstone family vineyard. There was nothing like a beautifully decorated vineyard, surrounded by snow in the middle of December.

Ahote had become the most doting father to Alo and dove into the work he did on the vineyard to escape the pain of losing Rachael. It broke Marie's heart every time she saw them together, and yet at the same time, it healed a little bit each day. Everyone grieved her loss, especially at the Blackstone household, but also in the town. Rachael had been loved by many.

Priscilla Augustine took her loss extremely hard. She had later come to explain she had a vision of sorts of what would transpire after Judson's magic was unlocked. That was how the coven was prepared and showed up in the forest to help Marie against Cynder when they had. Priscilla saw it all unfold, and they followed each step, waiting to intervene until after someone had screamed *No.* Unfortunately, in her vision she only saw the parts they were to follow step by step. She never saw what happened to make Marie scream. She didn't know Rachael had put herself between Cynder and Judson and risked her life. But still she felt responsible, as if she should have known all things.

Marie didn't blame her. She was grateful Priscilla did get the vision and that the coven did come. Marie wished she'd been granted the foresight to see the entire picture, but nevertheless, Priscilla's vision saved the rest of them. If the members of the Court and coven hadn't interceded when they did, they all would be dead.

"Marie?" Hank, her father, called from the other side of the door.

"I'm ready," she replied. She had originally planned for a fall opening party, but after losing Rachael, they took more time, and instead, it was the heart of winter. Marie was okay with that. Winter was a beautiful time where they lived up in the mountains. It was colder than anything she had ever experienced, but she liked it. The sharp brisk air that stung her lungs when she inhaled deep made her feel alive amidst the pain. It reminded her life did go on and she was blessed to be among the living. She opened the door and stepped out.

Her father's smile warmed her heart. He said, "I wish your mama could see you now. She'd be so proud of you and the woman you have become, Marie Marcella Blackstone."

Marie reached up on her tiptoes and kissed his cheek. "Thanks, Dad. Now let's go get this vineyard officially opened to the public." She winked at him and giggled.

They didn't have far to go, since the party was right outside their home. They had placed paper bags filled with sand and small candles along the edges of the vineyard and surrounding an area designated as the dance floor. Also in strategic places were barrels of contained fires to help keep people warm. Her brother Rodney had made an attempt at decorating the buildings with some cutout paper flowers and snowflakes he had made with his adopted nephew, Alo. His technique needed some work, but the effort warmed her heart and made her smile.

Unlike Marie's dream, she would not walk down an aisle of grapes at the vineyard, and she would not worry about the people being sucked into the darkness invading their town. Instead, she looked forward to the gathering of her family and friends to witness such a special time in the midst of the heartache and pain the last several years had held for everyone. Opening the vineyard would mark a turning point for the town, as it would bring in outside business, but also for them as a family.

She held the hem of her blue dress accompanied by light brown fur boots and a cream fur shawl to keep her warm. Her unruly blond hair was pinned high on her head, save the few pieces that refused to be bound.

Marie closed her eyes and slowly breathed in deep the crisp cold air, savoring every moment. They had done it. They built a new life, a new home, and a business to sustain them for years to come. She had planned and anticipated this very moment with Rachael by her side. Marie allowed a single tear to fall for her friend. Rachael would be missed, but Marie knew she was truly there in spirit.

When Marie lifted her head and opened her eyes, she gasped.

People. The area was full of people from the town. They had all been invited, but she didn't think they would come, due to recent events. They had created an aisle with unlit candles, leading her from the house to the outbuilding where they made the wine. Judson waited for her at a tall table they had made. Right where he was supposed to have been in the dream. On the table were glasses of all kinds, and the newly sealed bottles of wine ready for consumption.

All eyes were on her, waiting for her. And though it was the dead of winter, magically fireflies bobbed and weaved in the air above their heads. Judson extended his hand toward her, beckoning her to come. Her father led the way through the group of people— friends from the town. But unlike her dream, they were smiling, supportive, and happy to be there. Just as she wanted at such a special celebration of their new life.

"I . . . I'm speechless," she said. "It's beautiful. Thank you. Thank you all for coming." She began to move toward Judson, ready to start the party.

"Oh, wait, please," Judson said out loud with a hint of embarrassed panic. He stood tall and closed his eyes, breathing deep and attempting to relax himself.

Marie looked quizzically at her father, but he simply shook his head, indicating he didn't know what Judson was up to. All at once, the candles lining the aisle burst into delicate little flames. He opened his eyes and smiled with pride. Marie laughed, ditched the traditional atmosphere, and ran the rest of the way into his arms.

"You're amazing," she whispered.

"You're amazing," he returned, and kissed her forehead.

A throat cleared. It was her brother Rodney. "Let's start this party! We're freezing our arses off out here."

The crowd laughed, and the evening turned into a magical moment. Wine freely flowed. Music played, and people danced. Though the loss was felt, it was important to enjoy the moments of life and love and togetherness.

Before the night was over, the Trents approached Judson and Marie with an item covered under a blanket. Marie was so excited, she couldn't wait to see what they had made for Judson, but when she glanced at Judson, he seemed equally excited. Before she could say anything, Gregory Trent interrupted.

He explained how both Judson and Marie had each gone to them to create an item for the other, so they put the ideas together. Instead of making two items, they had made one.

Charlotte Trent pulled off the blanket to reveal the most beautifully detailed wooden box Marie had ever seen. They both gasped in surprise.

"Oh my," Judson said, at the same time Marie said, "It's beautiful." She couldn't help but run her fingers over the engraved scrollwork on the front.

Mr. Trent demonstrated by pulling open one of the drawers then clicking a lever and having the lid pop open. Deep red velvet lined the interior of the box. He showed them several other secret compartments and how to work the puzzle parts of it.

"This is truly amazing craftsmanship," Judson admired.

Mr. and Mrs. Trent left the box with them and bid them goodnight and congratulations on their vineyard, then left.

"This is perfect. I was thinking you could put your most special daggers or pieces of metal you work with in it," Marie admitted.

"And I hoped you could have a safe place for your dagger and journal when not in use."

"I think we should be able to accommodate all that and more in this box. There is more space than I thought there would be," Marie said with a huge smile.

"And I think we should keep it hidden in the secret vault in the armory in the basement to keep it safe," Judson said, deep in thought.

"But it's too pretty to hide away in the basement." Marie pouted.

"I agree, but I think it's important for future generations," he said, his face so serious that Marie agreed.

Anne-Marie and Sheriff Kasun approached Marie and Judson from the side so as not to draw too much attention to themselves. With them was Cynthia, looking extremely uncomfortable about being there.

"Marie and Judson?" Anne-Marie addressed them. "Cynthia wanted to say goodbye before she left."

Cynthia had been held by the coven in a magical prison of sorts to ensure the presence of darkness was completely gone. They continued to check her magic levels and were surprised to find she was currently a full witch, no longer only half. They could only conclude it had something to do with all the magic and the work Marie did on her soul simultaneously. But she had been growing stronger, and the uncertainty of it made them all uneasy, including Cynthia. During her time in the prison, she had told the Court where the other witches had been held. Sheriff Kasun and his pack found the handful of missing witches from their town, as well as a few others. Only one, from outside their town, was no longer alive, though the others had been completely drained of their magic and were in bad shape. After seeing the Luna Coven, they were all expected to make physical recoveries; sadly, the same could not be said for their magic.

"You're leaving?" Marie asked, surprised to just now learn this news.

"I am. My family is, too, actually. We decided we needed a fresh start somewhere else." She paused and hung her head. "Marie, I'm so sorry about Rachael. I . . . I . . ." Her words got choked in her throat.

Marie had no words, but hugged the girl and let her grieve and find forgiveness in that moment so they could all find some way to move forward.

After a minute or two, Marie pulled back with alarm. "I can't feel you, Cynthia. I mean, I can't feel your witch."

Anne-Marie placed her hand on Marie's forearm with understanding. "We bound her magic—at her request," she explained.

Shocked, Marie shook her head. "Why? Why would you do that?"

Cynthia shrugged. "I needed to start over. With everything in the past, I just wanted a chance to not worry about any of that. I'm really okay with it, Marie. But thank you for caring. Thank you for everything." She lunged forward and squeezed Marie so tight she couldn't breathe for a second.

"Goodbye, Cynthia."

Sheriff Kasun and Anne-Marie escorted her back out and to her family, who were apparently leaving that night. Marie felt bad, but she also felt relieved not to have to see Cynthia and have the reminder of what happened to Rachael every day. Marie truly didn't blame Cynthia, but she still wore the same face, and Marie couldn't unsee the petite girl throwing Rachael against the tree with her magic.

"You all right?" Judson asked, and kissed the top of her head.

Marie nodded. "But I could use a dance with my husband."

She smiled when he took her hand. Judson led Marie to the dance floor and spun her around a few times.

"What are you thinking, Marie?" Judson asked, placing his hands around her waist, drawing her close.

She sighed. "First of all, this is amazing. I'm so proud of the work everyone has done to make our vineyard a success." Her face turned down, and she gnawed on her bottom lip. When she looked back up at him, his warm gaze was so patient and understanding, she continued, "This is hardly the time or place, but I couldn't help but wonder now that Rachael isn't with us, what happens to the curse she put on Dante before we discovered this canyon?"

Judson frowned, deep in thought. He remembered how Rachael stood up to Dante when he faced off with Marie. To save Marie, Rachael cursed Dante in a way that would be the most detrimental to him. The curse would hide Marie and her family from his senses; he wouldn't be able to find them, no matter how hard he looked. And she cursed him to feel his humanity once again. However, by doing so, she tied her life to his. Meaning the curse would only remain in place as long as the one who cursed him remained alive. Now that Rachael no longer was among the living, Dante would regain his hunter side with a vengeance and come looking for Marie. Being where they were, and surrounded by the new wards their town was implementing, Marie would be hard to find. But Dante would never stop looking for her.

"Let's think on that another time. Tonight is for us." Judson encouraged her with a spin ending in a low dip.

They laughed and had the fun she had so anticipated for their opening ceremony. During a slower moment, she looked out at the people from the town who had come to celebrate with them. She watched Raffaele Augustine dip Priscilla to the point she giggled. The Bishops stood in the corner talking with Raffaele's brother while they drank punch she was pretty sure was laced with moonshine. The Trents' apprentice, Theodore Carver, took a turn on the dance floor with Betsy in his arms. Her father spun a couple different women around, and Marie laughed. Rodney and their cousins Caroline and Michael shoved special treats in their mouths. Other townspeople, including the Millses, Elsmed Fairchild and his wife, Ric and Gaby Kasun, Mihail and Irina Petran, Mr. and Mrs. Lancaster, and several others gathered about, mingling and having a good time. Ahote and Alo hesitated at first, but then she watched their faces light up when the father spun his son around in his arms and they allowed themselves to have fun. The sight was everything Marie wanted. She only wished Rachael could be there to see it too.

"I love you, Judson. I'm so grateful to have found a home with you," Marie said, and slowly kissed his lips.

Judson smiled from ear to ear. "I love you too, Marie. You did it."

"Did what?" She was suddenly confused.

"You followed your heart, chose who you wanted to be, found us a home, and called out the witch hunters to rise to the challenge of becoming something more."

Marie smiled. Yes, she did. She couldn't wait for the future generations of witch hunters to rise.

The dagger and its secrets remained in the family's protective possession for generations to come, and they continued to make weapons for the town. Judson and Marie weren't sure they would be able to have children with the seemingly combative traits between witch and witch hunter, but they did. Once their children—specifically daughters with the hunter's mark—began to demonstrate extreme challenges controlling their hunter side along with the witch magic, though, they asked the Luna Coven to bind the magic that flowed through them—at the children's request. The suppression was intended to be a blessing and a protection for their children and grandchildren. As the years went on and the generations continued, the knowledge of the magic in their veins was restricted, then lost . . . until there would eventually be one able to access the family journal in its entirety again.

We hope you enjoyed this story in the Legends of Havenwood Falls series featuring a variety of supernatural creatures. You may also want to read these other stories about the Blackstone witch hunters, all by Morgan Wylie:

Dawn of the Witch Hunters
Reawakened
Redefined
Rediscovered

ABOUT THE AUTHOR

Morgan Wylie is an award-winning and *USA Today* Bestselling Author with several genres published from YA fantasy to adult paranormal romance, as well as other stories in between. Morgan published her first novel, *Silent Orchids,* one year after moving across the country with her family on a journey of new discovery. After an amazing three years in Nashville, Tennessee, and the release of two more books, Morgan and her family found their way back to the Northwest, where they now reside. With a collection of twelve-plus titles, she passionately pursues working every day with great optimism. Daily, Morgan continues to embrace all things: Mama, wife, teacher, and mediator to the many voices and muses constantly chattering inside her head, where it gets pretty loud!

You can find her and news on her books at the following:
    MorganWylie.net
    Morgan Wylie Books on Facebook
    @MWylieBooks on Instagram (and Twitter)

ACKNOWLEDGMENTS

Thank you for visiting the 1800s with me and the Blackstones again! Creating a collaborative world like this takes a village of amazing authors and an even more amazing leader supreme, and we have that in Kristie Cook, founder of Havenwood Falls. Thank you, Kristie, for letting us continue to play throughout all eras!

Thank you, Liz Ferry, for your time and your expertise! Thank you, Regina Wamba, for the beautiful covers and graphics you create! And thank you to Ang'dora Productions for allowing me the opportunity to work with you.

Thank you, Kristie Cook, for the collaboration with Anne-Marie Beaumont and the Luna Coven. Thank you, Randi Cooley Wilson, for the use of Rodavan and Roman Bishop, Eric Asher for the use of Charlotte and Gregory Trent as well as Theodore Carver and Betsy, Kallie Ross for the use of Ric and Gaby Kasun as well as the Kasun Pack, E.J. Fechenda for the use of Elsmed Fairchild and his wife, Kristen Yard for the use of Martha Daryn and the Green Coven, and Amy Hale for the use of Lawrence Mills and family. It is always an honor to get to collaborate with such amazing and generous authors. Thank you!

THE DROWNING BRIDE

SEVEN JANE

~ A Legends of Havenwood Falls Novella ~

HAVENWOOD FALLS LEGENDS

THE
DROWNING
BRIDE

SEVEN JANE

For my part, I know nothing with any certainty, but the sight of the stars makes me dream.
—Vincent van Gogh

In loving memory of BB.

CHAPTER 1

The fall of 1993 was a particularly lovely one, even in Pensacola, where autumn didn't normally show its colors, much less announce itself with the usual splendor that it did in other parts of the eastern United States. With an average two hundred and twenty-four sunny days per year, northern Florida was a year-round blue-sky paradise, with temperatures that rarely dipped below ninety before late September and sometimes not even then.

It almost never got cold enough for a real coat, and you could forget about winter, which might have gone by completely unnoticed were it not for the holiday season that inspired people to deck palm trees with Christmas lights and play "Mele Kalikimaka" on every local radio station. In Florida, Santa wore swimming trunks and Ray-Bans when he came for his annual deliveries—and why not? This part of the country hadn't seen enough snow to turn anything fully white since the late seventies, and even then it only very barely qualified as a dusting—at least by New York standards, Stella's home state.

Now, in mid-September, other than a slight crisp in the evening breeze and a few blushing dogwood trees, it was nearly impossible to tell that the fall equinox was only a few days away, and Stella

Malley was trying to come to terms with the fact that this would be the first time she'd celebrate the coming of fall in a place that almost never bothered itself to be anything other than summer.

The thought cooled her in the way that a crisp autumn breeze would have, even if it did smell like saltwater.

"It's a hundred degrees outside and not a sign of fall in sight, and I'm still chilly," Stella grumbled to herself, brushing the palms of her hands down her forearms and wishing she'd had the forethought to keep a light jacket in her car, even though people would have teased her for doing so. She slid behind the wheel and cranked the engine to life, ready to drive home in the dark after work, alone with her radio and her thoughts. Music blared reliably from the speakers, but true enough, it was after midnight and the thermometer on the bank she passed still read 89 degrees—not a temperature that fell within her idyllic fall range.

Stella turned her mind toward happier things and tried to think cooler thoughts, but at the moment such a thing was a tall order, even for Stella, who was nothing if not a perpetual optimist.

It wasn't simply the lack of fall foliage that put a damper on her usually high spirits. Stella was already feeling seasonally out of place, and winter, she knew, was going to be truly bizarre by the time December came around. She'd be lying if she said she wasn't excited to spend the holidays buried in white sand rather than in the snow she'd grown up with in upstate New York, but still, despite how long she had dreamed of living on the beach and how happy she was to call Florida her new home with her fiancé Peter, Stella was still a little anxious about her first holidays in the Sunshine State. A deep aching had settled into her bones during the last days of August, when holiday decorations had begun appearing on the shelves in the department stores around town. She and Peter had moved halfway across the country over the summer, right after May Day. As a result, this would be the first year she wouldn't be able to partake in her family's seasonal celebrations.

Stella considered herself an independent, modern woman, but still she yearned for tradition and family, something she was moving toward but hadn't quite reached yet with Peter. She might have been twenty-two and ready to settle down and start her own life, but that didn't make the uprooting any easier, not even when she'd spent her whole life wishing she were somewhere warmer. Her mother was Nigerian by way of Haiti, and had inspired Stella with stories of sunshine and tropical climates, but her father was of Irish descent, and among the many mixed ethnic traditions celebrated in her childhood home, the spring and fall equinoxes had been her favorites. Her dad had called the fall equinox Mabon, a celebration that honored a moment of harvest, when the Welsh god Mabon performed his act of pure love with the cutting of the last grain and died until his return in spring.

"Fall is a season of balance," her dad had been fond of saying, his freckles lit up like fireflies with excitement as he taught Stella how to plait a sheaf of corn into a dolly. "This is the time of year that you reap what you sow, a harvest before we return to the darkness from whence we came to await the rebirth of the new year."

Her mother would scoff; her beloved Port-au-Prince was just as hot and humid this time of year as Florida, and she had never fully bought into seasonal change. But Stella had always liked her father's version best—that fall was the cusp of transition, when the old faded away so that something new could grow in its place.

That was another reason this year's fall season seemed even more special, and even sadder to miss celebrating in full: right now Stella was just a girl in love. Come spring, she would be a bride, and together she and Peter would begin their new life as husband and wife here in Pensacola, where spring and summer and fall and winter all melded into one season of sand and sea.

Thinking of it that way, Stella couldn't help but fancy herself as the god Mabon himself: prepared to perform an act of pure love and await the spring. She was giving up changing leaves and cooler weather for the greater good—for her future and for her fiancé— and come spring, it would all be worth it. Who cared about the weather when you carried the spirit of the season in your heart?

This year, she resolved, even if she couldn't see it in the balmy, perpetually summer weather outside or celebrate it in the usual ways, Stella could still feel fall in her bones. That, she figured, like the transformation that came along when the sun headed south over the celestial equator, was what was making her restless—unbalanced. All five foot nine of her wasn't just a woman at all, but a leaf, ready to transform her colors from bright summer green to crimson or gold or even deep, earthy burgundy. She was in the final stages of harvest and ready to be reborn—in a new place, with a new family and a new name.

Having found a way to knit together her worries and anxieties and turn the half-empty glass back to half-full status, Stella hummed along on her ride home, thinking cooler thoughts after all. She wasn't just a girl away from home and lamenting seasons lost, but a woman on the verge of becoming something new. She was preparing for the harvest of all she'd worked for in reaching both for her dreams and her future.

Now, she could feel it. The feeling of fall was a crisp breath on her wheatish skin and the sound of rustling, dry leaves in her ears. It was the warm scent of pumpkins and cinnamon blooming from the air freshener she'd picked up tonight at the Kmart on Highway 90 and hung from the rearview mirror of her Ford Probe that was the same powder blue as the sky at dawn. Stella flicked the little cardboard tree and twisted the volume knob on her radio up another notch, her voice rising to match as she sped toward home through the late-night darkness of near-midnight.

Elsewhere, deep in a forest edged by mountains, a single, crimson leaf fell from a branch above. It floated downward, wafting to and fro, and alighted on the surface of still water in a stone well, where a woman picked it up with interest and held it up in front of her face. She watched as the tender edges of the leaf began to frost and curl with cold, and then she shivered and cast the leaf away from her well.

Noelani, the Lady of the Water, slipped her toes back into the water and thought about love as a pair of young women, their arms laden with wildflowers, made their way under the moonlight to ask her blessing.

~

Stella's coupe had been an early wedding present from her soon-to-be husband, Peter Heilen.

It was her dream car—brand new, sleek and sporty, and Peter hadn't approved of the car any more than he'd approved of Stella adding the underbody lights or installing the subwoofer in the hatchback. He'd said it was overkill; that such behavior put her in the spotlight—the kind that would make men with bad intentions take notice of her when she was alone in the dark. But this didn't bother Stella one bit. With him beside her, she argued, what harm could possibly come to her? Besides, she loved to be in the light, particularly if she was the star shining in its center.

Peter knew that, too, and while he didn't particularly approve of it either, it was what Stella thought he loved her for most, even if he pretended otherwise.

"Do you really have to blare Mariah Carey at full volume every time you get in your car?" was a question he had asked on more than one occasion. Sometimes it was slightly modified to "every time you go to the beach" or "every time we run to Blockbuster," but no matter how he dressed up the question, Stella's answer was always the same.

"Absolutely, yes, I do," she'd say. "Mariah is a musical goddess, just like I'm going to be one day. And that's why you love me so much, remember?" She'd follow this with her best impression of the songstress's trademark high-pitched squeal and then warble off snippets of "Dreamlover," her favorite track off Maria's new album,

Music Box. The album held a special place in Stella's heart, since Peter had hidden her engagement ring in a beautiful blue, heart-shaped music box the night he'd proposed. She'd then punctuate the lyrics with kisses until he caved, which he always did. Stella thought Peter terribly cute when he pouted. She knew how to get her groom-to-be to turn his smile upside down, and so no matter how grumpy he got about her singing or her loud music, Stella knew that all it took were a few kisses and a little light teasing to bring Peter around.

He played at being all dark and broody, but she knew he had a soft spot in him too. She also knew that it was reserved especially for her.

"Stop," he'd protest, his not-so-earnest deflections weakening each time her lips brushed against his skin until his arms were wrapped around her and he was kissing her back, nibbling on her bottom lip as his fingers dug into the flesh below her shoulder blades. "You're such a handful," he'd tease her, calling her his little sea siren and tugging at her perpetually windblown hair that snarled her natural curls into tight balls of tangles. Stella would laugh and respond back, trying not to sound breathless with all his warm heat washing over her so she could get out the words "but you love me," at which he would groan playfully and admit, "I do, I do."

"You have the voice of an angel," he'd tell her, "even better than Mariah. It lights up the shadowy places of my soul."

Those words made Stella blush every time she heard them. She knew she wasn't anywhere near as talented as her favorite singer, but like Mariah, Stella thought that she was indeed one of those women who was born to sing. Her parents had instilled a love of song in her growing up, and Stella had parlayed that into early careers in school choirs and talent shows. She'd been captivated by the vocal talents of the women whose voices spun like magic out of her mother's big sound system that took up an entire corner of their living room—women like Whitney Houston, Chaka Khan, Paula Abdul, and Janet Jackson, strong and powerful black women with voices more beautiful than any instrument. When Mariah Carey—who had also grown up in a mixed-race home in New York—

arrived on the scene in 1990, she had instantly become both Stella's muse and her inspiration.

Like Mariah, Stella had that same kind of undeniable exotic beauty that everyone always agreed was beautiful without ever worrying over why. Perhaps it was because of the rolling gingerbread curls that fell midway down her back, or her large almond-shaped eyes that were precisely the same shade of burnt amber as fossilized tree sap. Or perhaps it was her tawny complexion, the perfect blend of her mother's ebony skin and full, shapely lips, and her father's pale, freckled flesh and angular features. Whatever it was, Stella had always felt too pale for her mother's people and too dark for her father's, a part of two worlds and yet belonging to neither, and despite her inborn talent, she'd always held back from putting herself out there as a real singer. She loved the spotlight, but sometimes found it too exposing. But watching Mariah sweep the Billboards, Stella finally felt not only beautiful for the first time, but like she could really be something other than a girl from Rochester who sang in her shower.

The first time Stella heard "Can't Let Go" from the *Emotions* album, she decided she couldn't let go of her dream to sing. She styled herself after her favorite musical idol, right down to the cropped denim shorts and knotted flannel shirt, and got her first real gig singing weeknights at a hole in the wall called the Skylark, which was a little less Cheers and a lot more Bar Fly than she would have preferred—but it was a start.

Sometimes all it took for something magical to happen was a little spark to start the fire.

It had been her voice that had led Stella and Peter to meet in the first place, too. One night after her set, right as the bar was closing down, a tall man with dishwater blond hair and piercing green eyes had come up and introduced himself. Stella's mother had warned her never to date a man she met in the bar where she worked, but he'd been charming, so she'd agreed to share a drink with him the following night. Three weeks later, Stella and Peter were engaged. They left New York the following summer. Her parents hadn't been too happy about it, but then Stella supposed most parents probably weren't happy when their children grew up, fell in love with a stranger, and moved a thousand miles away from home.

"You barely know him, Stella," her mother had admonished, making the sign of the cross over her chest, the way she always did when she worried about evil spirits or people with bad intentions. "No good can come from running away with a man you barely know."

"You barely knew me, Rachelle," Stella's father, Kieran, had countered. He ignored the clicking rattlesnake sound his wife made with her tongue when she was getting angry. What he'd said next had been enough to avoid Stella's mother's wrath and maybe even make her agree, though she would never have admitted it. "Follow your heart and your dreams," he advised. "Sometimes they lead to the same place. It might not be what you expect, but it'll get you there."

So far, they had, even though the path had been a little bumpier than she might have preferred. Stella and Peter were polar opposites in nearly every way, from food choices to fashion sense, but the couple was as madly in love almost a year after their engagement as they'd been on that first night in the lounge, and falling further every day. Peter wasn't really being critical when he complained about her music, and Stella knew that too. And his gloomy mood had nothing to do with the volume of her radio or the undercarriage lights on her car, or even how much hot water she wasted rehearsing her sets in the shower.

He'd been a little temperamental since they'd moved down near the beach. Peter preferred the tranquility of mountains and forests to the hot sun and the noisy rush of the waves breaking upon the shore, while Stella, naturally, felt the exact opposite. Mountains made her feel boxed in; they were so big and tall and overwhelming that she worried she might suffocate in their presence. In Stella's mind, the sounds of the ocean were just another form of music—the cry of gulls, the rush of waves, the sough of wind over the water—but Peter said being so near to the ocean made him feel on edge, like all those lovely noises were mocking him and he was going to be sucked out to sea and fall off the edge of the earth or something. He complained when the beach sand followed them into the house and bemoaned the constant application of sunscreen, but in spite of how much he claimed he disliked the beach, when Stella had been offered the singing gig at the jazz lounge in the heart of Pensacola Beach Boardwalk, she'd been prepared to turn it down until Peter had said his landscape preferences weren't worth her giving up her dreams.

So they'd gone.

And so it didn't matter that Peter was a habitual grump. Stella was calm and even-tempered with her lovable curmudgeon, and since her love had given up his mountains to take her to the sea, it was easy for her to be patient with Peter—and extra careful to keep the sand out of his side of the bed.

That was, after all, what Mabon had been all about, right? Sacrifice and pure love. And so no matter how dark it got—whether it was the waning, autumn-less end of year or Peter's moods—there was always light just ahead.

And Stella would be Peter's beacon, both on stage and off. She would rescue him from his darkness and bring him back into the light with her. Maybe then he'd learn to see the same beauty in the water that she did.

CHAPTER 2

Sitting on the back porch and thinking about how much he wished the whole damn ocean would freeze over, Peter heard Stella's car long before its wheels crunched up the sandy shell driveway of their rented beach house on Sandpiper Lane. Peter always sensed Stella coming when she made her way toward him, with a sort of tinnitus-like sound that was even shriller than his inner musings on how unsettled being so near to the open ocean made him feel—which was saying something, because he hated being so close to the water.

It made him feel exposed and gave him the uncomfortable sensation that something was watching him—waiting for him—and yet still he sat on the porch and glared at the waves, almost as if he were daring whatever watched him to come for him.

Peter, the water seemed to call as the waves broke upon the shore. *Peter, come to us.*

With a sigh, Peter set down the empty bottle of beer he'd been holding next to another empty bottle on the small outdoor table, and moved back inside the ugly little beach house. The landlord—a middle aged man with a feather earring and a seemingly endless supply of Hammer pants—had painted the small two-story building the rosy, optimistic color of a living conch shell, but with its spindly staircase and squat, layered frame, the house reminded Peter more of a petulant crab that had washed up on shore than a shell.

The house was ramshackle and could use a good bit of maintenance, but even with its current state of disrepair it was some sort of paradise to his fiancée, who refused to move to a more sensible apartment closer to the heart of town. No matter how much Peter tried to convince her that this place was less a paradise and much more likely to be in danger of being swept out to sea during a hurricane—a real and frequent threat in the Gulf, particularly during this part of this year—Stella wouldn't hear it. But then, he and Stella rarely ever agreed on much when it came to beach life, so that was to be expected.

"This place is a disaster waiting to happen," Peter had professed when she'd first shown him the unit for rent.

She'd laughed and responded with, "Don't be silly, Pete. It just has character."

He'd thought character looked a lot like disaster, but he'd signed the lease anyway. Anything to keep Stella happy.

That had been the normal course of life since he'd met her—Peter and Stella rarely agreed on much of anything, but this only had the odd quirk of making him love her even more. He was drawn to Stella like a moth to a flame, or the negative end of a magnet to her positive, or whatever other cliché saying made sense to describe the incredible power of attraction he felt to Stella despite the total polarities at which they existed. Stella was the only woman on earth who could drive Peter so often to the brink of madness while at the same time having the singular ability to allow him to feel such deep feelings of love and devotion that he had never felt about any other person before.

He loved her—for better or worse, he loved her with his entire heart.

Peter watched through the living room curtains as Stella's sporty blue coupe pulled into the drive and came to a stop. He waited for her to exit the car, his thoughts moving away from the water and the ugly little beach house and to his beautiful bride-to-be.

Even though she insisted on blaring her music at unreasonable volumes day or night, the sound of her booming stereo wasn't how Peter knew Stella was almost home, and the sound of her arrival didn't stop once her engine had cut off and the stereo gone silent. That was something . . . else. It was difficult to articulate it, and he'd never even attempted to describe it to another living soul—both because he couldn't and because to try would probably make him sound insane—but he could sense the woman's presence. It called him to her, and it had been what pulled him off the road in Rochester and drew him to that grimy little dive bar, the Skylark, effectively ending his plans to head up to Canada. He'd been on his way to Acadia, intent on losing himself in the forests and mountains that insulated him from the coast and abandoning himself to solitude for a while.

Peter had always considered himself a pretty average, decent guy, but something had changed in him around the time he hit twenty, and he didn't like the man he felt like he was becoming. He felt unsettled, antsy, and a depressive cloud had descended on him —and then there had been the accident.

Laura, Peter's ex-girlfriend, had drowned early the summer before, when the two of them had been on a camping trip down in Shenandoah National Park. Peter had never been able to fully understand what had happened that day. One minute, Laura was in the canoe with him, her bright auburn hair whipping around her head in the wind while she laughed and splashed him with water from her oar. The next, she was gone and he was soaking wet, clinging to the hull of the upturned canoe. As for what had happened between, Peter wasn't sure what was real or what had been filled into his memory in the series of nightmares he'd endured afterward. The rangers had found Laura's body floating on the other side of the lake. After a fruitless investigation, it had been assumed that something had capsized the small boat—maybe they'd been moving around too much, having too much of a good time splashing each other, and flipped. Peter must have been knocked out, maybe hit his head on the fiberglass siding and come to in time to fling himself back across the bobbing boat, but Laura must have remained underwater. She'd drowned and Peter had lived, but he couldn't help thinking that, somehow, he was to blame for what happened out on the lake.

No, he'd known he was. He just didn't want to admit it.

Peter, Laura's voice still sometimes called in the whisper of waves breaking on the sand—just another reason Peter hated the beach. In his dreams, he saw her face staring at him from beneath the water.

So Peter had fled, trying to get as far away from himself and that memory as possible, but his mood only seemed to worsen the farther he traveled up the eastern seaboard. Glimpses of coast constantly winked in and out of view along that drive, making it impossible for him to wrestle his thoughts away from the day at the lake. By the time he'd reached Rochester, Peter was already dreading crossing the bridge over Niagara into Buffalo, but then out of nowhere a weird feeling had come over him, calling like a siren to a sailor over water. It had possessed him to get off the highway and take up two parking spots at the Skylark.

The first thing his eyes had landed on when he stumbled into that dimly lit little dump was the source of the song itself, crooning her heart out up on a makeshift stage: Stella Malley.

From the first moment he saw Stella, Peter was smitten. Everything about her smoldered, from her amber eyes down to the long, long length of a pair of legs that looked every bit as strong and graceful as the tall pines he had loved to climb as a boy. He took one look at Stella and fell irretrievably into her gravitational pull, orbiting her from that moment forth as surely as a moon circles a heavenly body. He'd sat at a small, wobbling table in the back of the room and listened to her sing, knowing she was destined to be a star and just as surely knowing he'd follow her anywhere, which was at once both liberating and troubling.

He was a goner; she had him hook, line, and sinker—whether he liked it or not. He'd waited out her set and then approached the stage. She'd seemed shy but warm when she shook his hand, but he could tell she resisted, so Peter pleaded and did his best to charm her until she finally agreed to meet him for drinks the following night. He counted every single minute for the next twenty or so hours until their meeting time, and still couldn't believe it when she actually showed up, wearing a bright pink cocktail dress with little rhinestone buttons on the straps that made her eyes shimmer.

He'd bought the best diamond ring he could afford the very next day and kept it in a little glass music box in the glove compartment of his car. Whatever plans he had of taking the murky madness banging around inside his head to the Canadian forest were over. He might not know exactly who he was yet, but he knew he never wanted to be free of Stella Malley. As maddening as it was, marrying her was now the only thing he wanted to do.

Peter hadn't been happy about moving to Florida, much less setting up residence so close to the water that he could literally step into the surf if he wasn't careful, but having Stella come home to him every night made it worth it. Besides, as a freelance travel writer he could work from anywhere, and pieces about the beach sold as well as any, maybe even better. Everyone—everyone other than him, anyway—seemed to love being on the water.

That's what Peter thought of now as he watched Stella fuss with her hair in the driver's side mirror, trying to smooth down unruly curls that had been tangled into a frenzy from driving with the windows down. He laughed under his breath, admiring the view as Stella extracted herself from her car, barefoot and carrying her heels. She left every night dressed to the nines to sing at the club. Tonight, she wore a sleek red number with skinny satin straps that accentuated every single one of her beautiful curves and made Peter's skin flush with both desire and jealousy of what other men in the club might have thought while they watched his bride perform this evening.

The thought made Peter cringe, and the taste of envy soured his tongue. She was his.

Peter, the ghost of girlfriends past called. He ignored it.

Stella's curls were disheveled, and one of her dress straps had come loose over her shoulder, but to Peter she was the most gorgeous creature he had ever seen. He couldn't wait to take her in his arms.

Stella spotted him watching out the front window and smiled, waving so that the shoes in her hand banged against each other like the world's most awkward wind chimes. Peter smiled back and met her at the front door.

"You heard me coming again, huh?" She smiled, biting her lower lip in that way she did when she thought he might fuss. He didn't think she realized she even did it, which made him love it even more. Then again, he also didn't think he fussed.

"All the way up the road," he taunted, "maybe even the moment you got in the car after work. What was that tonight? Toni Braxton?"

"Janet," Stella corrected, naming both the artist—the "princess of America's black royal family," as quoted in *Rolling Stone*—and the album's title in one word. Janet, like Mariah or Madonna, didn't need a last name, according to Stella. Their first must have been powerful enough, he figured.

Nevertheless, Peter provided it, adding his own twist. "Ah, Ms. Jackson, then." He looped one arm around Stella and pulled her in for a quick kiss. "How about Mrs. Heilen?"

Stella snickered and wriggled free of his grasp, then tossed her shoes into the already huge pile at the door and began making her way to examine the stack of unopened mail on the counter. Peter tried not to wince. She was beautiful, his songbird, but not neat. If it were up to Stella, the whole house might become one giant unkempt closet and every dish in the kitchen would get used before a single one found its way back into the cabinet.

"If you're nasty," she shot back over her shoulder, completing the song lyric as she bit her lip again, and Peter instantly stopped caring about Stella's lack of domestic prowess. The urge to wrap her in his arms increased. He wanted to wrap himself around her, hold her as tight as he could.

"How about if I just ask really, really nicely?" Peter negotiated as he sidled up behind her. He rested his chin atop her head, breathing in her sweet, smoky scent and waiting for a response while she rifled through stacks of bills and junk mail. Stella was sorting the mail into two piles, those that Peter liked to think of as "junk mail Stella will scatter around the house for months and inevitably throw away" and "bills she'll plan to pay but will then promptly forget until the past due notice comes." Of course, he wouldn't tell her that. He'd just go through it again later and tidy up behind her.

Clutching—rumpling—a stack of mail in her hands, Stella spun on him, wedging herself between the counter and Peter in a way that pressed her body against his and made him stifle a moan. There was a mischievous glint in Stella's eyes that meant she was in a teasing mood, and her lips were curled in a devilish smirk that said very plainly that he would be the thing she'd be teasing. She must have had a great night at work. The sharp prick of jealousy flared again in the back of Peter's mind as he thought about how sexy Stella looked on stage. Instantly, he decided he'd go to work with her the following night and watch her sing. He hadn't done so in weeks.

"Really nicely," Stella repeated, stretching out the word in a singsong tune that sounded a whole lot less nice and a lot more naughty. She lifted her lips to his and that little ringing Stella soundtrack that always played when she was near reverberated through Peter's head.

It was loud, suddenly, too loud, and punctuated by a weird sound of rushing water, like a faucet turned on too high. Peter kissed her quickly so she wouldn't think something was wrong, then backed away to a safe distance. He must have had more to drink than he'd realized—two beers, maybe three, or had it been more? His insides were twisted. It felt like half of him wanted to kiss Stella and the other half wanted to . . . he didn't want to say, even in his own mind. The memory of Laura's auburn hair whipping in the wind flashed through Peter's thoughts, and he shook it out of his mind. The faucet ruckus decreased until it was just the sound of Stella still shuffling through mail.

It had to be the water, Peter thought. He shouldn't have sat outside and toyed with it. His nerves were fraying. Maybe they could take a trip up to Georgia or maybe over to Alabama, get lost in the woods for a little bit and away from the damned beach. There were deciduous trees there, and the temperatures would be cooler, too. Stella would get her fix of fall. It'd be a win-win.

"How was work?" he asked, desperate to move on to happier—drier—subjects.

"Oh, you know," she muttered dismissively, oblivious to Peter's inner turmoil as she flipped the pages of a clothing catalog. "Same old. I sing, they clap, and then everybody gets bored and the drinks dry up. It gets late, and they all go home. I need a change of scenery, just for a night or two. Maybe I can audition to sing at that place over the bridge, in Mobile."

Peter cleared his throat, ready to grasp the opportunity that had magically offered itself up before him. "You sound upset," he goaded, hoping she'd say she was. "Do you not like it here?"

Stella was more open to change—and more impulsive—when she was unhappy. Maybe he could finagle his way into more than a trip; maybe he could talk her into moving away from this stupid beachy hellhole.

A change of scenery could be good for both of them. He still wasn't sure why he'd agreed to Florida in the first place.

Stella looked at him for the first time since she'd started examining the mail, and her eyes were thoughtful, free of teasing. "Not upset, but maybe a little . . . I don't know . . . tired," she admitted. "I think it's the season, or rather, the lack thereof. It feels like home here every other day but today, no matter how I try to reason it out in my head. I love Pensacola, but I do miss the cooler weather and the colorful leaves. It's just not fall without that, you know?"

Oh, do I ever, Peter thought. This was not the first time Stella had complained about missing fall. He could agree on that point. The only color Peter ever saw here was his least favorite: blue.

"Maybe we should start thinking about our honeymoon," Stella suggested, her voice light around the edges. "We could look into going up to the mountains or something. Maybe the Poconos? I've heard about a resort there that's just for honeymooners."

"Our wedding isn't until spring," Peter reminded her, trying to keep on the subject of right now rather than derailing into wedding planning. He was a guy, after all, and could only tolerate so much talk about gowns and flowers and cakes. "That's a long way away, and definitely after fall. I don't want you to be unhappy all winter."

Stella countered. "I know, but this place I'm thinking of isn't just a fall resort. There's tons to do in the spring and summer, too—hiking, horseback riding, canoeing." Peter cringed, glad he'd never told Stella about the accident on the lake. "Oh! There's even spas in every bridal suite, and they're, like, shaped like martini glasses, so you have to climb a little ladder to get in. How diva is that?"

Peter knew exactly what resort Stella was talking about—Cove Haven—he'd found a brochure stuffed inside one of her bridal magazines in the bathroom. It sounded kitschy and overpriced, but there was one thing attractive about it: it was in the mountains. Peter was just about to agree, thinking that the Pocono Mountains in Pennsylvania weren't far from New York, and if he could just stick it out through winter, then maybe once they were married and already so far away from the beach, he could wheedle his way into convincing Stella that the city would be a cornucopia of opportunity for a budding songstress, when her voice—eager this time—interrupted his thoughts.

"Oh my gosh, Pete, did you see this?" She waved an oversized glossy postcard from the bottom of the mail pile in his direction. Her eyes scanned it again, and then she did that little bouncing thing that all girls seemed to do when they were excited about something. "It's an invitation to some place called the Haven Saloon in Colorado. They've invited me to come and sing as a special guest!"

Well, this was just too good to be true, Peter thought—like the invite had arrived by magic.

"Where in Colorado?" he asked. Colorado was nice and landlocked. Perfect.

"Someplace called Havenwood Falls." Stella shrugged and passed the postcard to him. "I've never heard of it. Do you think it's real, or one of those scammy junk mail things? Like I'll get there and have to pay to sing or something?"

"I think it's fate," Peter said, examining the postcard. On the front was a view of sweeping, snow-topped mountains surrounded by dense forest of bushy evergreens and vibrant, fall-flowering trees. Nestled in the heart of a box canyon was what looked like a quiet little town, the kind beloved by tourists and rich people who had spare homes to go with the seasons. On the back, just like Stella had said, was a short message written in smooth cursive:

Dear Stella Malley,

If you're up for a trip to Colorado, we'd love to have you at the Haven Saloon. We think you'll find our peaceful little town a magical place to share your voice. We have room here just for you.

Too good to be true or not, that was all it took for the perfect plan to arrive in Peter's mind. He wanted mountains and serenity, Stella wanted to sing, and both of them were tired of waiting for their wedding day. Peter took one look out the window, at the waves slapping around under the moonlight, and tossed the postcard on the counter. He swept Stella up in his arms, swinging her from side to side in time with the tingling in his ears, and for the first time since they'd moved to the beach, loving the musical sound of his little songbird's call.

"Pack your bags and tell your boss you're taking the next couple of days off," he told her between kisses. "I'm ready to marry you, my little sea siren, and we're eloping to Havenwood Falls."

CHAPTER 3

$\mathcal{E}$loping wasn't something Stella ever thought she would do. Ever since she was a little girl, she'd dreamed of having the big, traditional wedding—the white dress, the tiara, the crystal champagne flutes—all the trimmings that would make her feel like a princess on her big day. She'd had visions of walking down the aisle with her father and serenading the man waiting for her at the altar—the man who would be her husband at the very moment she said "I do." An iconic love ballad would play during her vows. Whitney Houston's rendition of "I Will Always Love You" had been at the top of that list, or better yet, Etta James's "At Last."

She'd built dream boards and collages of weddings, scrapped together with magazine pictures as she assembled the Perfect Wedding Day. When she and Peter had gotten engaged, Stella immediately started thinking about things like where to set up her wedding registry and making bridal fitting appointments for her and her eleven closest girlfriends, all of whom she planned to dress in pale shades of lavender. But the move to Pensacola had thrown a kink in wedding planning, and she'd had to rethink everything from the flowers to the venue.

The truth was, she hadn't made much progress on the actual plan itself so much as she had on daydreaming about making the plan. When Peter suggested they take advantage of the mysterious invitation and elope to the unknown town of Havenwood Falls somewhere in Colorado, though it was apparently too small to be mentioned on any map, it was hard to say no—and not just because it was her first real invite to sing or because there would be actual fall in Colorado.

Stella knew that a big fancy wedding, regardless of where it happened or how many attendants they had in the bridal party—a number that, despite her protests, Peter had already whittled down to no more than two apiece, and even that had been a hard fought victory—was not what her beloved truly wanted. And, she decided, it was something she could live without if it meant Peter's happiness. Mabon, she reminded herself. Sacrifice.

And so Stella packed a suitcase, making sure to include both her best performance dress and the glass music box that had once contained her engagement ring but now held both of their wedding bands, and boarded a flight to Denver International Airport with the hopes of making a stellar debut at the Haven Saloon before getting married under the brilliant canvas of autumn treetops she'd been longing for. She didn't need the big, fancy wedding with the dress and tiara and crystal. All she really needed was a place to sing her vows to the man of her dreams, and if she could do it somewhere beautiful with real falling leaves, then right now there was nothing else she wanted more.

Maybe an autumn equinox wedding was just what all her craving for fall had been leading her toward anyway. It was change. A new season. An opportunity for her and Peter to put away their old lives and spend winter cocooning for the spring of the future.

Either that or she was just being selfish, and this would all be for nothing. Stella had the odd feeling that the invite to the Haven Saloon had been a solo one—"We have room here just for you"—and not a couples invite, but there was no way she was leaving Peter behind, so she hadn't even given voice to that thought.

Now, sitting beside her, even with his brow furrowed in confusion as he scoured the state map of Colorado, hunting for the telltale dot that would identify Havenwood Falls somewhere between Grand Junction and Durango, Stella could see relaxation had already softened the rough edges of Peter's expression. His sharp green eyes had mellowed to the color of jade, and she could see the dimples in his cheeks now that he'd stopped clenching his jaw. It had been a while since he'd looked so at peace.

Maybe moving out to the beach had been a bad idea after all. Stella loved it, but Peter's hatred for living on the water seemed to be more than a landscape preference. They would both have to learn to compromise and communicate better—that was the bedrock of relationships that lasted, wasn't it?

"You're sure this is the area it's in?" Peter asked for what must have been the hundredth time that morning. He was holding the map closer to his eyes now, like he might be able to make out a teensy, tiny dot if the paper were close enough to his face.

"I'm sure. The guy I talked to at the Haven Saloon said the closest town we'd probably see on the map is Grand Junction, which is about a two-hour drive north. Montrose is closer, but it's smaller," she said, visualizing the space in her mind. "Durango is south." Stella repeated this easily, quoting the directions the saloon's owner, a laid-back dude who'd introduced himself as Brent, had given her over the phone. Stella didn't mention that Brent didn't seem to have any recollection of sending her the postcard or inviting her to sing at his saloon, but he'd covered this up with a laugh that sounded like he'd been spending some time with Mary Jane, and said that things worked a little differently sometimes in Havenwood Falls.

If she'd gotten an invite to sing, well, then she was welcome to come on down and sing.

"I just don't know why it's not on the map. It's like it doesn't exist," Peter mumbled, mostly to himself. "Weird."

The captain announced their final descent, and Peter folded the map he'd picked up in the airport convenience store, then tucked it into the seat pocket in front of him. Stella braced herself for another round of questions about the location of a town not found on any map, but instead Peter leaned his head back on the headrest and sighed contentedly. Even though eloping was his idea, Peter had been unsatisfied with the amount of information he'd been able to find on the town. It hadn't been much. Mostly what Stella had discovered when she'd phoned the few places referred by other places to set up their trip in a sort of telephone tag—a place called Whisper Falls Inn, where she had booked a room for their stay, and the local courthouse, where they'd be able to pick up a marriage license. Peter, who liked to plan everything down to the nitty gritty details, had mercifully stepped aside to let Stella plan the trip, and though she was completely out of her element, Stella thought the spontaneous trip to the mysterious town was the height of good fun.

Peter's hand found Stella's and gave it a quick squeeze. He lifted her knuckles to his lips.

"At least if there's a shuttle, we don't have to know where it is, right, babe? We just look for the bus stop, wait for it to show up, and climb aboard. Did you ever find out how often the shuttle runs?"

Stella sucked her teeth, anticipating a rebuttal. "No, I didn't. I forgot. Sorry."

"Well, if it's the preferred way into town, it must be pretty often, right?"

"Right," she agreed, stifling a yawn. Brent hadn't said what time the shuttle ran, but he had said the ride into Havenwood Falls from the Denver airport was a good five- or six-hour drive, depending on road conditions. The complimentary shuttle would take them the entire way, no problem, but she'd totally spaced on asking what time it actually showed up. Hopefully it wouldn't be a long wait. Peter had booked the first flight of the morning out of Pensacola, and between the early flight and the time difference, Stella was looking forward to taking a nap on the long drive up into the mountains. If all went well, they'd arrive in town sometime in the early afternoon, which was just enough time to check into the inn, get a quick bite to eat somewhere local, and show up nice and refreshed at the Haven Saloon for her inaugural performance.

Peter nuzzled against Stella's ear as the plane's wheels touched down in Denver. "I can't wait to get my arms around you in this secret little town," he teased, his voice purring darkly against her skin. "This trip is going to change everything, babe. Just wait and see. This gig in Havenwood Falls is just the beginning. It's all up from here. Once you sing one night, no one will ever forget your name. You'll be a legend."

~

A few hundred miles away in Havenwood Falls, Noelani shivered.

Ever since the first leaf fell the day before, she had noticed the fall that bloomed in the trees surrounding her meadow in the forest seemed chillier than usual. The wildflowers kept their petals closed even at noon, and the water of her well—which no matter what season or time of day always stayed as warm as if the sun still shone brightly upon it—had begun to grow icy. Goose bumps prickled along her skin, and frost had begun to form in the lengths of her hair and spiderweb along the stones of her well when she sat atop its brim. But it wasn't just the outside that had begun to change; her heart, too, seemed to be freezing inside her chest.

She felt weak and vaguely ill, as if the magic inside her had begun to fade away.

"Are you all right, my lady?" a young girl's voice spoke over her ear as Noelani sat, swirling her finger idly in the water and wondering what had caused her well to run cold. It was a difficult task, for naiads had very little sense of time and rarely concerned themselves with things that did not directly affect them, which was nearly all things.

Noelani closed her eyes and shook her head without turning. She hadn't sensed the girl approach, and even on her best days didn't allow just anyone to catch more than a glimpse of her before she disappeared beneath the waters of her well. It was unwise, particularly when she did not know well the heart whose eyes looked upon her. Her water she would give freely; she never turned away a wish for love made in good faith and gave her blessings to humans and supernatural creatures alike, to the town's residents and visitors, men and women who loved other men and women regardless of the conventions of the times. But for someone to see her would mean that some of her magic would stay with them, tucked safely inside the memory of that sight, to be carried in their hearts for the rest of their days. For that kind of blessing, she had to be sure the desire for love was pure. Otherwise, even her magic would sour and turn dark within them, and she would share the blame in whatever evil it did.

"Yes, sweetheart," answered Noelani, slipping beneath the cool surface of the water. "You may drink of my water, but I am tired. I must rest."

Something dark and cold was coming to Havenwood Falls, and for the first time in centuries, Noelani was afraid.

Under normal circumstances, Stella might have been surprised to find a tall, willowy man with pale skin, long black hair, and even longer black fingernails holding a sign bearing her name at pickup in Denver International Airport, but goth subculture was in, and she never liked to judge someone else's fashion choices. Besides, in spite of the thick eyeliner around his deep-set eyes and the sharp, glinting points of various piercings in his face, he had a kind smile and a serenity about him that put Stella instantly at ease. She'd always thought the whole goth thing made people look angry and unapproachable, but the air around this guy was magnetic with an undeniably positive energy.

She hurried eagerly toward him.

"I'm Stella Malley," she introduced herself with a handshake, after triple-checking that the name written on the sign really was her own, which it indeed was. She was surprised to find she was out of breath, partly out of excitement and partly, she assumed, because of the thinner air this high above sea level. "And this is my fiancé,

Peter." She gestured in Peter's direction and gave a nervous sort of laugh that made her face flush. "I'm sorry, I hope we didn't keep you waiting. I didn't realize someone would be picking us up. I just assumed the shuttle ran on a schedule."

"It's not a problem at all, Stella," the man replied. His voice was serene and faintly dismissive, but the way he said her name was familiar—not overly familiar in a creepy sort of way, but in a way that almost felt like they knew each other from somewhere else, though Stella certainly thought she would have remembered meeting someone as unique-looking as this guy. She'd never met someone who wore more jewelry than she did before—at least, not a man who did. The pendant around his neck was particularly interesting, though—an hourglass that had sprouted angel's wings.

In quick, precise movements, he folded the sign and then tucked it away deep within the folds of his long black trench coat. His eyes made a quick dart to Peter and then returned to her as his lips curved into a small smile that gave Stella the impression it was meant just for her—and didn't include Peter. "We've been looking forward to your visit."

The flush on Stella's face warmed a little bit more, and she was glad that her skin tone was dark enough to hide the occasional blush. It made her feel both embarrassed and excited to be recognized, even if it was for a shuttle reservation she didn't remember making.

"I'm sorry," she said, "but have we met somewhere before?"

Stella ignored the sting of Peter's eyes in her peripheral vision.

"No," the man answered, "but it is a pleasure to meet you now, Stella. We're so glad you accepted the invitation."

"We?" Peter's voice, a little tighter than normal, cut in beside her.

The driver's smile flattened into a soft line as his eyes shifted away from Stella's. "Havenwood Falls, of course. It's nice of you to come along, Peter. Perhaps you will find something you are looking for in our little town, too."

Stella could sense Peter stiffen beside her, and the temperature in the space around him decreased by a few degrees. When Peter slipped into a foul mood, it was like he could suck all the air out of a place. She wrapped herself around his arm, sliding her hand into his to squeeze his fingers. "Kinda neat, huh, Pete? It's like the red-carpet treatment, just for us."

"If you say so." Peter's tone didn't hide his skepticism.

Minutes later, they were on board the shuttle, headed for the mysteriously hidden town of Havenwood Falls.

The driver, who'd said his name was Cicada, like the sweet-singing insect, didn't say much as they drove up into the mountains. His quiet wasn't unpleasant, though. Normally Stella enjoyed chatting up strangers, especially strangers who were as interesting-looking as Cicada, with his dark edges and multiple piercings. She wanted to know what the pendant around his neck meant—time with wings, she mused—but she was sleepy from the early morning flight. Soon the shuttle's smooth vibrations lulled her into an easy sleep as it chugged upward into the heart of the Rockies.

A few hours later, Stella awoke as the shuttle bumped its way past a stone welcome sign with beautiful black metal lettering that announced their arrival in Havenwood Falls. Her ears popped as the shuttle continued to climb for a few more minutes, curving a bend and cresting a ridge, before a gasp escaped her lips, stirring Peter back to consciousness in the process. He grunted sleepily and burrowed his head in her shoulder, but Stella moved to peer out the window.

From her new perspective, she could see all of Havenwood Falls spread out below as Cicada navigated down into the town. Excitement fluttered in Stella's chest as she took in the beautiful colors of fall that painted the town in vibrant hues of crimson and gold. She saw mountaintops and waterfalls, and the thought occurred to her that she might never again want to leave this place.

Perhaps that was what the pendant around Cicada's neck symbolized for her—it was time for her to fly.

CHAPTER 4

*I*t didn't take long for Peter to come to terms with the fact that Havenwood Falls was not going to be the quiet mountain respite that he'd hoped it would be. He'd feared this much the moment the strange shuttle driver had collected him and Stella, unannounced, from the Denver airport, and by the time he set foot in Havenwood Falls, he knew it to be true. He hadn't felt great about that Cicada character, either.

What was that weird symbol he wore around his neck, anyway? It gave Peter the impression that time was running out, which was not a pleasant thought. Between that and the weird makeup and black-on-black attire, the guy had the look of a grim reaper come to call.

Not comforting.

As the pair made their way through the town square, a strange thought struck Peter: if he let this town, it might drown him. It wasn't a happy thought, and not the first time such uninvited dread had invaded his mind. He'd managed to escape it for a while, but he seemed to be having a hell of a time avoiding it now.

The difference was that, this time, he wasn't going to listen.

For all its beautiful fall foliage and stony canyon walls—lovely, insulating geographic features that should have made him impervious to the uneasy sensation he felt around water, since there was so little of that here—Peter felt just as exposed in this hidden mountain ski town as he had on the wide expanse of sand and sea at his and Stella's home on the edge of the ocean. It wasn't the demanding, confrontational sort of sensation that had hounded him and made him lock himself away inside the ramshackle beach house that Stella insisted on renting. This was more of a surreal sort of feeling, one that shouldn't have made sense but was too real to ignore.

Peter indeed felt oddly suffocated, the kind of feeling one might get if they suddenly found themselves buried underground and were trying to claw their way up. Here he was, tucked inside the heart of a box canyon set deep in the Colorado Rockies and surrounded by mountains and dense forest—not a speck of open water in sight—and still Peter couldn't shake the feeling that he was being watched. Not by anyone in particular, but by everyone and no one. It was like dozens of little imps hid, hissing at him from their hiding spaces of rock and leaf and forest, their voices trickling to him in the sounds of the waterfalls that whispered in the distance.

No matter where he went—no matter how deep in the forest or how high in the mountains—the sinister voice of the water always found him. Even—and perhaps most especially—here, in Havenwood Falls. It was almost as if by going farther away from the voice, he'd come to its very source.

It seemed to like it better when Peter hid from it, too. It was too easy to taunt him when the thundering of waves could pound relentlessly against his thoughts like the hammering of drums, banging their way into his head night and day and day and night. Here they could whisper instead, teasing him from the rush of the waterfalls that gave Havenwood Falls its name in hushed, hidden voices that echoed sinisterly in the back of his mind and wound snakelike through the streams of town. It made Peter question whether the voice he heard in his head was theirs or his own.

Peter, the watery voices echoed, rushing back and forth like the sound of stirring liquid as they tumbled over themselves. *Peter, come to us.*

Then, more strongly, *Bring her to us.*

Peter shook his head, but the more the voices called, the harder it was for him not to listen. The sense of being watched closed in around him, pulling him under. He hadn't felt this way in over a year. Not since the accident—since Laura.

Come to us, Peter.

Peter shook his head, this time not to quell the water's voice, but to free himself from the memory of that day on the lake—the dreamy, maybe real memories he had never told another living soul.

Peter, the water called again, and this time it was Laura's voice that reached his ears.

Peter, help me, Laura cried, her voice shrill above the roar of the water. He saw her face again, pale and white beneath the blue. He put his hands over his ears, trying to block out the sound. Her lips moved underwater. *Pete—*

"Pete? Are you okay?"

Stella's bell-like voice broke through the maelstrom, and Peter turned to see her, smiling up at him with an expression of total innocence. His heart fluttered. He loved Stella, loved her more than anything or anyone he ever had. And that was what made her so dangerous to him. If he wasn't careful, the water would take her, too. Just like it had taken Laura. He wouldn't survive Stella's voice in his head, though. It would eat him alive.

"Yes," he self-corrected, forcing his lips into a smile. He squeezed her hand reassuringly and then pulled it away to rub at the stubble on his jaw. "Sorry, babe," he continued. "Just a little jet-lagged, I think. What were you saying?"

Ever patient, Stella smiled again, and Peter's heart thumped a little harder, grounding him solidly back beside her. Suddenly his head was clearer, whisper-free, and the soundtrack of Stella ambient in his head. Maybe what he'd told her hadn't been untrue after all—they'd barely had any sleep and were a couple hours behind their usual time zone. It was mid-afternoon in Colorado, but close to dinnertime at home. Bedtime was creeping up, and they still had a long day ahead of them. Stella's first gig was tonight.

"I was saying this place is just so pretty, isn't it?" Stella repeated, oblivious and talking excitedly. "I never would have guessed I'd love being in the mountains so much, not when I've always fantasized about living at the beach. But it feels so inviting here, like it was the town that invited me here more than the saloon. What about you? Do you like it?"

"It's great," Peter fibbed. "As long as you're happy, I'm happy."

Peter hated to lie to Stella, but as usual, he didn't have it in him to disappoint her. Though the town had escaped mention on every map he'd consulted, since he and no one he'd asked had ever seemed to have heard of it, it did feel disturbingly familiar now that he'd arrived. Stella had taken one look at the town and fallen—as was her habit—instantly in love, seeing only the quaint, picturesque storefronts and scenic landscape. Peter, on the other hand, had seen only a stretch of small businesses that looked like any other mountain tourist trap. It was funny how the same thing could look totally different when observed through another set of eyes.

Stella laughed and slipped her hand into his, tugging Peter onward down the sidewalk. He shifted his duffel bag to the opposite shoulder and took the handle of her suitcase so that she was free to peek, unencumbered, in every shop window they passed. Cicada—which Peter sincerely hoped was an unfortunate nickname that would be less permanent than the ring through his septum—had delivered them to the heart of the town square with a vague gesture in the direction of Whisper Falls Inn. The inn was located at the intersection of Eleventh and Main and, as the woman who'd taken Stella's reservation by phone had told them, would be the best place to drop anchor for their stay in town. It was centrally located and charming, and the luxury suite in the third-floor turret, Cicada added knowledgably—though Peter spied no obvious signs of a wedding ring on the man's finger—was a great place to spend a honeymoon night. The Haven Saloon was on the south block of the town square, at the western end. Cicada promised the walk between the two ends would be well worth their time after they checked in. That's where they'd find all that the town had to offer in its collection of bookstores, trinket shops, and eateries. After giving some recommendations on where to grab dinner if they wanted something more substantial than bar food, Cicada had disappeared back into his shuttle almost as mysteriously as he'd appeared.

Now, her hands cupped around her eyes as she peered into something called Madame Tahini's Potions, Lotions, Palm Readings, and Other Extra-Sensory Services, Stella's excitement was enough to shimmer in the air around her.

"Isn't this town just the most darling place you've ever been?" she gushed as Peter retrieved his fiancée from the window, guiding her gently on the route toward the inn. "I don't think I've ever seen a place that felt more like fall—fall and magic. It's even more beautiful than Rochester. This is the perfect place to start our happily ever after."

"Sure is," Peter agreed halfheartedly. It was easier than being disagreeable. He didn't mean to sound so sour, and he should have been happier—he was with the woman of his dreams, she'd agreed to marry him, and he planned to make her his while they were here in this beautiful little town she was so captivated by. He would have to get over the rest. It was all in his head, anyway. What else could it have been?

After a few more minutes of walking, Whisper Falls Inn appeared. It was, as Cicada said it would be, the quintessential small-town resort—it even had the kitschy gingerbread trim to prove it. A three-story Victorian-style manor, the large home-turned-inn sat diagonally on the lot, its wraparound porch facing the southeast corner of Town Square. It had turrets and bay windows, and the expanse of well-manicured lawn that stretched between the main building of the inn and the cottages behind gave it a well-loved appearance: old but not run down, comfortable but not pretentious.

Peter heard Stella's intake of breath beside him as her eyes landed on the inn.

"Wow," she cooed, mostly to herself.

The door chimed as they stepped in, and a woman behind the counter turned away from a small television set placed behind the counter to greet them. Peter glimpsed what looked like a cheesy Hallmark Hall of Fame flick—Glenn Close and Christopher Walken, wearing dusty colonial garb, argued over how to ensure their family survived a drought and then kissed with all the carefully choreographed passion a PG-rated romance movie could muster. Peter rolled his eyes.

He could seriously go for a drought right about now. Or a drink. Whichever came first.

"Welcome to Whisper Falls Inn. I'm Irina Petran," the woman behind the counter introduced herself. She had dark hair and green-grey eyes, and was cradling a baby in her left arm while she gathered registration paperwork with her free hand. She set the papers on the counter in front of Peter, then leaned forward to show off the child to Stella, who responded with precisely the reaction Peter would have expected. So far, his future wife hadn't brought up children—in fact, Stella had said she didn't know when, or if, she'd be ready for any—but that didn't keep her from gushing every time she saw one. "And this is Michaela," Irina introduced her daughter. "You must be Stella Malley"—her gaze drifted to Peter, pausing as if to drink him in and decide she didn't like the taste, then brightened—"and Peter Heilen."

Peter thought her voice was noticeably harder when she said his name.

"That's right," Stella said, her cheeks reddening. "That's us."

Irina smiled warmly. "It's about time we got a new singer at the saloon, and like I told you on the phone, there's nowhere better to stay in town than at the inn. You look like a singer," she added, her eyes sweeping over Stella. "If you sound half as much like Mariah Carey as you look, you'll be a star."

"I just hope I don't disappoint anyone," Stella said, blushing harder. "My first performance is tonight."

"I have a feeling that you will be spectacular," Irina said matter-of-factly. Peter got the distinct impression the woman was ignoring him. He didn't love it. "How long do you plan to stay in Havenwood Falls, Stella?"

Before Stella—or Peter, who had clearly been dismissed from the conversation—could answer, a group of people barged into the inn behind them, large cardboard boxes brimming with decorations in tow.

"Where do you want the banners, Irina?" one of them asked. Another flipped the lip of one of the boxes and pulled out a large fall garland of brightly colored silk leaves wound with sparkling copper tinsel. The third carried a sign that boasted the name Mara Blackwood in glittery calligraphy and her candidacy into something called Miss Teen Havenwood Falls.

"Anywhere you want to put them—go wild," Irina answered, motioning them back out the door. "Sorry about that," she said as she returned to her guests, accepting the registration paperwork from Peter without touching his fingers. "The whole town is preparing for the annual Founders Day festival this upcoming weekend. It's a big to-do, so everybody starts setting up days in advance so there's plenty of time to get it all done. We don't get a lot of visitors this time of year, though. It's mostly locals, so you two will be in for a treat."

Stella was obviously intrigued, though Peter would have much rather plucked out his own eyelashes than attend a local town festival in a town where he already felt out of place—and weirdly unwelcome. "What kind of festival is it?"

"Oh, a fall festival," Irina explained. "Vendors and games, that sort of thing—if you have time before going to the saloon tonight, you should explore the town square a little, watch everyone setting up. We crown one of the local girls as Miss Teen Havenwood Falls. Not sure who it'll be this year, but my bet is on Mara Blackwood." She peered down lovingly at the babe in her arms. "Not too long now and it might be you, huh, pretty girl?" she cooed to Michaela, who yawned as if festival pageants were the furthest thing from her mind.

"That sounds like a lot of fun, doesn't it, Pete?" Stella said, elbowing Peter in the ribs. Peter grunted. "You see, we're not just here so I can sing at the saloon—we're getting married, too—the sooner the better. So we'll have something to celebrate at the festival. Right, babe?"

Peter avoided Irina's eyes. Their color was, like everything else in town, just a little . . . off. Not totally normal. "Right."

"In that case," whispered Irina conspiratorially, leaning over the counter toward Stella while simultaneously sliding a room key in Peter's direction. He noticed it was for the turret honeymoon suite, even though they hadn't specified. "You might want to visit our wishing well, too."

"Wishing well?"

Irina nodded. "There's an old custom around town for young brides to visit the Lady of the Water that is said to inhabit an old wishing well out in the forest. If you visit her and wish for love, she will bless your marriage. Some people have even claimed that they've seen her, too. They call her Noelani—the mist of heaven."

"Oh, that sounds fun," exclaimed Stella, clapping her hands together. "Pete, we should go!"

Peter's response bordered on rude, though he tried to keep his voice even. "You want to go stomping off into the forest to ask a forest nymph to bless our marriage? Stella, babe, come on."

"Well, I think it would be nice," Stella insisted. "Not every newlywed couple can say they've been blessed by a Lady of the Water, you know. It would be so me, too—you know how much I love the water, Pete."

Peter knew. Somewhere in the back of his mind, he thought he heard that voice again, calling, calling. Dripping like a leaky faucet somewhere behind his eyes.

Irina smiled, but it didn't reach her eyes. She leaned closer in to Stella, so close that Peter couldn't clearly hear what she said next, but whatever it was made the sparkle in Stella's eyes dull just a little. Peter thought it must have been about him—why else would it be kept a secret?

Peter, help me, Peter, the phantom Laura voice cried again.

Irina was upright again, far away as if she hadn't just been whispering in Stella's ear. "Yes, you should visit her," the woman said in farewell as she turned back to her Hallmark movie, shivering as she pulled a blanket from the back of her chair over her shoulders so that it covered most of her and nearly all of the baby, "maybe sooner rather than later, too. There's an unnatural chill on the air. I think it might a cold autumn this year."

CHAPTER 5

*H*avenwood Falls was everything Stella had hoped it would be.

More, actually.

She'd known the town would be special when she first received the invite to sing at the Haven Saloon, and had kept her mind occupied before the trip by imagining what the town might look like. It had been a challenge, considering Stella had spent most of her life in upstate New York and had never even heard of a box canyon until she'd looked it up in the encyclopedia on Peter's bookshelf. But what she'd seen when she arrived had been so beyond her expectations that it felt like a dream, because places this beautiful surely didn't exist in the real world. While New York certainly knew its way around an autumn kaleidoscope, even the colors of the red oaks, maples, and river birches of her home state didn't compare to the phantasmagoric colors of this place. It was as if every season and color had added its essence to the town at once, with its vibrant fall hues set against the backdrop of silver mountaintops and distant waterfalls from which fell water bluer than the sky.

The mysterious little town hidden within the mountains felt like a secret; its off-the-map and out-of-the-way seclusion made

Havenwood Falls seem almost magical—a place of endless possibilities if only you knew where to look. Not to mention everyone she'd met so far had been so incredibly welcoming, as if they thought she belonged there.

Havenwood Falls, Stella was coming to believe, was a place where dreams might come true—where *her* dreams might come true—and she was more anxious than ever to find her happily ever after. A few hours in, she was beginning to get the feeling she might never leave Havenwood Falls.

Peter was—predictably—less than enthused. Stella could tell her sweet-but-grumpy fiancé was hesitant to let himself fall in love with the town like she had, but then he was always more reserved than her. The poor guy never seemed truly at home anywhere; sometimes Stella thought he looked out of place even in his own skin. He'd come around, though, she thought. He always did. Stella was the dreamer—the one with her head lost in the sky. Peter was her tether. Together they could see the stars without losing their footing. That reminded her of what Irina—the lady at the inn—had whispered in Stella's ear when they'd checked in: "Keep your eyes open," she'd said, "and your heart free. Beware of those who would hold you down."

After they'd checked in at Whisper Falls Inn, they unpacked enough to feel settled, showered, and—after a good bit of begging and more than a few pleading kisses—Stella had convinced Peter to take up Irina's suggestion and visit the town square. She wanted to take a peek at the Founders Day Festival preparations before introducing herself at the saloon and getting ready for her set. She hadn't been able to convince him to visit the wishing well. They had plenty of time, though—in fact, they had forever.

And Irina had said that young brides went, not young couples. Maybe she'd go by herself tomorrow.

On the short walk from where the shuttle had dropped them off, Stella had peered in through the windows of most of the shops on Main Street, but there was one in particular that had caught her eye—Callie's Consignments. The moment her feet hit the pavement outside the inn, Stella beelined to the store, Peter in tow behind her. As soon as she stepped inside, Stella forgot all about the beautiful natural scenery that formed the backdrop to Havenwood Falls and found herself instead immersed in what must have been a trip back in time to some other exotic corner of the world.

The store was a gypsy caravan gone retail. Like a mystical tent, the inside was much larger than the storefront had led her to believe, comprising two stories of mostly vintage clothing, furniture, and accessories. It was decorated top to bottom just as eclectically as would be the home of a wanderer who had collected treasures from all over the world over many lifetimes, with the peculiar furnishings and decorations as enticing and mesmerizing as the wares themselves. From the rugs that covered the floors to the interesting assortment of light fixtures and the lush, colorful fabrics covering the walls, no two items seemed to be the same. Everything was unique, as if the store had a mind of its own and it liked collecting things.

Stella was in heaven. If the town was magical, then this would definitely be the place she'd find her own pair of glass slippers or a dinglehopper or some other equally divine and powerful object. She'd brought her best dress, which she planned to use both as her debut dress at the saloon and as her wedding dress, but it seemed suddenly plain compared to all the curiously lovely pieces in Callie's.

Suddenly, she saw it, as if it had heard her thoughts and jumped out to surprise her.

Clinging to a mannequin at the edge of an aisle was the loveliest dress Stella thought she'd ever seen—and being a nightclub singer, she'd seen and worn a lot of sparkly dresses, from cheap prom dresses she'd picked up at thrift shops to cocktail dresses she'd snagged off clearance racks. This one looked like someone had spun the Milky Way into fabric and stitched it into an ombré-print dress with an angled bodice, banded empire waist, and full skirt. It was deep indigo with a layer of glittering pale pink, pinned with sequins that twinkled when they caught the light. This wasn't just a dress for a gig—and it wasn't even white—but it was something Stella could see herself getting married in.

It was prettier than anything she'd ever glued on her dream board, too.

"See something you like?" A rich, sensual voice vibrated in Stella's ear, making her start and then giggle nervously, embarrassed by her own jumpiness.

The woman the voice belonged to was as exotically beautiful as everything else in the store, olive-skinned with waist-length dark brown hair and curious hazel eyes. She was draped in silks and other textured fabrics that billowed around her slender frame as she moved, and she wore so many bracelets and necklaces that she jingled when she walked, as if she moved to her own music. A small tattoo peeked around the edge of her neck. Stella couldn't tell what it was, but she was sure it was just as interesting as everything else about the woman.

"I didn't mean to startle you," she said, edging closer. "I'm Lily Montgomery, owner and fashion consultant. Welcome to Callie's."

"Lily, like a calla lily?" Stella asked. Then, she got it. "Oh, calla Lily's—I get it!"

"Yes." Lily smiled, and the room seemed to warm with her. "My grandmother was the original owner of this story. She was Calla Montgomery, and it would seem the moniker stuck through the generations. But lilies symbolize luck and love, and so I would say there are worse things to be named for."

Nodding, Stella agreed. "My name is Stella."

"For the actress or the play?" Lily winked.

"Neither." Stella laughed. "For Stella Obasanjo, the political activist from Nigeria. My mom's people are from Nigeria, and she named me for Stella, because of her humanitarian work. I don't think I quite live up to it, though, or any of those other Stellas. I'm not a star like the Stellas that were actresses or the playwrights or even politicians. I think I was born to sing—just to sing. That's why I'm here, actually. I'm singing at the Haven Saloon."

Lily ran her tongue consideringly along her top lip. "There are different types of stars; they just all light the sky a little differently. Namesakes give you something—or someone—to be inspired by, but they don't determine the type of inspiration you can be. Besides, songs have their own kind of magic, don't they? They're just as important as the rest. They can lift you up, bring you down, inspire you . . . People need music. Giving it to them must be your gift—your own starlight—right?" She began to unbutton the dress, draping the fabric over her arm as it slid off the mannequin. She held it up, twisting the material so the dress sparkled in the store's ambient lighting, and then held it approvingly against Stella. "Either way, you need a statement piece, and I think this dress may have been destined for you."

Stella beamed as she regarded her reflection in one of the long dressing room mirrors that lined a nearby wall. "You think so?"

"Absolutely," Lily replied. "It's one of a kind. I look at this dress and I can see the stars—almost like a song itself. I think it suits you perfectly."

Stella and Peter left Callie's Consignments with the dress safely wrapped in a sleek clothing box, along with a pair of silver stilettos. Stella hadn't meant to buy the shoes, but when she'd put them on her feet, she'd felt like she was walking on starlight, and so it had been as impossible to leave the store without them as it had to pass up the dress. Peter had said she looked lovely in it, but worry lines still framed his eyes when he'd pulled his credit card out to cover the cost. Stella hoped she made enough tips to put his mind at ease.

The shopping excursion had taken longer than expected, and so it was nearly time for Stella to take the stage when they finally arrived at the Haven Saloon. She wished they'd had longer to explore the town, though, and her stomach was rumbling with hunger. Just as Irina had promised, Main Street was abuzz with vendors setting up their wares for the Founders Day Festival. Callie's had added a fall flourish to their windows, and, despite the

For Sale sign in its window, a coffee shop called Coffee Haven had added festive signage to their doors, similar to the garland banners that Irina had been hanging at Whisper Falls Inn. If the activities that went along with the decorations were any indication, the festival was going to be the best place to be in town very soon.

A woman with short brown hair was arranging a station that offered temporary tattoos and tarot card readings on a table outside of the Haven Saloon. She was pale and pretty, wearing layers of flowing fabrics and a large crystal pendant around her neck. She instantly reminded Stella of Lily. Like Irina, she was nursing a baby in the crook of her arm.

Stella stopped suddenly at the table. Peter grunted as he collided into her back.

"What are you doing, babe?" he asked, curling his fingers gently around her forearm as he attempted to maneuver behind her to open the saloon door. "We don't have time to stop here. You're going to be late."

"Hang on," Stella shushed him, stepping nearer to the table while her eyes moved from the array of tattoo inks to the deck of tarot cards and the baby cooing in the woman's arms. "It seems like everyone in Havenwood Falls has a baby right now," she said by way of greeting to the woman at the table.

The woman's laugh sounded like windchimes. She stroked the child's cheek proudly. "What can I say? Life in Havenwood Falls goes with the seasons. Things bloom here in spring just like in the rest of the world. This is Addie."

"Oh, she's beautiful," Stella cooed. "Isn't she, Pete?"

Peter barely looked, but managed a small smile that looked passably pleasant. "Sure does," he agreed. He tugged gently on Stella's arm. "You're going to be late for your first night, Stel."

The woman with the baby shifted her gaze to Peter, and she didn't smile until she looked back to Stella. "Late? You must be Stella Malley, then? Welcome to Havenwood Falls. We're all very much looking forward to hearing you sing. I'm Lyra Beaumont. It's nice to meet you."

Stella felt her cheeks turn pink the moment Lyra recognized her name. Just like she hadn't expected the town to be so beautiful, neither had she expected such a warm welcome. So far, all the women she'd met had been as kind as family, which made Stella miss her mother even more than usual.

"Thank you so much," she said. "I'm so excited to be here."

Peter tapped his foot impatiently behind her.

"And right in time for the Founders Day Festival, too." Lyra swept her hand in front of her, ignoring Peter's obvious irritation. "How about a free temporary tattoo as a welcome gift?" she asked. "For both of you. Free of charge, of course. And it won't take long," she promised, looking over Stella's shoulder at Peter. "I promise."

"Oh my gosh, that would be amazing!" Stella exclaimed, thrusting out the inside of her wrist without hesitation. She already knew what she wanted. "Could I have a treble clef?"

"You got it," Lyra said. Handling the baby as naturally as if Addie were another appendage, Lyra spun a bottle of bright purple henna ink into the handle of her tattoo gun and began to trace the shape of the musical note freehand on Stella's skin.

It was a little warm, but didn't hurt. When it was done, Stella showed the mark to Peter, who rubbed nervously at his skin.

"Your turn, Pete," she said.

"Oh, I don't think so. Not for me."

"Come on, Pete," Stella begged. "It's only temporary—and it doesn't hurt a bit."

"That's right," Lyra agreed. "It's only temporary," she added.

Peter took another step backward, motioning toward the saloon. "Stella, your set begins in less than an hour. We really don't have time for this. Maybe we can come back tomorrow."

"Peter, please," Stella begged again, drawing out the r sound in his name. She batted her eyelashes and stuck out her bottom lip in her most pleading pout. When she noticed him start to soften around the edges, she gave a little squeal of delight, then reached out and wrapped her arms around him, shoving him forward toward the table. Oh, how she loved her handsome stick in the mud of a fiancé!

Grumbling, Peter stretched out his arm in acquiescence.

"Small," he instructed Lyra, and when she raised her eyebrow meaningfully at him, he added a "please" so as to not be rude.

Lyra changed the ink in her tattoo gun, swapping out the purple for a darker color that looked like a muddy brown.

"Any requests?" she asked, her tone expectant but curious.

"Dealer's choice."

In just a few minutes, Lyra was finished.

Peter lifted his forearm and glanced at his wrist, a quizzical expression turning his features. "A horseshoe?" he asked. "And a moon? Isn't that for good luck?"

"Yes and no," Lyra said, putting away her supplies. She turned back to working on her table as if the matter were settled. "The horseshoe is indeed a symbol for luck, but it has other uses as well."

"Like what?" asked Stella.

"Protection," Lyra answered without elaborating. Addie cooed agreeably.

Peter was still studying the mark on his arm like he didn't like it. "Protection?"

"Yes, protection." Lyra laughed, the windchimes stirring again. "It comes from a practice in ancient England, back before the years numbered into four digits even. There was a blacksmith named Dunstan, who was later canonized. Anyway, legend says that he nailed a horseshoe to a horse, only it wasn't any old horse—it was the devil in disguise. The horseshoe caused the devil great pain, and he made a deal with Dunstan: if Dunstan removed the shoe, the devil would never enter a house that displayed a horseshoe. And so it became a symbol of protection from evil . . . which I guess you could say is one of the greatest tokens of luck."

Stella clutched Peter's arm and gazed at the symbol with newfound appreciation. "And the moon?"

"Ah, the moon," Lyra continued, raising a finger toward the sky. "Well, that's where Artemis comes in."

"Artemis the Greek goddess?" asked Peter.

"Artemis the moon goddess," Lyra corrected. "She was the patron and protector of young girls, and was worshipped as a goddess of childbirth. That was Addie's addition, wasn't it, baby girl?"

Lyra jostled her arm, and the baby giggled as if in agreement.

Stella expected Peter to grump about being given a tattoo that had anything to do with having babies, but to her surprise, he laughed. "Well, the good luck I appreciate, and how could I turn down the protection from evil? But the moon and childbirth? I think your daughter might have misjudged her audience."

"Oh, maybe." Lyra shrugged. "But not all tattoos we get are for ourselves, are they? Even the temporary ones. The question is, Peter —are you the one giving the shoe, or the one who should wear it? And what would the moon see if she should look down?"

CHAPTER 6

*P*eter had been distant and temperamental all afternoon, but luckily Stella had been too distracted with exploring the town's tacky stores and gimmicky festival setup to take notice. He couldn't believe he'd let her talk him into getting a tattoo, though, even if it was a temporary one. Peter hated tattoos, almost as much as he disliked the water, and he wasn't too sure how he felt about being branded with a horseshoe or a moon. But Stella was like that—once she got an idea in her head, it was nearly impossible to get her off of it. It was easier just to give in.

Like always.

Anything for Stella. Stella, his bride to be. Stella, the girl of his dreams. Stella—

Peter.

Peter swiveled at the sound of his own name whispered darkly over his shoulder, but the only thing behind him was a door, and it was closed.

The moment they'd entered the saloon, Stella had glimpsed the sign for the ladies' room with the uncanny knack that most women had for finding that particular safe space in places like pubs and bars, where men had the habit of lurking about like sharks eager to feed. She'd been bubbling with excitement and, muttering something about dreams coming true, had taken off to change into her new dress—the one that cost nearly as much as her engagement ring—before introducing herself, leaving Peter to stand around alone, holding on to her handbag lamely like a fish pulled out of water and plopped in the bottom of a boat.

Why hadn't he just stayed at the inn, Peter wondered to himself. No, he had to be here for Stella's first night—he wanted to be here. This was her big shot, right? The first time she'd been invited to sing somewhere, rather than throwing herself on the mercy of dinky pubs and off-the-beaten-path taverns that paid her in peanuts and leering glances. Though, if he was honest with himself, while Peter wanted to be around for Stella, he'd rather be anywhere other than here—a sentiment which applied both to the Haven Saloon and the entire geography of Havenwood Falls. The scant hour they'd spent in their honeymoon suite at Whisper Falls Inn had been a merciful reprieve from the foreboding sense of doom that had followed him from Florida and descended in earnest once they'd arrived in town. The whispering, watery voices he'd been hearing had attacked again with renewed vigor when he and Stella had set about the town square, and they seemed to grow louder and more insistent every time they edged nearer to the falls or the forests.

It might have been a figment of Peter's imagination, though he'd never had a terribly good one and didn't know why he'd start now, but he'd imagined that the voices had grown loudest just before that Lyra woman had etched a horseshoe on his wrist. He could barely remember anything that had happened in the clothing shop before pulling out his wallet, but his head had gone mercifully clear the moment he'd been tattooed. Branded, like some common animal. Or at least it had been clear, lasting a full five minutes until he'd heard his name on the breath of nothing. And Stella had been wrong: the tattoo was weirdly painful; it seemed to hurt worse now than it did during the application.

Peter.

Peter shook his head and resisted the urge to look behind him again.

The Haven Saloon was just like everywhere else in town that he and Stella had seen thus far: a blend of weird and bizarre that tiptoed the balance between quaint and touristy. The place wasn't nearly as seedy as most of the joints Stella sang in, but it wasn't exactly the Ritz either. They way Stella reacted, though, one would have thought it was the Taj Mahal. The two large windows that flanked the entry had already been plastered over with flyers for local happenings—most of which were concerned with the upcoming Founders Day Festival that Peter was already sick of hearing about.

What little light was left of the afternoon sun filtered in through slanted windows, which looked like they hadn't been cleaned in a while. Peter suspected this might have been intentional to add to the saloon's mystique, rather than just sloppy housekeeping. The bar itself was clean enough to reflect the glow from the few pendulum lamps and wall sconces that illuminated the otherwise dark space. The décor was something between rustic and industrial, devoid of the exotic flair that had given the vintage clothing shop its personality. Compared to Callie's, the Haven Saloon seemed downright glum—dim and smoky and just a little sad.

And it reeked of pot.

The cherry on top, though, was the owner, some dude named Brent that Peter just couldn't—insert sarcasm—wait to meet. Peter was beginning to sense a theme developing around the inhabitants of Havenwood Falls: all the women wore flowy clothes and were preoccupied with babies and oversized jewelry; all the men gave themselves terrible nicknames.

Peter scoffed, feeling momentarily superior for reasons he didn't want to think too deeply about. He eyed the horseshoe on his wrist and wondered why that woman had really chosen that symbol.

Because you are different, Peter. The water's voice breathed almost invitingly this time against Peter's ear, like it offered better company than the pitiful handful of people in the saloon. *Come to us.*

With another shake of his head, Peter moved farther into the bar, away from the dirty windows where someone—something—outside might see him. Then, without deciding to do so, he tugged the sleeve of his shirt down over his wrist, cupping his hand to keep the fabric pinned safely beneath his fingers. He never should have let Stella talk him into that silly tattoo. He didn't like the burning sensation where it was on his skin, either. Maybe he was having an allergic reaction to cheap ink or something.

"Hey there," called the man behind the bar, Peter's sudden movement having caught his attention. "Can I getcha a beer?"

Resigning himself to what he could only assume would be an absolute bore of an evening, Peter perched on a barstool, as far away from the other single occupant of the bar as he could without coming off as rude, and eyed the labels of the bottles behind the man's long mane of dirty blond, shoulder-length hair. There was an insane amount of vodka, particularly the flavored kinds—colorful bottles containing every flavor from apple to zucchini lined the bottom row of the liquor shelves.

Peter grunted in disapproval. He still hadn't figured out why flavored vodka had become a thing, much less why the fad had taken off with such a vengeance. What was so wrong with plain vodka? The rest of the shelves were lined with wine bottles bearing the label of someplace called Stone Falls Winery, which Peter had never heard of but thought was probably local—and probably made by a woman in a flowing dress and her man, Wicked Willy, or something.

Peter cracked his neck, hoping he could break the bad mood along with the pressure in his joints. Between the early flight, lack of sleep, and general moodiness, he was even getting on his own nerves.

"What'll it be, man?" the guy behind the bar planted his palms on the bar top, and a bold wave of cannabis infiltrated Peter's nostrils. He exhaled away the stench, but had no doubts about its origin. The guy certainly had the look of a stoner, outfitted in layers of flannel and featuring glassy, slightly pink-tinted eyes.

"Moosehead if you've got it, Miller Lite if you don't," Peter decided, trying not to sound glib. The bartender pulled a bottle of Heineken from under the bar—of course they wouldn't have anything non-domestic—popped the cap, and set the bottle and a frosted glass in front of Peter. "Thanks."

"New in town?" asked the bartender. Still feeling unavoidably irritable, the question struck Peter as annoyingly invasive rather than friendly bar banter.

"Just visiting," mumbled Peter. He took a swig of Miller Lite, then another, tapping the bar top to signal he'd need a second. At least the beer was cold and tasted normal. Peter felt a little guilty for being so standoffish. No wonder the women Stella had met so far in town seemed perfectly content with acting like Peter didn't exist—like if they ignored him well enough, he'd just fade away completely. He didn't exactly want to become friendly with anyone, but it was sort of nice to be acknowledged. "My fiancée is singing here," he said, inviting further conversation. "She's just getting ready now. Know where we can find the owner?"

"Right here," the bartender grinned dopily, pointing two thumbs backward at himself. "I'm Brent. The locals call me Bent Brent. Welcome to Havenwood Falls, man."

Peter swallowed his reaction in a bigger-than-necessary gulp of beer. *Of course you are*, he thought.

Just then the sound of heels tapped their way up behind Peter. Half a second later Stella's warm hand was smooth and reassuring on his arm. Her touch soothed him in a way the beer never would, and he felt the tension coiled in his body ease just a little under her hand as her voice swept over his shoulder like a lullaby.

"Hi, Brent. I'm Stella," she introduced herself, having apparently overheard the exchange. "Thanks so much for inviting me. I hope I'm not late."

Brent's glassy eyes sharpened instantly, and the single other patron sitting at the bar turned his head and—at least in Peter's approximation —made a point of taking in his view of Stella with all the subtlety of a hungry wolf who'd just stumbled across a tasty morsel alone in the woods. Anger flared in Peter. He could barely tolerate the women they'd met, whispering secrets in Stella's ears; he definitely didn't appreciate the men eyeing his soon-to-be wife like some kind of delicacy.

Stella's finger squeezed into his shoulder, and he resisted the urge to jerk away from her. He knew what she'd say if he shared his thoughts with her—and no, he wasn't imagining things.

Above his head, the evening was moving on without him.

"That's right!" Brent palmed his face and then grinned, extending a hand across the bar and breaking Peter's view of the man at the other end. "Almost forgot you were coming in tonight, silly me." Brent laughed like he found his own forgetfulness hilarious. It wasn't. "But glad you're here. Welcome."

He gave Stella's hand a quick shake and then he swept his arm over the open expanse of empty tables and sagging booths. "It's a little slow yet, but night'll be picking up soon. Lots of the crowd that hangs in here doesn't get out much until the sun goes down— but then we got ourselves a real party." He jerked his head in the direction of the other man. "Ain't that right, Rusty?"

The hungry wolf at the other end of the bar, whose name apparently was Rusty, raised his beer in agreement. He smiled, and it might have been a trick of the light, but Peter could swear the guy gave him a mocking wink. His vision went red.

"You're welcome to get your bearings up on stage," Brent went on, pointing toward the small stage at the opposite end of the room. "Mic's all set up and whatever music you want, I'm sure we can queue up for you."

"I brought my own," Stella's voice returned from Peter's side, where the indigo fabric of her dress sparkled in his peripheral vision. He felt pressure on his arm as Stella dug around in her handbag, which Peter had forgotten was still hitched on his shoulder. He flopped it onto the stool next to him right as she lifted out a handful of cassette tapes and a few slim CD cases.

"Then the stage is yours to command, my lady. Let me know

how I may be of service." Brent offered a playful salute. "Go on and settle in. We can sort the paperwork later."

All three men at the bar stared after Stella as she made her way to the other end of the room, a vision in her sparkling starlight dress. Even Peter held his breath as he watched his bride-to-be tinker with the stereo system and fuss around with the derelict-looking sound equipment. He hated to admit it, but that gypsy woman at the dress store had been right—the dress did look like it was destined for Stella. It fit her perfectly, the fabric hugging and flaring in all the right places, and the blues and pinks of the material made her lovely caramel skin all the more creamy, the dark curls of her hair all the richer and more vibrant. The lipstick she wore tonight was the same pink as the top layer of her dress, and Peter yearned to kiss it away from her lips.

Peter sipped his beer as he gazed at Stella, forgetting entirely his overwhelming desire to be surly as he drank in the view of the most beautiful woman he'd ever seen—until he noticed he wasn't the only one staring at Stella with stars in his eyes.

Bent Brent had returned to doing things that bar owners did—scrubbing down bar tops and polishing glass and not cleaning windows—but the man at the other end of the bar was looking at Stella like he might want to take her home. His dark eyes tracked her every move, and with each flicker Peter felt his temper kindle, then ignite, and then begin to flicker hotly within him.

Peter sized up the man—Rusty, wasn't that his name? Peter's theory about the men of Havenwood Falls and their nicknames fluttered into his thoughts. He noticed Rusty's hair was the same reddish-brown color as oxidized iron itself, and wondered briefly if his moniker was just another unfortunate nickname. Either way, this guy was no walking goth stereotype like Cicada or pothead like Bent Brent. Peter considered Rusty. He looked like he was probably close to Peter's age and his own six feet in height, but where Peter had earned most of his muscles from the gym, this guy looked like the kind who'd earned them outdoors, especially if his jeans, hiking boots, and flannel shirt that looked like they might have been borrowed from Brent's closet were any indication.

If it came down to a fight—and if the burning sensation at the back of Peter's throat was any indication, it might—Peter wasn't sure he could win.

"Something I can do for you?"

For a second Peter thought it was the water talking, until he realized that Rusty's lips had moved. Once he realized this, he became aware that, just as Brent had said, the bar had become suddenly populated. Not just populated, but crowded. He even caught a few familiar faces. Lyra—who had neither her tattoo gun nor her baby—and the woman from the dress shop were both looking intently in his direction, staring at him, Peter thought, the same way he'd been boring holes in the side of Rusty's head. Lyra turned to whisper in Lily's ear. She nodded in agreement with whatever the other woman said. Both moved closer to the stage— toward his Stella. He got the impression they were trying to cut her off from him, to keep him away.

Peter.

Peter recovered quickly, and returned his attention to the more pressing problem. Women could gossip all they wanted, but if this guy thought he was going to get between Peter and his fiancée, he was dead wrong. Raising his voice so that he'd be heard over the din of excitement that had begun to fill the air as the bar's new patrons chatted and clamored amongst themselves, Peter did his best to mark his territory. "I was just about to ask you the same thing. Noticed the way your eyes were feasting on my fiancée."

"By the moon!" Rusty exclaimed. "I'm not looking at your girl, friend."

Peter did not like being called names any more than he liked bad nicknames. "I'm not your friend, friend."

The temperature in the room fell to subzero as Peter made as if to stand up, but that was the moment when Stella began to sing. The effect was as if the room had spun into orbit, and her voice was gravity. It rang out, loud and confident, over the crowd, capturing everyone's attention instantly.

"By the moon!" Rusty of the hungry eyes exclaimed again, and Peter had to agree.

His Stella was a star. And she would always, always be his.

CHAPTER 7

*N*oelani sat in the underground cavern that was her home, counting the flower petals she had collected from the offerings brought by those who visited her well. She arranged them in various manners as she considered the ways the coldness had altered them. Some had curled edges; others still wore frost spots in their centers. Such a sudden change, she knew, meant that something was coming. This was the way of natural things; the cycles of seasons both figurative and literal.

Change was positive or negative, but very rarely neutral. The cold made Noelani nervous. It meant, at worst, that the chill of death was coming. An ending, cold and final. At best, it implied stasis—a form of debilitating stillness or an otherwise abrupt and lasting pause.

Neither was a terribly promising omen, and Noelani was not accustomed to such dark thoughts. She only wished she knew what it was for certain, but since she almost never left her well and rarely had any company whom she might ask, she knew little about what went on in the world around her. For the most part, that was just fine. But since the unseasonable cold had found its way to her well, she could not escape the worry that the change that was upon Havenwood Falls was intended for her. There was a new imbalance in the box canyon, and nature would correct it even if magic could not.

Noelani thought of this and grew even colder as she counted the petals, and as she did, she heard something that sounded like music, high in the sky above her well.

It was not the singing of birds or the strumming of an instrument, but something even more beautiful—a tune with a quality she had not heard in ages. She tipped her head to the side and listened.

It was not music at all, but song.

A woman's voice, as elusive and melodious as the chime of brass, carried bell-like on the wind from the epicenter of Havenwood Falls, somewhere amid the town square, from which Noelani caught the faintest whispers of voices and music, and sometimes magic. The sound filtered down through the cold, dark waters of Noelani's well. It filled her ears, delicately, and with it came a rush of warmth that stole away the chill in her heart.

Despite her lamentations, Noelani liked what she heard. She floated to the top of her well, pulling herself up on its stone brim where she sat, listening intently.

The musical quality of the woman's voice reminded her of the celesta, a French instrument with a name that shared meaning with Noelani's own. Her namesake was the mist of heaven. The celesta's name was derived from the French word celeste, meaning heaven itself. It was as fitting a name for the instrument as for the voice that breathed warmly against Noelani's heart, melting the frost in her hair and smoothing away the goose bumps on her flesh.

"Celesta . . . celesta." Noelani enjoyed the feel of the word as it played on her lips in time with the woman's song, and then another slid from her tongue.

"Stella."

CHAPTER 8

*B*y some strange twist of fate, Peter grew more tense and agitated at the exact same rate at which Stella became happier and more enchanted with Havenwood Falls. At some point, possibly very soon, she worried they'd both go so far around that they'd swing back in the other direction—and either crash into each other or die of whiplash in the process.

The couple had been in town barely three days, and the polar opposite ends at which they normally orbited had never before felt as far apart as they did now. What had been a quirky, opposites-attract type of relationship—the kind Paula Abdul had famously sung about—now felt empty, stretching endlessly between the two of them in a black, ugly void that grew wider every hour. Stella had felt the tension starting to grow the moment they'd stepped off the plane in Denver, but she could almost put a timestamp on exactly when the distance had started: the moment Cicada had greeted them at the shuttle.

Peter had begun slipping away from her during the drive into the mountains, and by the time she'd walked out of the ladies' room at the saloon and touched his shoulder, the man she loved had felt like a stranger beneath her hand.

She remembered how he'd felt. Hard and foreign. Almost

untouchable, like the mannequin that had worn what was to be her wedding dress before she'd bought it at Callie's.

The old wisdom Stella's mother had shared with her before she and Peter had left Rochester the summer before had come back to haunt her. "You barely know him," her mom had warned. "No good can come from running away with a man you barely know." With those words, worry wormed its way into Stella's bones. She and Peter had only been together a little while, in the scheme of things. She deeply loved him, but did she truly know him?

It wasn't something she'd ever considered, but now that she had, Stella didn't think she did. She knew what Peter liked for breakfast (poached eggs on an English muffin) and how he took his coffee (black, two sugars). She knew what papers he liked to read (the *Times*) and how he looked fresh out of the shower (perfect). But she knew little about his past, nothing about his family—she wasn't even sure why he'd pulled off the road and wandered into the Skylark the night they'd first met, much less what he'd been driving toward—or away from. She'd asked once and he'd said, "Nothing," and they'd left it at that.

Suddenly that nothing felt a lot like something, and Stella had been trying to shake that feeling ever since she'd first realized she felt it. She'd drowned herself in songs day and night to keep her heart from growing heavy from the burden of worry, like she always did when she felt out of her element. So far she'd gone through four sets of batteries and her voice was growing hoarse.

And it wasn't working. She was sinking quickly, and Peter was not only falling away from her, but he seemed to be pulling away. Like he was trying to get as far away from her as possible.

"This town creeps me out," Peter had said when they'd returned home after her first gig. "I feel like everybody here is watching me —like they know something about me that I don't or something. And it's bad."

"You're imagining things," Stella had protested. "Everyone is so nice and welcoming."

"To you," spat Peter. "But then you're the star, aren't you? I'm just the dumb horse you rode in on." Here he'd brandished the temporary tattoo Lyra had given him at her like it were an exhibit in a courtroom.

Peter hadn't joined her last night for her set at the Haven Saloon, where Stella had worked her way through the songs that were her staples—several of Mariah's, Vanessa Williams's "Save the Best for Last," and even a number by Celine Dion called "Water from the Moon," which Stella had never sung before, but it called to her when she saw it in the saloon's song index.

The lyrics asked if the singer must do the unthinkable—find water on the moon—to make their lover's heart come back to them. When she'd sung that, it felt like the words were her own—the ones she'd been searching for and trying to say to Peter but hadn't known to put together.

She'd never even heard the song before, but the words had hurt when she'd sung them, and any relief she'd found from the burden of her newfound unease dissolved. It wasn't that she thought Peter didn't love her—no, it wasn't that at all. It was something else. Between the aching feeling of disconnect and the niggling doubts spurred by her mother's words, Stella couldn't quite put her finger on what was wrong, but even not knowing exactly what bothered her didn't stop the worry from chewing at her insides. She felt constantly queasy, on the edge of losing her cookies.

When Peter worried, he got angry. Apparently, Stella got nauseous.

None of this not knowing had ever bothered her before. Stella had always been of the mind that she and Peter were creating a future together, not reliving their separate pasts. But as Peter's mood continued to sour, the words Irina Petran had whispered in her ear when they'd checked in two days ago—keep your eyes open, and your heart free—no longer felt inspirational, but more like a warning. Cicada's necklace, the hourglass with wings, likewise suddenly didn't feel like dreams taking flight, but time flying away. And even though Stella was happier than she might have ever been, a chill had begun to seep in through the pores of her skin—turning everything, from her upcoming wedding to the songs she picked for her set, cold.

Now, not only did Peter feel like someone she didn't know, but she was beginning to feel afraid, as if not only was he a stranger, but a dangerous one. Cold feet were one thing, but this wasn't at all what love, and dreams coming true, was supposed to feel like. That much, at least, she did know.

Stella thought again of the wishing well in the forest, the one she'd been told belonged to Noelani, the Lady of the Water who could bless their love. Every time she'd tried to bring it up to Peter over the past two days, he'd only gotten angrier and more frustrated. It began with statements that she should focus on practicing new songs for her ongoing engagement at the Haven Saloon, a practical, if useless, argument—Stella easily knew at least a hundred songs by heart. Eventually, Peter began to make strange comments about getting lost in the woods or falling into a stream, but these were odd, paranoid types of things that were utterly contrary to the avid outdoorsman she knew Peter to be. In the time they'd been together, he'd never met a mountain he couldn't climb or a trail he couldn't trek.

But when he'd raised his voice and yelled at her—something he'd never done before—she'd given up asking altogether. He'd just not been feeling well, he said. Headaches and the like, he'd insisted while clawing at his own head. She'd dropped the subject faster than she expected Mariah Carey to dump her manager-turned-husband Tommy Mottola.

As Stella watched the sun rise through her window where she lay beside Peter in their hotel bed, she shivered. The autumn morning waking up outside didn't look crisp and beautiful like it had when they'd first arrived in Havenwood Falls. It looked cold and rainy and gross. But even if the weather wasn't perfect, Stella told herself, today was the Founders Day Festival, which meant that tomorrow was the day they'd planned to get married. With this thought firmly in her mind, Stella hesitated only briefly before she pounced on Peter, peppering his sleeping profile with kisses.

She'd also reached a decision: she'd go to the well on her own to ask the Lady of the Water to bless their love. Stella wasn't particularly superstitious, but then she wasn't the type of girl to ignore such a nice idea, either. And who knew? Havenwood Falls was magical enough; maybe there was something real to the legend. Maybe all Peter needed was just a little bit more love to pull out of his darkness.

"Wake up, sleepyhead," Stella said softly, working her way from Peter's jaw to his lips. "It's festival day. Wedding eve."

Moaning in his sleep, Peter wrapped his arms around Stella and rolled her under him, attempting to cuddle her into submission. "Let's just stay here," he mumbled, voice thick with sleep. "Go back to sleep."

Stella wriggled away from him, only to climb atop him, straddling his body as she kissed her way down his throat to his chest. He moaned again, but even though his eyes stayed closed, other parts of his body were definitely waking up beneath her. That kind of reaction Stella recognized, and when one of Peter's eyes peeled open to gaze up at her, she felt a little silly for thinking he could ever be a stranger. His eyes were the color of fresh grass in the morning, nostalgic and refreshing at the same time.

"Are you sure you want to go back to bed?" she teased, drawing out the words while she tickled her fingers along his ribs. She pulled at the waistband of his pajama bottoms, pulling away and then flicking the elastic band against the solidness of his abdomen.

Peter's moan turned into a throaty growl. His left eye opened just a little and his hands slid upward to cradle her hips. "Well now I think I just want to stay in bed. With you."

"Oh, you do, do you?" Stella laughed. She slid her body lower onto his so that she could press her weight against him.

"I do." His voice was breathy. It was the first time since they'd gotten to Havenwood Falls that he sounded like her Peter again.

"Too bad, mister. It's the Founders Day festival today," Stella reminded him. "And you promised we could go, so let's go. Up and at 'em."

Peter's mood instantly shifted.

"I don't want to go, Stella. I don't want to go out there." His voice was hard and flat. He nudged her off of him and slid from the bed, disappearing silently into the small washroom. Stella waited as he took care of his morning business and then came back into the room, moving right past her to the small desk on the other side of the suite, where he lowered himself into a chair without so much as looking in her direction.

Any enthusiasm Stella had dared allow herself to feel evaporated instantly. She pushed herself upright, shivering again. This time she tried to rub the cold—and the irritation—out of her skin with her hands, but her fingers were like ice on her already cool skin, and the whole exercise just made her colder. Like Irina had predicted, the temperatures outside had indeed grown cooler —unseasonably cool, even this high in the mountains—and, like the widening gulf between them, seemed to have a direct correlation to Peter's bad mood. Stella bundled herself in an extra layer of blankets as she glared across the room at Peter, who sat, shirtless and totally comfortable, and as distant from her as the moon.

"Why?" she asked, when it was clear that Peter wasn't going to bother to explain himself—or say anything at all. He had a strange expression on his face, and when he did finally look at her, he blinked a few times, as if he hadn't recognized her.

"Why do you even want to go so badly?" he snapped. "It's not like this is our home. That woman downstairs said it was mostly locals at the festival anyway. If you haven't noticed, we don't live here. We don't belong."

Stella huffed. "We may not be locals, but we're here, aren't we? We've met people. We've made friends—or at least I have. You seem to want to fight everyone who looks at me for some reason."

Peter's left eye twitched. He glowered at her but didn't say anything. A shadow moved across his face.

"I don't want just to go to the festival, Pete," Stella sighed eventually. "I want to go with you. I want us to have a great day together. We're getting married tomorrow, and right now I sort of feel like that's not what you want anymore."

"I never said that. Of course I do." Peter's voice cracked like his tongue was under the tremendous strain of things unsaid.

Stella twisted her engagement ring on her finger. She'd done it so much that the flesh was starting to get raw and crack. "You didn't have to. If you've changed your mind, you can tell me."

"I already told you: I don't feel well."

"I just don't get it," Stella confessed, not ready to let the issue go until she zeroed in on the source of the problem. Now that she'd gotten him talking, maybe she could get him to actually tell her something. "You were fine before we left Pensacola. It was your idea to come here—to come with me. But ever since we got here, you don't want anything to do with this place. God, Pete, it's like you don't even want to have anything to do with me. You say it's not that, but what else am I supposed to think?"

On the other side of the room, Peter had the audacity to roll his eyes. Stella considered grabbing her robe and storming out, but two heartbeats later, Peter beat her to the tantrum. He flew out of his chair as if attacking the air between them, his fingers splayed as his hand reached toward her.

"The whole reason we're here is for you, Stella. The whole reason I'm still here is because of you. I can't get away from it. And I hate what it's doing to me—do you have any idea what you are doing to me, Laura?"

Stella flew backward in the bed as if he'd hit her. Who the hell was Laura, and what exactly was Peter so desperate to get away from?

An hour later, Stella stood at the edge of the forest, thinking dark thoughts and willing her heart not to break in her chest. She clutched the glass music box in her hands and the gold of their wedding bands glinted in the sunlight.

She and Peter had never had a fight before. Not a real one. They'd bickered a lot, and occasionally one or the other had gotten snappy, but Stella couldn't remember a moment when she'd ever felt so miserable with Peter. An argument she could chalk up to wedding jitters. Maybe even a small fight could be written off to the stress of being in a new town, away from home, and pent up together in a hotel room. Perhaps Peter did feel sick. It could have been something he ate, or the thin mountain air this high above sea level.

But none of that made him calling her by another woman's name in a fit of rage anything near acceptable. If he'd been anyone else, Stella would have ripped the jewel off her left ring finger and flung it straight out of the window, or flushed it down the toilet. In any case, it would have been off her hand and she would have been out of there, headed right back up to Rochester, where she could tell her momma that she'd been right. Nothing good had come of running away with a stranger—just a lot of hurt and heartache and disaster.

It might even make a good song, Stella considered. Heartbreak was always a chart-topper.

She had been so angry that she could barely speak when she asked Irina directions to the wishing well before she left Whisper Falls Inn on foot. So angry that she'd barely heard Irina's response, or whatever had come after it. She seethed the entire taxi ride to the forest, arguing with herself through every possible recourse to that thing in her hotel room who had stolen her fiancé from her. Just who in the hell did he think he was? It wasn't like he had a secret identity that had sprung loose the moment they got to Havenwood Falls, although it sure as hell felt like it.

Eventually, Stella's anger had given way to despair, and then, by the time the town square had faded into the distance behind her, to guilt. Was this her fault, Stella wondered. Had she asked too much from him? After all, it was she who had received the invitation to come to Havenwood Falls. Maybe he hadn't been meant to come.

Maybe this was her journey, and Peter never should have

followed her here. She loved him—that wasn't in question, even now. But maybe she should have taken the gig and enjoyed the fall alone—kind of a bachelorette party before the wedding where she could have one last thing for herself.

But she hadn't done that, obviously. Peter had come, and whatever was troubling him—whatever it was that was "doing something" to him was her fault. Or at least, it wasn't not her fault.

By the time she'd been dropped off at the edge of the forest with simple instructions on which trail to follow to find the wishing well, Stella had almost abandoned the whole trip through the forest. She'd not-so-briefly considered that she should get right back in the car, drive right back to Whisper Falls Inn, collect her things and her love, go home, and put this whole thing behind them. She stood and stared at the brilliant colors of the forest unfolding before her, and the only thing she wanted more than the blessing of the Lady of the Water was just to go home. It wasn't a blessing that she needed anyway; it was to go back in time.

Half a dozen songs queued up in Stella's head.

Stella laughed to herself. There truly was a song for every occasion. She'd just assigned a third meaning to Cicada's pendant, too. If she saw him again, she'd have to ask which one was right. She turned to begin the walk back to the town square and stopped, frozen in her tracks.

There was a wolf—a large, shaggy animal with fur the color of rust—standing right there, in broad daylight, staring at her. It didn't growl or appear particularly menacing, just watched her, its tail wagging ever so slightly. Even odder, it looked familiar, and Stella was positively certain she'd never met a wolf before.

Something that sounded like *oh my god* tumbled out from between her lips. Stella swallowed and took one step backward. Two. The wolf stepped forward. Three.

"Nice wolf," she tried, patting the air in front of her in supplication, hoping that the animal would turn and walk away, go back to doing whatever wolf things wolves typically did during daylight hours. The hardness of the asphalt driveway under her feet gave way to the soft crunch of dew-crisped grass. Peter's eyes flashed into her memory.

Stella swallowed again, her mind not letting her forget that the wolf stood, unmoving, between her and civilization.

"Nice wolf," she tried again. "Now go on; go ahead and run away. Leave me alone."

The wolf cocked its head to the side as if curious, but it didn't turn away. Instead, it took another step forward.

Stella hummed as she tried to quickly sort out her next move.

The wolf growled. It lunged.

Stella turned and fled into the forest.

CHAPTER 9

*H*e couldn't believe he'd called her Laura.
Couldn't. Freaking. Believe it.

Of all the things he could have said to Stella—all the things he arguably should have said—anything would have been preferable to that. Why that? He was losing it.

Peter, the water's voice whispered, grating against the inside of his mind like nails on a chalkboard. He could no longer differentiate the ghostly whisper of the woman he'd accidentally—no, not accidentally—yes, accidentally—drowned in the lake in Shenandoah National Park any more than he could the falling of water from the faucet in the bath or the rain that fell endlessly from the sky. He'd loved her too, Laura, hadn't he? Not as much as Peter loved Stella, but he had loved her.

He hadn't wanted to hurt Laura. He still couldn't believe—wouldn't believe—that he had. It hadn't been him. Not really. It was the water. Yes, the water was to blame. It called to him, told him to do terrible things. Forced him. It whispered to him whenever it was near, and no matter how much he tried to ignore the sound of its call, it forced its way into him. It changed him, turned him into something else—something that he never asked to be. He'd been running from it since.

A gross shiver of pleasure raced through Peter as he remembered the reflection of Laura's face shimmering below the water as it drank her up. The look in her eyes. The memory swelled in him, excited him as it stirred deep in his body and dark in his heart. Desire flooded through his veins. Peter gasped, horrified and delighted at his own reaction. He hated what he had done, and craved it with a longing he did not have the words to describe.

Come to me, the water called. *Bring her to me.*

"Shut up," he commanded, pressing both hands against the side of his head so hard, the pressure made his jaw ache. The horseshoe tattoo on the inside of his wrist flared painfully. He wanted to scratch it off his arm, scratch at it the way Laura's hands had at his face when he'd held her just far enough below the water that she couldn't reach him, one hand atop her head, fingers curled tightly in her pretty red hair. It had been so quick, lasting just for a moment —scratch, scratch, scratch—and then her body had gone soft and her hands had slackened. Then she had fallen away, drifting downward, slipping into the water's throat as it swallowed her.

Peter forced the memory away. That was long ago now. Far away. He'd been running from it—from the water—ever since. He'd been trying to get as far away from the water, from himself, as possible. But now it had found him, here, of all places—deep in the mountains of Colorado. It had tracked him down as slowly and surely as a river found its way back to the sea, and now it wanted her, too.

Stella.

Peter hadn't meant to lose his temper with Stella. He wasn't even angry with her. He was the very opposite of angry: terrified. He couldn't make the voices stop, that constant rush of moving water that beat like waves and whispered like puddles and pinged like raindrops inside his head. It raged and swelled like a storm over the ocean, and Peter was powerless to do anything other than be flung about like wreckage in the maelstrom, tossed to and fro on the waves as they rocked him.

The water wanted Stella, and it wanted him to give her to it.

But he wouldn't. No. She was his! Peter wouldn't let the water take Stella! He would keep her safe . . .

He would keep her safe. He just needed to keep her away from the water, that was all. He needed to keep her somewhere dry, yes, and more than anything, he needed to get out of Havenwood Falls. It had been a mistake to come here. This wasn't an ordinary town; he'd known that the moment they arrived. There was something else here. Something that knew what he was—

A monster who fed his loves to the water.

All his life, Peter had heard stories about such creatures. Myths about sinister beasts that could adopt the shape of animals and would drag women down into the depths, drowning them. They had been given many names in many lands, these beings. Some were seen as mischievous, others as playful and sometimes cruel, but only one was seen as truly evil.

The horseshoe on Peter's wrist burned. He heard the sound of hooves pounding like drums inside the roar of the ocean.

Bring her to us, Peter . . . Peter . . .

Nykur.

He regretted letting Stella walk out of the hotel room more than any other terrible thing he'd ever done the moment the door shut behind her. She'd stormed out—rightfully so—and to add salt to the wound, Peter hadn't even bothered to chase after her.

Not at first, anyway.

For a while he'd just sat right back down in his chair and stared at the space on the bed where Stella had been. She'd been right there, with tears in her eyes as she'd practically begged him to come to her, just as earnestly and beautifully as the water had been begging him to come to it.

And oh, how he'd wanted to! He'd wanted to take her up in his arms, to cover her in kisses and assure her that everything was fine. Everything would be okay. They just needed to leave this place, that was all.

But he hadn't, had he? No. He'd looked at her, and the hate he'd felt had been every bit as strong as the love. It was her fault this was happening, Peter knew that, even if he didn't want to believe it. It was her voice that had lured him off the road, she that pulled him into her gravity and would not let go. She'd tricked him into loving her, and now he was addicted to that love. He saw how brightly she shined, how everyone around him looked at her, as if she were every star in the sky and he was nothing more than the backdrop of darkness that gave her space to shine. If it hadn't been for Stella Malley, Peter would never have let himself fall in love again, and if he'd just avoided that, then he wouldn't have to suffer.

Well, if Stella insisted on making him suffer, then he would have to make her suffer too. He'd wash the shine from her. Dull her light so that it wouldn't blind him.

Peter.

The tattoo on his wrist flared and stung, the mark coming to life as if Lyra's tattoo gun was hot upon his skin, stabbing the horseshoe into his flesh. The pain was so strong, it pushed the voice of the water out of his head.

In the sudden silence, the heat receding from his wrist, Peter flung his arm out over the desk, sending the table lamp and phone book clattering noisily to the floor. This was madness! Peter wasn't sure what was going on in his head. Stella had suggested it was wedding jitters. Maybe it was the lack of oxygen. Maybe it was both, or something else. Peter didn't know. He just knew he needed to get to Stella—to make her his before he lost her forever.

The woman at the front desk of the inn hesitated before telling him that Stella had gone to that blasted wishing well in the forest—the one where the fairytale lady in the water supposedly granted wishes to young brides.

"Perhaps you should wait for her here," Irina suggested. Her eyes landed purposefully on the mark on his wrist, like she'd known its meaning all along. "Or maybe you should leave Havenwood Falls altogether. Stella is happy here. We will keep her safe."

"She's not in danger," Peter snarled, furious at the implication that he was the danger, though deep down he knew it was true. "And she is mine to protect."

He left the woman with her baby, stumbling through the town square that was decked out for the festival. It seemed like everyone in Havenwood Falls was there, packed into the small area so that he had to weave his way around the bodies of the town's residents. He caught glimpses of familiar faces—the woman from the dress shop, the bar owner, the woman who'd given him the tattoo.

Peter recognized their faces, but couldn't remember their names. His head was full of noise that he could no longer hear clearly, and his senses were overwhelmed to the point of overload. The scents that infiltrated his nose didn't make any sense. Everywhere he turned, pushing through the throng of Havenwood townies enjoying their festival, he smelled animal—things furred, feathered, fanged. He scented things, too, that had no smell. Things he shouldn't have even been able to discern as there at all found their way to him, and Peter got the feeling that all of these were working together, trying to trap him amongst them.

Trying to keep him from getting to Stella.

At one point Cicada appeared before him, but Peter shoved the man aside and kept going.

Pete. It was her voice he heard now, calling him to her the same as it had done the night he'd pulled off the road in New York.

He wasn't sure where he was going, but his feet carried him steadily toward the water. The thought of traipsing out in the woods —of being anywhere near any sort of water, even if it was a well— did not sit well with Peter, but if that was where Stella had gone, then that was where he would go.

It was freezing, but Peter barely felt the cold as it wrapped around him. The deeper into the forest he walked, the more frigid the air became, blowing against his back as if it were following him. When the cold had become so unbearable that his muscles clenched and his bones began to ache, Peter saw her, standing with her back to him.

He could see Stella's profile as she whispered into the well, and then he saw it.

The water.

It lapped over the edge of the well, running in cool lines down the stone sides just the same as the tear that slid down Stella's profile.

Peter saw the water, and it saw him, and everything he had been running from caught up with him.

Nykur.

The tattoo on his wrist scorched as if a red-hot brand had been laid against his skin, but even the excruciating pain of the mark was not enough to overcome that which spread suddenly throughout his body. His arms and legs stretched into long, muscled limbs beneath him, and his blond hair turned as white as the cold around him as it fell in shimmering waves like sea foam down his skin. The agony was excruciating as his body reformed, his bones cracking and reshaping even as his mind screamed out for it to stop, and by the time Peter's hands rested upon the ground, they were no longer the hands of a man, but hooves of a horse.

CHAPTER 10

The second the wolf had lunged at her, Stella fled into the woods, all thought of abandoning her trip to the well forgotten.

Since then she hadn't stopped running, the rubber soles of her sneakers finding purchase on the earth as her feet carried her deeper and deeper into the densely packed foliage of Havenwood Falls. The forest passed in a brilliant flash of colors around her—blushing sweetgums, blazing chokecherrys, golden aspen with white trunks—but Stella saw none of it. For a while it had felt like she would never stop running, even though she had long since ceased to hear any signs that the animal still chased her. There was no growling, no padding of paws on the ground, nothing that should have compelled her to keep running, but nevertheless she could sense danger pressing in behind her back, and so she ran.

Stella ran, and she hoped whatever it was didn't catch up to her.

In her fright, she hadn't paid attention to where she was going. The smooth, well-trodden path of the trail had long since given way to uneven, unblazed terrain that was peppered with jagged edges of sharp rock and roots that stretched upward like hungry fingers from under the earth. Branches grabbed at Stella, scratching her face and arms. Twigs tore at her clothes. She fell once, but ignored the sting in her knee and kept going, wincing through the pain. Even when stitches stabbed her sides and her breath came in great, ragged plumes of frozen air, she kept running. She ran so far and for so long that the silver walls of the mountains that surrounded Havenwood Falls began to loom up before her, deepening the canopy of trees into shadow, and she knew eventually she'd run out of space to flee.

Eventually the walls of trees broke apart into the slim shapes of spindly, uneven aspens through which she could see sunlight, and at last even these gave way to the tall, brushy grass of a wildflower meadow. Stella kept running, more slowly now so that her own momentum carried her. At last, when it felt like she couldn't take one more step, the vision of the well rose up before her, and the forest bloomed into color and scent again. It was cool here, not cold as it had been in the forest, but the crisp, inviting kind of coolness that one might feel as they slipped between fresh sheets on the first night of spring.

Stella's feet slowed beneath her. She moved more cautiously now, more out of anticipation than fear, setting one foot tentatively in front of the other. Her hands grazed the tops of the wildflowers as she walked amongst them, her fingers pulling petals until she had to cup her hand so they didn't spill from her fingertips. The forest was quiet around her, but not still—she could hear the tinkling sound of water, like the babbling of a brook, before her. And then, very faintly, she thought she heard a woman's voice, singing somewhere on the wind. It was the most beautiful sound she'd ever heard, befitting for a Lady of the Water who dealt in love and blessings.

The well, as it stood before her now, was just as Stella had imagined a real wishing well might be. A peaked cedar canopy hovered above a yawning mouth of gray stone, and with the bright midday sun shining down, the unassuming round shape appeared carved out of sunlight. It glittered like gold, and Stella shielded her eyes with one hand as she leaned against the well, angling her body so that her feet anchored her to the ground but she could still bend forward far enough to see the water all the way to its bottom.

"Noelani," she whispered into the water, when her pulse had slowed and she breathed evenly again. "I am here to see the Lady of the Water. I am here to ask for your blessing."

Stella peered into the water of the wishing well and let the petals tumble one by one from her hand into its depths in offering. Their sweet, heady scents seeped into the water, and the fragrance rose up to meet her. For a while, though, Stella saw nothing, and her heart sank. Had she really expected the legend to be true—that some lovely creature truly inhabited these waters and granted blessings to those who wished for them?

Yes, she had, because it was the only thing left she knew to do. She had to believe, because she now knew that the man she so desperately loved was falling away from her, and this was the only thing left she could think to do to save him.

"Please," Stella pleaded, her voice cracking as the first tear slipped from her lashes. "Please, Noelani, if you're there, please hear me. I really need your help."

When it seemed that it had all been for nothing and Stella finally loosened her grasp on the stone brim of the well's edge, something stirred far below. A shape, red and white like strawberries and cream, floated to the top and hovered just below the surface. For a moment, a cloud of crimson billowed like ink dropped into a pail of water, and then it cleared, bringing into view a woman's face.

Stella gasped at the sight. The woman in the water was beautiful, like something out of a dream that was too perfect to be real but still undeniably there.

"I am the Lady of the Water," her lips said, and though Stella couldn't hear the woman's voice, she could feel it washing over her, warm and comforting like bathwater. Stella felt something pass between the two of them as she stared into the woman's emerald eyes—a sort of peaceful knowing and shared secret that instantly connected them in an unbreakable way. "What is your wish?" she asked.

Stella lifted the music box that was still clutched in her hands. She had kept her fingers curled tightly around it as she ran, and it was almost painful to loosen their hold.

"I am to be married," she explained, "but my fiancé, Peter . . . something is wrong."

Noelani's face turned sideways in question.

"Wrong?" she echoed.

"It's like, he's the sky, right? Only where the sun used to be, there's a dark cloud that's passed over it. Peter is still there, trapped behind it—I know he is—but the cloud has taken away all that was warm and bright and made it cold and dark and distant." Stella fumbled for words to explain the darkness that had come over the man she loved. She'd barely even acknowledged this, and the words to describe it hadn't even formed completely in her head yet, much less her mouth. "Something is bothering him, but I don't have any idea what it is. I can feel it, and whatever it is is dark. Dangerous," she admitted. The sensation of being chased fell over her again, and she shivered.

Noelani said nothing.

Stella licked her lips, feeling silly but strangely resolved. She held out the music box to Noelani but kept it just above the surface of the water so as not to damage the mechanism that made the box chime. "The lady at the inn where we're staying told me that you give blessings—that you bless people's love. I was hoping that you could bless ours—mine and Peter's—and we might be happy again."

"That is true," Noelani's lips moved again. "But my magic blesses love that already exists. It makes it brighter, stronger . . . but I'm afraid it does not change love."

"Change love?"

"If darkness has crept into your love's heart, even when it is clear that you love him so strongly and so brightly already, then I fear nothing I can give you will help," she explained. "I cannot grant love, and I cannot make love that is received different than what is given."

"But he loves me," Stella insisted. "I know he loves me—just as much as I love him. I just need him to remember—to come back to me."

Noelani nodded, and she rose a little higher so that her features were more sharply defined and Stella could see clearly the outline of her lips as they broke just above the water. Her voice was a whisper. "Not all love is pure," Noelani warned. "Some love is dark. Some love is drowning. You must run away from it, Stella. Run away—do not let him trap you in a love that is, above all else, loveless. Keep your heart free."

Keep your heart free.

Stella opened her mouth to say something, but as she did, she saw Noelani's face twist into fear. The Lady of the Water pushed back below the surface, descending swiftly into the safety of her well. Stella heard the crunch of grass behind her, but before she could turn to see what brought the shadow that had fallen over her shoulder, she had time for one more thought—Peter—and then the world swallowed her and all was icy, cold, and dark.

CHAPTER 11

*N*oelani's heart ached at hearing the hurt in Stella's words. This was the imbalance that had come to Havenwood Falls—the change that had turned her waters cold.

Stella was pure love—bright, shining, and blue—but even her light was not enough to illuminate the darkness of the man she loved. It wasn't exactly magic, but love that powerful had a way of transcending into something that was very much like it. Noelani didn't know how any darkness could be so bleak as to be impervious to such a blinding light as what Stella's love offered, but whatever it was, it was tainted and cruel, a darkness that could only come from a very black sort of soul.

Noelani knew instantly why the magic of Havenwood Falls had called to Stella. It had been trying to save her, to call her home where she might shine brightly without being smothered. And she had come, but the darkness had followed her, clinging to her in the nasty way that shadows always clung to the edges of dawn. Stella had come to Noelani's well to ask for her blessing, but for the first time she would not be able give it. It was a test for them both—for Noelani to understand the boundaries of love, and Stella to know when to love herself more than to give her heart away to someone—something—that did not deserve it.

Noelani had known this, and so "Keep your heart free" was what she told Stella when the woman asked for her blessing.

Stella dropped her head in resignation, and then she parted her lips to say something as a shadow rose up behind her, eclipsing her as totally as a moon sliding across the sun. Whatever she might have said was lost. Her eyes went wide, and she was shoved so quickly and so suddenly into Noelani's well that her scream filled the water.

"Peter! Peter, stop!" Stella cried, her voice growing at first more panicked and then strangely sleepy. When her throat had filled too fully with water to form words, it was simply the sound of her grief that carried on the water, and the feeling of such pain and misery pierced Noelani's heart even more sharply than Stella's words had.

Stella's scream shattered the peace of Noelani's well, and Noelani screamed with her. She could taste Stella's grief, but could do nothing but watch in horror as a dark figure forced Stella's head beneath the water. It held her there, rigid and unrelenting, as she screamed and thrashed, her arms and hands tangling in her own hair as they fought to free themselves of the thing that held them trapped underwater.

Noelani screamed again, calling out for all those magical in Havenwood Falls to hear. To come. To save Stella's light from being extinguished, and to rid the forest of the darkness that had followed her here.

But no one came. It happened so quickly.

Stella stopped screaming. The silence was deafening, and then a sound . . . The music box had slipped from Stella's hand and opened, spilling the pair of wedding bands into the water. A haunting melody chimed from the box as it sank to the bottom of the well.

"Let her go," Noelani yelled, choking on Stella's grief where it polluted the water. Exhaustion overtook her as she reached for Stella. Noelani pushed all that she had—all the magic she could give—into the water's essence, not to bless Stella but to save her. To give her life, breath, anything that would allow her to escape from the monster at her back.

Mouth gaping, Stella's final words were a whisper in the water. "I loved him," she confessed, as the rich amber of her skin paled into milky white and the sparkle in her eyes burnt out. "Peter."

The moment Stella died, the water began, finally, to freeze. Her body went slack and then toppled completely into the water, pushed into its depths by the monster who'd drowned her. Fury wrapped itself around Noelani as she gathered up Stella in her arms and held her body against hers, clinging to the brilliant, beautiful star whose shine had been blown out so violently.

Stella was gone, and even though Noelani had known her but minutes, the weight of that loss destroyed her. But even worse was what she saw next, staring down at her in the depths where she clung to Stella's drowned body and waited for the cold to claim her. At first Noelani saw the shape of a great beast, white-hot with rage, and then it moved, shimmering in the way the vision of an oasis might glimmer in the desert. When she blinked again, it was not a beast that she saw staring into her well, but a man.

Noelani saw him, Peter Heilen, fair of skin and hair but black of heart, and she knew what he was. She could smell the scent of animal and knew exactly what sort of beast drowned women who loved them.

"Nykur," she growled up at him, glaring at his downturned face. "What have you done?"

Drips of water still fell like falling tears from his fingertips as Peter's eyes locked on her. "I didn't mean to. I didn't . . ." He fumbled for words, looking momentarily lost before the weight of satisfaction fell over him. "She made me," he insisted. He wiped at his face and then abruptly jerked his eyes upward. "I had to drown it out."

Noelani tried to look away, but it was too fast. He saw her, his eyes spearing hers where she stared upward at him, still clinging to the body of Stella Malley, and just as Stella's last words had been the name of the thing that drowned her, the face of Peter Heilen was the last thing that Noelani saw.

CHAPTER 12

*W*hen Peter came to on the now-frozen ground beside the well, he knew what he had done. Worse, he knew now he would do it again if given the opportunity—not because the voices made him, but because he had liked doing it. He had enjoyed the feel of holding Stella under, of feeling her love for him as it bled out of her into the water. Still, he was filled with self-loathing. He had loved Stella, loved her every bit as much as he had loved killing her.

It was in his nature, the evil inside him as much a part of himself as the part that loved Stella so fiercely. He had never meant to harm her, but it had been foolish to think that he would not. His love, no matter how well-intended, was twisted and cruel, and Peter resolved in that instant never to love again—and to never, ever again put himself near enough that he would hear the call of the water. He might not be able to resist its call, but never again would he let it claim someone he loved.

"Stella." He said her name one last time and then ran from the forest, the limbs of the trees scratching at his skin as he fled on bare feet back to the town. When he broke through the last barrier of trees, he was surprised to find a congregation of familiar faces awaiting him, as well as others he did not recognize.

They looked expectantly at the tree line, and it was impossible to miss the grief and disappointment that washed over them when they saw it was Peter who emerged from the forest, and not Stella.

Lyra Beaumont was the first to speak. "Where is Stella?" she asked.

The others—Rusty, Lily, and Irina, as well as an older, severe-looking woman—stared at him, their malcontent evident in their eyes. Peter didn't know what to say, so he said the only thing he could. "In the forest. At the well."

He didn't bother to clarify that she was now *in* the well, and—mercifully—no one challenged him. It's not like they would find her body anyway, not without dredging the well, and he doubted the . . . *thing* . . . that lived in it would allow such a thing.

Irina turned her head into Lily's shoulder, and Lyra's face went white. "I had hoped the magic I put into your tattoo would be enough to restrain your evil from coming loose before Stella could seek the wisdom of the Lady of the Water," she said. "And I hope now that her magic may be strong enough to heal what is broken between you.

"The magic in the tattoo?" asked Peter, remembering the way it had burned and stung on his arm, as if it had been a brand. "What are you, some kind of witch?"

Lyra glared at him. "Some kind of witch, yes."

"And we know what you are," added Rusty. "And what you are capable of doing."

"You have taken magic tonight. Magic that was not yours," Lily cut in, touching her fingertips to her forehead as if seeing by an inner eye. "It is the magic of the Lady of the Water. She has blessed you?"

Peter felt his eyes narrow. Again, he did his best to evade the question. "The woman in the water. I saw her."

"Yes, Noelani." Lily looked to Lyra.

"What does this mean?" Lyra asked. "We had expected her blessing to go to Stella, not Peter."

"It is difficult to know, but it cannot be a good thing."

Peter was quickly losing the thread of the conversation. The women talked amongst themselves, but Rusty's eyes remained locked on Peter. Peter had the impression that if he made a run for it, it would not go well for him.

"What happens now?" he asked eventually.

For a moment, the congregation of people barring his escape from the forest stared silently at him, and then the other woman, the one whose name Peter did not know, spoke sternly. "You were never meant to come to Havenwood Falls, Peter Heilen," she said. "The invitation was for one. Stella will stay with us. You will leave this place now, and you will never return. And the magic you have stolen, every bit as much as the love that you have blackened, will haunt you for the rest of your days. Eventually you will wither and dry out, and become as starved for love as the women whose hearts you've drowned with your own evil. Now go."

One by one, they cleared a path for Peter. Cicada waited at their backs, the shuttle door open behind him. Peter saw his bags had been brought from the inn and were waiting on one of the seats.

Unsure of any other action, Peter moved toward the shuttle. He set one foot atop the first step of the shuttle's stairs, and only then did he move his eyes up to face the man who would ferry him away from Havenwood Falls. So tall that he still rose above him even on the shuttle's step, Cicada didn't speak, and he didn't smile. Whatever warmth had animated the man when they'd first met was long gone. He seemed little more than a statue now, cold and indifferent, though he still wore the same strange pendant around his neck that had been there when he'd first delivered Peter and Stella to Havenwood Falls three days before.

The hourglass no longer stood on its base, but was turned on its side.

Peter had to clear his throat twice before he could speak. "What does it mean—that thing around your neck?"

Cicada's black eyes drifted upward to Peter. "It means time, at least for some, has stopped."

Peter gulped in fear. An unfamiliar and decidedly uncomfortable sensation shot like fire in his veins.

"I am a nykur," he admitted, speaking the word aloud for the first time. He jerked his hand in the direction of the people still watching from the edge of the forest. "One of those women is a witch. And there was a woman living below water. I don't know about the others, but they're definitely not human." With every word, the fear dug deeper into his bones, burning him in a way that the tattoo never could. He could barely force the next words off his tongue. "What are you?"

Cicada grinned then, the smile slicing apart his lips and curling far too high up on his gaunt face to be anything other than terrifying. "One day you will find out. One day I will come for you, ready to drive you to another place, the place where you truly belong. But today is not yet that day, Peter Heilen. Not yet."

EPILOGUE

*I*n the wake of the events at the well, a dark curse was born.

A vicious cold spread fast and violently in the little corner of the forest that had belonged to Noelani, the naiad who once gave blessings of love and light from her waters. When it did not thaw and none of the spells cast could warm it, that area of the forest was erased from maps and guarded by the protection of the Court of the Sun and the Moon, the town's governing council, so that no innocent soul would wander into the woods and find themselves lost in the dark. Noelani's well was abandoned, and what was left of the Lady of the Water was no longer a thing of love and blessings, but a monster of darkness and decay.

She became the rusalka, and all—at least for a while—was lost. Noelani would wait in the darkness for a light bright enough to burn through the never-ending dark. One day the magic of her well would return, but until then she would wait, and dream, and wait. No one disturbed her, not even to recover the body of Stella Malley, because sometimes it must be from the very ashes of loss that something new can be reborn.

Peter's deceit was eventually discovered, and though he had already fled, the wards were sealed off behind him so completely that even if, on some long-away day, he remembered the magical little town in the heart of a box canyon high in the mountains of Colorado, he would never be able to return.

And so it was, and for many years, so it would remain. In the days to come, Peter's black heart would wither and dry within him, and Noelani would wait. Still, though the love of Stella Malley was gone, it would not be forgotten. She would shine on, a single star in the darkness, until one day, from the very unlikeliest of places, her light would break through the curse of the drowning bride.

We hope you enjoyed these stories in the Legends of Havenwood Falls series featuring a variety of supernatural creatures. The series is a collaborative effort by multiple authors. Find out what happens with Noelani in *Of Salt and Stars* by Seven Jane.

Also try the signature New Adult/Adult series, Havenwood Falls, and the YA series, Havenwood Falls High
Stay up to date at www.HavenwoodFalls.com

Subscribe to our reader group and receive free stories and more!

ABOUT THE AUTHOR

Seven Jane is a bestselling author of dark fantasy and speculative fiction. Her debut novel, *The Isle of Gold*, was published by Black Spot Books in October 2018. She is represented by Gandolfo Helin & Fountain Literary Management and supported by Smith Publicity.

On Facebook, Twitter, and Instagram @sevenjanewrites or at www.sevenjane.com.

ACKNOWLEDGMENTS

Many thanks are due to Kristie Cook, Regina Wamba, Liz Ferry, and the team at Ang'dora Productions, as well as to the many wonderful authors whose stories have contributed to the incredible world of Havenwood Falls—most particularly Kristie Cook, E.J. Fechenda, Susan Burdorf, and Randi Cooley Wilson, whose characters welcomed Stella into Havenwood Falls 1993. I am so grateful and proud to be a member of this fantastic community.